Night
of the
Tyger

Night
of the
Tyger

David
Klass

St. Martin's Press
New York

Design by Amelia Mayone

Library of Congress Cataloging-in-Publication Data

Klass, David.
      Night of the tyger / David Klass.
          p. cm.
      ISBN 0-312-04397-X
      I. Title.
    PS3561.L247N54 1990
    813'.54—dc20   89-78024
                                          CIP

First Edition

10 9 8 7 6 5 4 3 2 1

For George Culver
and Andrew Xerxes Kuritzkes.

And for Lezra.

Part One

In Memoriam

I held it truth, with him who sings
To one clear harp in divers tones,
That men may rise on stepping-stones
Of their dead selves to higher things.

But who shall so forecast the years
And find in loss a gain to match?
Or reach a hand through time to catch
The far-off interest of tears?

Let love clasp Grief lest both be drowned,
Let darkness keep her raven gloss.
Ah, sweeter to be drunk with loss,
To dance with Death, to beat the ground.

—Alfred, Lord Tennyson
from "In Memoriam A.H.H."

Chapter 1

Alyssa hurried along High Street on her way to read about ancient Carthage.

It was ten-thirty on a Thursday evening, and as she crossed the campus, she had to swerve to avoid a few intramural squash players on their way home from a late match at the Payne Whitney Gym. Their laughter made her speed up a little. She was anxious to leave the world of her peers for a much quieter world of books. At last she reached the imposing library entrance and slipped inside.

The vast main hall of Yale's Sterling Library glittered before her. The statuettes and murals and high ceilings and strictly enforced silence gave the hallway an almost religious atmosphere, like the nave of a hallowed cathedral. She hurried to the stacks elevator, got in, and the gray doors closed behind her.

On the twelfth floor, she moved quickly through the murky stacks toward her cubicle. The silence of the stacks had a peculiar resonance, as if the thousands of aged volumes were both filtering out the sounds of the outside world and whispering to each other in their own secret language. A faint moldy odor of very old paper and the sweet scent of leather bindings pervaded the air.

Alyssa's heavy legs clomped along the familiar dusty stone floor. The ceiling lights gave off a faint yellowish illumination that cloaked the walls and pillars and shelves with a soft veil of shadow. She turned into a study cubicle built into a far corner, switched on the desk lamp, plopped Polybius down on the wooden desk, and heaved a sigh of relief and pleasure. Soon she was two thousand years in the past.

Alyssa had the gift of history. Ancient history to her was not a dead thing, cut off from the present by an impenetrable curtain of centuries. Rather, she slipped back through the millennia with sure steps, repeating a journey she had undertaken hundreds of times before. Her Carthage was the Carthage of daring ships in a deep harbor, of one-eyed Hannibal raging at the walls of Rome, and of human sacrifices offered to propitiate the dreaded thirst of Moloch.

She had been reading for an hour with no interruptions, when she first heard footsteps. Engrossed in Polybius' account of the battle of Cannae, she was aware only of Hannibal's invading army of fifty thousand men set in brilliant formation by the master tactician, his Spanish and Celtic horse on the left flank by the Aufidus River, his prized African heavy infantry held back to spring a trap on the Romans when they charged in blindly . . .

Then she heard it. . . .

She looked up at the sound—a scraping sound. No, make that a shuffling sound—footsteps. She pushed her black-rimmed eyeglasses up the slope of her nose. The murky emptiness seemed unbroken. Shelves and shelves of books rolled away into the shadows, a vast sea of secrets. Nothing else.

Back to the plains of Cannae. Opposing Hannibal's army were the Romans, more than one hundred thousand of them, commanded by the foolhardy Varro. When the battle started and the Carthaginian line began to give way, to fall back to create a cunningly planned concavity with the African infantry on either side, the Romans plunged right in. The trap closed around them and their maniple formations broke down as Roman soldiers turned to face enemies on every side.

The scuffling sounds came again, closer now. They didn't exactly sound like footsteps—they sounded more like a person dragging himself slowly along. They stopped and started again, closer and louder.

Alyssa put down her book and stood. "Hello," she called in a hesitant voice, "is someone there?"

The books muffled her question.

She felt afraid, and hated herself for that silly fear. Her imagination had always been too vivid for her own good. *Jaws* had ruined a summer vacation in Florida, for instance, when she hadn't dared to go in the water, and *Halloween* had made her miss her last few years of trick or treating.

Kids stuff. Alyssa forcefully reminded herself that she was older now, more mature—a Yale student, for God's sake—and this was the main library of a great university. Nothing was going to happen to her here worse than a book falling on her head. She sat back down at the desk and tried to regain her concentration.

How many men had the Romans lost? At least seventy-five thousand. And Hannibal? Fewer than six thousand. Which proved that if you were soldiering in the ancient world, it paid to have a good commander.

Alyssa became conscious of the smell. It was a musty, doggish odor. She glanced up again—could it be an animal, a dog or a cat? Or maybe rats or a raccoon?

Silence. Even the smell seemed to fade.

She forced her eyes back to the page, but her concentration was really focused on waiting for the sounds to begin again.

Silence. She waited.

Suddenly footsteps disturbed the silence. Alyssa realized that the footsteps kept getting closer and then fading away because someone was circling her at a distance, moving around the shelves of books, watching her, drawing closer. . . .

"I know you're there. I can hear your footsteps. C'mon, don't joke like this."

Silence.

"Say something."

Silence. Footsteps. Silence.

"What do you want? This isn't funny any more."

There came a sound that could have been low laughter, but was probably just deep breathing.

"I'm gonna call security." Her voice cracked.

She glimpsed a shadow, perhaps fifteen feet away. It moved and then disappeared.

Alyssa began walking briskly toward the nearest exit. The scuffling footsteps followed her, the breathing sounds coming closer.

She knew there was a campus security phone by the stairwell. It couldn't be much farther, unless she had turned wrong in this maze of bookshelves.

The books were all around her, smelling of age and blocking out the light. Faint lingering thoughts of what she had just been reading flared up on the fringes of her panic as she hurried between the tall shelves. Cannae—Hannibal—Varro. She had studied the strategies and compared the lists of casualties, but only now did she hear the far-off clamor of the slaughter, the agonized wailings . . . calling to her as she began to run, faster and faster.

Alyssa sprinted for the stairway door. The pudgy young woman ran between the shelves, her glasses askew, her short legs pushing her forward faster and faster.

As she whipped past old tomes that had sat on their shelves for decades, buried in layers of dust, the footsteps followed her. Faster. Closer.

Fifty feet. Her side cramped but fear pushed her forward. Thirty feet. Twenty, and she managed a final burst of speed.

The bright-red campus security phone hung on the wall near the stairwell. She reached for it. But as her right hand closed around the receiver, she felt herself being seized from behind in a grip so tight that it ripped the breath out of her lungs, and the desperate scream she had been saving was smothered by the first massive wave of shock and pain.

The girl died without even a gasp to echo with her down the long plummet.

> *And as quietly as she went, it quieted. The silence was peace and the peace was layered and as smooth as the skin over the neck where her blood still beat close. . . .*

> *Pumping . . . pumping . . .*

> *Blood, still warm, on the insides of fingers and on cheeks, and on the books, pressing in more and more tightly, as they had and as they are and as they will forever and ever.*

> *It was sweet to be rid of the demon. As always, when the demon was vanquished the other voice came with questions.*

> *Is she dead?*

> *For now. Hush.*

> *Is it over?*

> *Hush. When one is chased by a demon, can there ever be such a thing as over? Now she is driven away and all is still in heaven and earth, and it is time for silent haste.*

> *Soon she will be back.*

Kevin Malloy Randall, professor of romance poetry at Yale University, was shaken out of a drunken sleep by the rattle of a jackhammer splitting the pavement beneath his window. At first he wasn't sure whether the pounding was going on inside or outside his head, and he kept both of his eyes tightly closed. When the jackhammer shut off for a second, Kevin managed to open his left eye and take in first, the empty bottle of Laphroaig, then the sunlight streaming through the half-open window, and finally the clock on the wall. It was nine forty-three. In seventeen minutes he was due to give a lecture on Arthur Henry Hallam to nearly a hundred bright and eager undergraduates. He climbed out of the armchair and stood tottering for a second, hung over, disgusted with himself, and tempted just to chuck the whole thing and go back to sleep. Then, forcing his feet to move, he headed for the bathroom.

The icy shower cleared his head. He stood there for a full five minutes until the skin of his arms began to take on a faint bluish color. When he stepped out of the shower he dared a quick look in the bathroom mirror. His eyes were red but not bloodshot or puffy. He checked his watch. Seven minutes. There would be no time to shave. He slipped on a pair of pants, a clean but wrinkled shirt, and a tweed jacket badly in need of pressing. He was out the door on the top step, preparing to bolt off into the Connecticut morning, when a glance at the headline on the front page of the *New Haven Register* stopped him cold.

For a long minute he stared at the newspaper, gasping like a fish that has suddenly been hoisted out of the water. He bent down and grabbed the paper, and tried to hold it steady in his shaking hands. "GIRL KILLED IN LIBRARY" the headline ran. The article was poorly written and the details were sketchy—the police were not releasing much information. Much of the article focused on how the university was going to step up security.

Kevin's eyes devoured the newsprint, and even in his daze he was shocked that the article made no mention of the library murders two years earlier. He stuck the paper under his arm and set off at a brisk run through Trumbull Courtyard. Suddenly all of Yale University seemed to vibrate at once as the bells of Harkness Tower chimed the new hour. He quickened his pace.

Kevin's long strides carried him across Elm Street in a bounding rush, and as he turned onto High Street and ran directly beneath Harkness Tower the chimes were still ringing. He entered Linsley-Chittenden Hall through the back entrance, dodging late students as he made his way to the lecture hall. He stood outside for a second to catch his breath, then entered the auditorium and hurried down the rows toward the stage. The hall was already nearly filled with students, and many of them turned to look at the infamous professor as he entered. His chronic lateness, drunken life-style, and ill preparedness for his lectures were becoming notorious, and rumor was that the university was seeking an excuse to revoke his tenure. Two hundred eyes watched him as he mounted the stage, walked to the lectern, and mopped his forehead with an already damp handkerchief.

The students gradually quieted. Kevin grasped the lectern for momentary support as hangover nausea made him fear he might be sick in front of everyone. The nausea passed. Absently he spread the *New Haven Register* out on the lectern and glanced down at it while the class waited expectantly. Then it dawned on him that he had forgotten his lecture notes and would have to speak for fifty minutes from memory.

"Today's lecture will be on Hallam," he began. "Arthur Henry Hallam. To some of you he may seem an obscure subject to devote an entire hour of a survey course in romantic poetry. After all, he was most definitely not a major poet. I would not even call him a minor poet. There are those who would contend that he was not a poet at all. Some even whisper that he was a talentless sham."

Kevin stopped and mopped his brow again. The nausea expanded inside his throat. He gazed out at the vast sea of bright faces, and for a moment he was overwhelmed with the thought that the majority of them would become lawyers and stock brokers. And here he was trying to interest them in Hallam! What a well-behaved crowd they were compared to the students of even five years ago.

They seemed to dress more neatly—especially the boys. They fidgeted less and took more notes.

The high ceiling light sparkled off the sandstone walls. The stained-glass windows kept out most of the sunlight and lent the room a dim richness. As Kevin inhaled deeply three times, he saw that the students in the front rows were watching him with concern.

Breathe, he told himself. Pace yourself. Sweat soaked into the collar of his shirt. He heard himself droning on about Hallam the prodigy who wrote credible dramatic poetry at four, Hallam the marvel who translated Dante's "Ugolino" into Greek iambics at fourteen, Hallam the Cambridge wonder boy whose own teachers were dazzled by him . . .

Dizziness, again. Nausea choked off his voice. He stood silently, trying to pull himself together.

As Kevin fought to keep his feet, his eyes swept down across the *New Haven Register* and the front-page headline. And I can stand here and babble on about Hallam with this knowledge in front of me, he marveled in the corner of his mind that was still functioning. The dizziness melted away a bit. He forced himself to continue.

Teetering time and again on the edge of collapse, he somehow managed to fight his way through the fifty minutes. Thoughts about the murder kept swirling around in his mind, destroying what little concentration he could muster. His first stop should be the police station. Lt. Patterson would probably chuck him out on his ear, but it was worth a chance. . . .

By the time he reached the conclusion, Kevin had managed to turn what could have been a debacle into a reasonably competent lecture.

"So what are we to conclude about Hallam?" he asked. As always when there were only five minutes to go, a surge of restlessness swept through the auditorium. They're ready for a break, he thought, and God knows so am I. "Was he a fraud? At Cambridge Hallam tried three times to win the Chancellor's Medal and failed in every attempt. He did not get a degree. His legal studies after 1823 were irregular. The fragments of his verse that have come down to us are far from impressive.

"And yet, who are we to judge across the distance of centuries? Throughout their lives the best of his age looked back on Hallam as the true genius of the nineteenth century. Gladstone and Brookfield, both superb judges of men, never wavered in their great admiration of Hallam. And to Tennyson, the true towering figure of his age, Hallam was enough of a burning presence to inspire *In Memoriam*. Surely the ability to inspire one of the greatest elegies in the English language is an irrefutable proof that Hallam had something special. In our next lecture we will look at *In Memoriam* and see how young Tennyson mourned the early death of his friend and hero."

There was no applause but there were also no boos. As the students began to file out, Kevin remembered. "One last thing," he called. They stopped and turned, puzzled. "This may seem like a strange thing for an English professor to tell you, but I would like to encourage all of you to limit your use of the libraries to the daylight hours." Some students stared at him as if he had gone mad. He guessed they were unaware of the murder. Still, he continued. "And if you must study in the library at night, please bring a friend. *Do not* study alone."

Lieutenant Romano was a hard man who worked in a bare room. His bald head glistened in the light cast by a naked bulb. A single memo sat on his desk top. As Kevin entered, the police lieutenant was studying it with great concentration. His eyes flicked up quickly to glance at the intruder and then returned to the piece of paper in front of him. "My desk clerk tells me you're something of a pain in the ass," he said in a gruff voice.

Kevin waited in vain for him to look up again. Romano took a yellow marker out of a desk drawer and began highlighting the memo as he talked.

"She says you've been waiting to see me for three hours and you won't leave. Won't talk to anyone else. You gotta tell me something about the library murder and it can't wait. Okay, talk."

Kevin hesitated. When it became clear that the lieutenant had no intention of looking up again, he said, "You don't remember me?"

Romano looked up quickly and examined him with care. Kevin stared back at the quick blue eyes imprisoned in the rock-hard, angular face. The lieutenant's high forehead was a cliff that ended in double overhangs above two deep-set eyes. His lips were thin and his teeth were regular and yellowing. A small circular glass ashtray, which sat in the right front corner of his desk, held the remains of three cheap cigars. "I don't remember you," he admitted. "And I'm too busy to play games."

"I came as soon as I heard about the murder," Kevin began. A slight tension creased the skin around Romano's jaw.

Kevin gave up on waiting for an invitation and sat down in the chair directly across from the lieutenant. It was hot in the office and his shirt was sticking to him beneath his tweed jacket. He could smell alcohol on his own breath, and hoped the policeman didn't notice it. "My name is Randall," Kevin said, as if that explained everything.

"I don't mean to be rude, but this has been a hell of a day, Randall, and I'm not known as a patient man to start with." Romano's voice was suddenly so dry that every syllable sounded as starched as his clean white shirt. "I gotta mount an investigation, help Yale out with extra patrols, and dodge everyone from reporters to campus women's groups demanding to know what we are doing to prevent another such killing. I don't have time to waste today."

Kevin took a deep breath. He knew what he had to say next, and it conjured up her memory so quickly, concretely, and painfully that when he finally spoke his voice was frail. "My wife was Anne Randall. I talked mostly with Jack Hobbs during the investigation two years ago—" He stopped and fought his way through the wave of emotion that swelled up and broke over him as he spoke his dead wife's name for the first time in months. "I gather you've inherited Patterson's job. I've come to help."

Romano nodded slowly and dumped the cigar ash from his ashtray into a metal garbage can. "Yeah, I remember you now, Professor Randall," he acknowledged. "Patterson didn't just quit, he had a coronary, and I wouldn't be surprised if you weren't half to blame."

"Patterson was a fool. He was after the wrong man and I wouldn't let it drop."

Lieutenant Romano smiled for the first time, and there was something very menacing about his smile. "Patterson and I were partners for years," he said in a soft voice. "He was no fool. And you had no call to keep after him the way you did. Letters to the mayor, complaints to the city council—he chased down his suspect and the murders stopped."

Kevin suddenly found himself on his feet looking down at the lieutenant and speaking much too loudly. "There was no hard evidence that the man who died in that car chase was the man who killed my wife and the other girl. No proof at all. Not then and not now!" He paused and regained a bit of control. "Look, I don't want to fight. Time has proven me right. Now I just want to help."

"Then sit down."

Kevin sat.

Lieutenant Romano leaned forward. "I'm sorry about what happened to your wife," he said seriously and sincerely. "I remember. And maybe time has proven you right. We don't believe yesterday's murder was connected to the ones two years ago, but it's a possibility we're investigating. You got in here because you said you had some info for me. Let's hear it."

"I want to help," Kevin said lamely.

"You think there's some connection between the killings two years ago and the one yesterday? Tell me, what's the connection?"

"They all occurred in libraries. Young women were the victims. . . ." Kevin's voice trailed off.

"You're wasting my time," Lieutenant Romano told him, standing. He was a much bigger man than Kevin would have guessed. His bald head seemed to almost brush the white ceiling. "This is a police investigation and we can't have amateurs blundering around—"

"You did a great job with the last police investigation," Kevin shot back, jumping to his feet to stare directly into Romano's eyes.

Romano flashed his smile again—his menacing smile. "Get that alcohol off your breath and someone might take you more seriously. You think we chased down the wrong guy two years ago?"

Kevin nodded.

"What? The real killer maybe went away on a two-year vacation—a round-the-world cruise—and he just came back?" The lieutenant's own breath was rank with the odor of cheap cigars.

"I don't pretend to know what the connection is," Kevin admitted. "But I know the old case backward and forward, and I'm here to help."

"Then let us do our job," Romano told him. "Don't interfere, you'll only cause trouble. If you get any bright ideas, talk to Jack Hobbs. I'll tell him I spoke to you."

"You'll damn well do more than that," Kevin found himself shouting, "because we both know there's somebody out there, a crazy maniac, and if you think I'm gonna let another dumb hard-ass cop squander human lives—" He stopped. He felt dizzy and was breathing with difficulty—the morning's hangover spread itself back over him like a net. He swayed and almost fell over.

Romano stepped to his door and opened it. All the warmth and sympathy had vanished from his hard face. "Get out." He bit off each syllable. "And don't you ever, ever swear at me again."

Kevin took two steps toward the doorway, and then turned. "You can reach me at the English Department," he said. "If you have any questions at all about the old murder, please let me—"

"OUT!" Romano's face had clenched like his fists.

A cold midnight drizzle had crawled in from the North Sea, spattering the rooftops so that water trickled down the spouts and ran off at the edges of the garden. Midori clasped her heavy cotton *ukata* tightly around her throat as she peered in through the narrow window at the other young woman. The sleeping girl's head was less than ten feet from the bedroom window, and each time she cried out in her sleep Midori trembled in the outside darkness.

From the east gate came the sound of a faint masculine call and a response from the guard on watch. The voices were followed by the throaty barking of dogs as the sentries changed shifts. Midori knew the guards worked in three eight-hour stints. She pressed her body into the shadows, as she stood at the open window studying the girl she loved. The barking of the guard dogs always frightened her but she knew she was in no real danger—security at Cheltenham was designed solely to keep outsiders from penetrating. The guests, with all their eccentricities and psychoses, had the run of the place.

Midori was from one of the richest families in Japan. Her father, a shipping magnate, had paid millions of yen for her nearly nine-month stay in England at Cheltenham Castle. No one would dare interfere with her noctural adventures.

A barn owl stitched its hunting call into the fabric of blackness. The drizzle quickened. Inside, on the chair beside the desk, Midori saw the silken robe that Jennifer always unbuttoned and slipped out of before she climbed into bed. For a week now Midori had stood at this window and watched the tantalizing ritual. Jennifer's fingers started at the neck and unbuttoned their way down the length of the garment, and then lifted it off so that her lissome figure, suddenly bared, was illuminated by the lamplight behind her and the moonlight filtering in through the window. A few times Midori had feared that Jennifer had seen her in the moonlight, and she held her breath, waiting for the girl to shout for help. On other nights, Midori was just as sure that the darkness totally concealed her from view. Lately she had begun to suspect that Jennifer was aware of her presence, but continued her nightly disrobing anyway, without giving the slightest sign of reaction. This possibility intrigued and excited Midori.

Another sob. It was a quick whimper, and the body on the bed cringed slightly. Midori stepped to the sill. She did not know much about the American girl. Whatever it was that had driven Jennifer into seclusion still tormented her. Her clothes were expensive, her demeanor well bred, and no one at Cheltenham Castle who did know—not the administrators, nor the doctors, nor even the higher staff—would say a word about her. She ate alone, she went out for her long walks alone, she retired alone at an early hour to her room, which was by far the best and most private at Cheltenham, the most costly and exclusive rest home in all England. Beside the fact that Jennifer played the cello beautifully and always slept with a lamp on, Midori had no definite information about the young woman onto whose window ledge she now lightly stepped.

For a torturous week the window had been a barrier. Now Midori was through it in an instant, her small feet barely making a sound as she swung herself into the bedroom and moved across the stone floor to the side of the bed. Jennifer's breathing was shallow and uneven, and as Midori watched, it was clear that another pained sob was welling up. With a quick movement Midori bent to the bed and brushed the chestnut hair back from Jennifer's forehead. Jennifer stirred but did not wake.

Taking the corner of the coverlet, Midori slowly drew it back, inch by inch, uncovering the naked sleeper. Jennifer's throat was laid bare, then the valley and hill of her neck and right shoulder, and finally the creamy mounds of her breasts with their crowns of pink nipple. Midori bent down low over the sleeping girl, letting her shadow explore the soft places that she so longed to touch, hoping even that the lovemaking of her shadow might lift Jennifer from the prison of her bad dreams to a more tranquil place.

Jennifer shifted on the bed, moving as if by instinct away from the shadow. Midori drew the blanket back yet further. She uncovered the gentle stepping-stones of ribs and the arching lift of the right hip. Her eyes traced down the slope of that hip to the flat desert of stomach with its oasislike indentation of navel. Below that navel, the tawny triangle of pubic hair pointed Midori's gaze toward the two long lithe legs that shifted restlessly on the white sheet.

Slowly, carefully, Midori got down on one knee. She moved her face closer and closer to Jennifer's own, until the sleeper's shallow breathing entered her mouth and Midori expelled it back again at Jennifer. Then her lips grazed Jennifer's lips, and the stolen kiss was so pleasant that Midori could not break the contact. Her soft kiss became firm, then inquiring, and almost immediately Midori felt Jennifer's eyelids open and her body stiffen with fear.

Midori stood up, waiting. Jennifer stared up at her in surprise. She opened her mouth as if to cry out, but no sound came. Moving quickly and with a dancer's grace, Midori untied the sash of her *ukata*. In a heartbeat it lay around her ankles and she stood naked, proudly revealing her taut nineteen-year-old body. Without being bidden, she lay down on the bed so that she faced Jennifer.

For a long moment they stared at one another. In the depth of that charged silence, as the two young women eyed each other in the faint lamplight, Midori wished fervently that English had honorific forms the way Japanese does. She longed to choose a way of speaking that would instantly show how respectful she was of Jennifer, and how passionately she admired her. Without such subtleties of politeness and positioning, how could one carry out a dignified seduction? In the end all Midori could do was to drop her gaze and lower her voice to whisper, "You were crying in your sleep. You do it every night but tonight was especially bad."

Jennifer shivered.

"Something happened in America? With a man?"

Jennifer gave a very small nod. Her body was tense, her spine rigid with nervous energy.

"You've never been with another woman before, have you?"

Again the head shook from side to side, and there was a tremulous uncertainty at the edges of her eyes.

"Did you know I was at the window? Watching you?"

"Yes," Jennifer whispered back. "I knew." And then, unexpectedly, she leaned across the space that separated them to kiss Midori lightly on the lips and whisper, "Tonight, please, just hold me."

Midori pulled the quilt up over them and held Jennifer in her arms. Their skin touched down the length of their bodies, and Midori found the contact so delicious that she could not sleep at all. She was awake when Jennifer's breathing leveled off into a troubled sleep. She felt Jennifer shiver and cringe as the horrible dream took hold once again. And all that long night as Jennifer trembled and sobbed, Midori held her and tried to imagine what awful experiences or knowledge could be responsible for such terrible dreams.

Chapter 2

The New Haven drizzle beat a steady tap-tap-tap on Kevin's window as he settled into a chair near his phone. He opened a bottle of Glen Morangie and poured himself a generous drink. Letting the smooth single malt coat his tongue, he savored the rich, strong, nuttiness of the fine scotch. Then he put the glass down and dialed the *New Haven Register*.

"News desk," a woman answered.

"This is Dr. Kevin Randall of Yale University." He gave his voice a rich academic gloss. "I'm calling regarding your article in the paper this morning about the murder in Sterling Library. I would like to speak to the reporter who wrote it—Ron Christopher."

"I'm sorry," she said. "He's out of the office."

"When will he be back?"

"He's working on a story." Her tone was stiff and direct—her job was to protect reporters by screening calls, and apparently she didn't like to be pushed.

"This is very important."

"What is it regarding?"

"It's about the story he's working on. Look, either help me or connect me with your superior. Now!"

She gave in gracelessly. "He sometimes comes in at five o'clock on his way home. You might try then." There was a *click* as she hung up the phone.

Kevin sipped the scotch and glanced out the window. The rain was turning York Street into a glittering black ribbon. Two coeds exited Yorkside Pizza and tried to fit under one large yellow umbrella as they hurried toward the graduate school. The road crew that had been drilling early in the morning had quit for the day. The holes they had dug gaped like open scars in the smooth skin of black roadway.

Kevin flipped through his address book and dialed Jack Hobbs. "Yale Police" came the receptionist's voice.

"I'd like to speak to Sergeant Hobbs."

A minute later Hobbs's deep voice flowed across the line. "Jack Hobbs here."

Kevin knew the reaction would be bad, so he tried to sound as friendly and enthusiastic as possible. "Jack, this is Kevin Randall. The English professor. You remember . . ."

"Yeah," Hobbs said grimly, "I do remember."

"So how are you doing?" The silence was long and hostile. "Your wife well? Sons still ripping up football fields?"

"I know why you're calling so you can cut the shit," Hobbs muttered. "I expected you to call. I was wondering why it took this long."

"I just read about it in this morning's paper," Kevin said. Then, in a low whisper he added, "You know this makes us right."

"No," Hobbs said. "We were wrong. This doesn't change a damn thing."

"You were the only one who understood," Kevin replied. "And whatever you say now, you know we were right."

Hobbs's voice was filled with anger when he responded. "Yeah, I understood. I fought the fight with you. Kicked up a fuss. Kendrick warned me not to make waves, but I knew better. And when he retired last year, they brought in some new guy from the outside to run security. 'Cause I was a troublemaker. I don't want anything more to do with you, Randall."

"But we were right. We are right."

There was no answer for a long time. Then: "Look, Randall, I'm busy setting up extra patrols. What do you want?"

"Dinner tonight," Kevin said. "At the Old Heidelburg. It's on me. Drinks too. I need your help."

"You're not gonna get my help."

"Lieutenant Romano said I should call you."

"He doesn't tell me what to do."

"Please, Jack. We were friends once."

"My mistake," Hobbs said gruffly. "Look, if I let you buy me dinner all it means is that I want a free meal."

"Fine, let's just talk. Meet you at six."

"Seven." There was a loud thud as Sergeant Hobbs slammed down his receiver.

Kevin tilted back the Glen Morangie and emptied the glass. He poured himself another drink and kicked off his shoes. Putting his feet up on the coffee table, he closed his eyes and allowed the wave of memories that had been building up all day to break over him.

"Anne. Anne." As his lips pronounced his wife's name, his thoughts raced back over ten years to the night in England when he had first met her. It had been on St. Agnes' Eve.

Another long pull at the Glen Morangie helped him slip back in time to their first meeting. He saw the courtyard of Christ Church, perhaps the most famous of Oxford's colleges. Tom Tower was all lighted up so that the outlines of the dome and tower twinkled and shimmered high above the yard. The pale grass stirred slightly in the bitter wind.

He was twenty-three years old and considered a brilliant young Rhodes scholar. That night he was making his way through the courtyard with the long, quick strides athletes save for cold and nasty nights. Most of the room lights in the fortresslike structure were off. The wind made a faint ghostly whooshing sound as it wrapped itself around the high ramparts. He had just passed the Fountain of Mercury and was heading out toward Porter's Lodge and the main gate.

The date was January 20, traditionally the coldest night of the year. According to English legend, St. Agnes, the patron saint of virgins, would grant a special boon to virtuous maidens on this night. A maiden who observed the ritual of St. Agnes would see a vision of her first lover-to-be in a dream. Kevin had just finished several glorious weeks of studying Keats and marveling at the young poet's magically prolific year of 1819. Now, crossing the diagonal pathway, he began to recite Keats's poem "The Eve of St. Agnes" aloud to himself. His deep, musical voice half spoke and half sang the lovely first stanza into the cold night air:

> *St. Agnes' Eve—Ah, bitter chill it was!*
> *The owl, for all his feathers, was a-cold*
> *The hare limped trembling through the frozen grass,*
> *And silent was the flock in woolly fold:*
> *Numb were the Beadsman's fingers, while he told*
> *His rosary, and while his frosted breath,*
> *Like pious incense from a censer old,*
> *Seemed taking flight for heaven, without a death,*
> *Past the sweet Virgin's picture, while his prayer he saith.*

He was about to begin the second stanza when he suddenly became aware that he was not alone. Light but steady footsteps sounded ten feet or so behind him. He turned quickly and saw a young woman all bundled up against the wind so that all that he could tell was that she was of a pleasing shape and size. He turned away, slightly embarrassed to have been caught reciting Keats to himself.

Then her gentle voice picked up the next stanza of the poem and tossed it back at him like a playful love offering. He slowed as she recited and savored each sweet syllable. Clearly she loved the music in Keats's poetry, and her fine voice became an instrument thrumming the sweet words out on the cold night air. She stayed a small distance behind him and the space between them lent their poetic flirtation a tinge of mystery. Though he longed to stop and turn, he savored knowing her only through the poem.

Kevin took the third stanza and she took the fourth. Her recitation was perfect and sure—she knew the long poem as well as he

did. And as they walked and took turns reciting, the cold wind blew
up around them. They had the whole length of the yard to themselves. High above the glittering tower and dome, the full moon cut
a yellow circlet through the thick winter clouds.

When she came to the wonderful sixth stanza she hesitated a
beat, as if a thought had suddenly entered her mind and broken the
spell. Then she recovered and recited it. He heard a playful laughter
in her voice as she told of virgins and their visions:

> They told her how, upon St. Agnes' Eve,
> Young virgins might have visions of delight,
> And soft adorings from their loves receive
> Upon the honeyed middle of the night,
> If ceremonies due they did aright;
> As, supperless to bed they must retire,
> And couch supine their beauties, lilly white;
> Nor look behind, nor sideways, but require
> Of Heaven with upward eyes for all that they desire.

Then she broke off suddenly and, moving quickly, caught up with
him. He stopped and they faced each other. "I'm sorry," she said, "I
won't be able to finish. I have to run off."

Sitting in New Haven on a rainy day with the taste of scotch in
his mouth and ten long years between now and that night, Kevin
could still remember the pure pleasure he had felt at the way she
spoke. She managed the rare trick of using a very aristocratic English accent without sounding cold or stuffy. On the contrary, her
voice bubbled like champagne.

"I'm Kevin Malloy Randall."

She hesitated several beats. "Anne Barrington-Mayfield."

They were now close enough so that Kevin could see her face
in the moonlight. She had brilliantly luminous blue eyes that sparkled over a small and perfect nose. Her full lips turned up slightly in
cautious playfulness. The moonlight revealed an aristocratic poise
and rather stiff decorum, though her smile was warm and friendly.

She had long black hair that seemed somehow darker than the midnight.

"Are you rushing away to meet a man?" Kevin asked her.

She nodded, her smile betraying nothing.

"Anne," Kevin said then, "life is long, but the chances of me meeting another girl while reciting 'The Eve of St. Agnes' in the Christ's Church Yard are very small. Such things don't happen twice in one lifetime. Forget the other guy, whoever he is. Let's go somewhere together."

"You Americans." She laughed, delighted. "Always in such a hurry to be in love, or feel angry, or grow jealous." Then her face and voice softened. "Have no fear—you have no rival. The man I'm meeting tonight is my father. Now I must go."

She took a step away before he stopped her with his question. "How will I find you again?"

"You won't," she said. "I'll find you." And then she turned and hurried away. Kevin watched her, and even though he was standing face into the wind he suddenly felt warmed by an inner glow. The warmth started in his chest and in his head, and quickly spread out so that all of his extremities were tingling. "Good-bye," he called after her, but his words were battered by the angry wind. "Good-bye, Anne." She disappeared through the gate without a backward look.

There had followed a week of intense investigation with very little result. As a scholar he was an eager and diligent researcher, and he had had no trouble finding out who she was. She had left out a few names and titles, but he soon identified her as the daughter of Lord Barrington-Mayfield. Some English friends who occasionally mixed in royal circles informed him that she was a famous beauty, and that her father, a very rich and powerful man, kept a close watch on her. There the information stopped. Kevin could not find out her phone number, or where she lived, or even what she was studying at Oxford. She seemed to be in a special category where all personal information about her and her whereabouts at Oxford was regarded by the university as an important secret. After a week, Kevin had expended a great deal of energy and found out almost nothing.

Then one evening, she appeared at his door. He had been studying late, reading the essay on Keats in Swinburne's *Miscellanies*. A low fire burned on the hearth. The knock sounded firmly three times, and he hurried to open the door and there she was.

Silently he stepped aside as she entered. She walked close to the fireplace and the flames dancing between the coals sent red and white demons chasing each other across her cheeks and forehead. He waited. She warmed herself for a few seconds, then looked up at him. He had not glimpsed her full beauty the night he had met her in the yard, but he saw it now and it awed him so that he could barely return her gaze.

"I tried to stay away," she said. "I've been taught not to go to men's rooms alone."

"I couldn't find you," he told her. "Lord Barrington-Mayfield keeps you well hidden." Then: "Why did you come tonight?"

She walked a step closer to face him. She took off her coat and folded it neatly. Under it she was wearing a long scarlet dress that brought out all the soft curves of her young figure. She looked him right in the eye. "I dreamed about you the night we met," she said. "I dreamed that you were there, in my bedroom, with me." She spoke quickly and managed not to blush.

"And you know what that means?" he asked her. "To dream about a man on St. Agnes' Eve?"

This time she reddened a little bit but she still answered in a smooth, steady voice. "I know."

"How was the dream?" he whispered.

She looked down at the firelight and then back at him, and this time her whole face blushed red. "It was the best dream of my life," she said. Then she went to him and he took her in his arms and held her while the wind blasted at the tower and the fire sizzled and died in the grate. When the first rays of the sun crawled through his high bedroom window to stroke her sleeping face, he looked at her and knew his search was over. They had found each other and they would never more be apart.

Kevin slammed his empty glass down on the table, then picked it up and slammed it down again so hard that it cracked. He sat in silence for several seconds, fighting the urge to kill himself. He had felt it before, dozens of times. The cold New Haven drizzle slanting down against his windowpane gave a rhythm to his desperation. It would be so easy to just end the pain once and for all.

In the mornings, with the sunrise, he missed her eyes opening next to him. In the evenings, it was impossible to walk the streets in the long twilight and think that such beauty and blissful quiet could envelop the world without her being at his side to share it with him. He drank at night, when the loneliness became a small animal burrowing furiously into the most closely guarded storerooms of his memory with razor-sharp teeth. But beneath everything else and at all moments of the day and night, he felt her absence as an aching of his soul, as deep and steady as his own heartbeat.

He still had the antique dueling pistols her father had given him. In three minutes he could be with her in death. The awful torment of the two years he had spent alone recurred to him all at once in a montage of things he could no longer find any joy in. Keats was gone for him. Oxford, and indeed all England, was painful for him to even think about. Most of Mozart was torture to listen to. He couldn't bear to drink champagne or wine, and had to get by on scotch and beer. Crowds of couples at parties or theaters drove him to despair. Even his first love, the saber, was lost to him—he hadn't fenced once since Anne's death.

He took out the pistols recalling the day Lord Barrington-Mayfield had presented them to him. They had spent the day fox hunting, and Anne's father, impressed by Kevin's horsemanship and feel for the hunt, had given him them almost as a reward.

Kevin loaded one of the pistols and held it in his hand. The polished oak pistol stock felt wonderfully smooth in his palm and gleamed as he turned it beneath the light. As he moved his wrist, he glimpsed his wristwatch and saw that it was five o'clock.

Five o'clock. Kevin stood still for a few long minutes, then returned the pistol to its case. His heart, which had been pounding wildly with suicidal thoughts, began to beat more normally.

It was time to call Ron Christopher at the newspaper. The trail that he was about to follow—beginning with the reporter and Jack

Hobbs—might lead him to the focus of all his rage. Someday he might be revenged.

Kevin picked up the receiver, dialed the *Register,* and asked to speak to Christopher. When Kevin promised to shed some light on the case, the reporter agreed to stop by on his way home from work. Kevin poured himself one last drink and put the bottle in the cabinet below the bookshelves.

Chapter 3

Ron Christopher turned out to be a slightly built man in his early thirties with very short sandy blond hair and a nervous habit of checking his watch every few minutes. When Kevin offered him a beer he explained that he was a Mormon and didn't touch alcohol, but that he would love some juice.

Kevin got him a glass of apple juice, threw a longing look at the six-pack of Pilsner Urquell on the top shelf of his refrigerator, and poured a second glass of juice for himself. When he returned with the drinks, he found the reporter settled into an armchair, reviewing some notes in a small black notebook.

"Thanks," he said, accepting the juice. He took one sip and then put the glass down carefully on a corner of Kevin's coffee table. "Now, Professor Randall," he began in a tone that was friendly but brusque, "you have some information for me on last night's homicide?"

"I have some information for you on several murders," Kevin told him.

"The police are investigating only one."

"Maybe, but they should be investigating three. The one last night and two that happened two years ago. I can tell you anything you want to know about the old murders. And what I'd like in return is some facts about the new one." Kevin met the reporter's eyes and held his gaze. "Your article lacked hard details. I need to know how the girl died, exactly where and what time the killing occurred, and what direction the police investigation is taking."

Ron Christopher's thin face twisted in puzzlement, his nose wrinkled upward, and his lips pursed together. He looked like a confused ferret happening upon an unexpected smell. "I'm familiar with those two other murders," he said finally. "But I wasn't with the paper then. It was a long time ago . . ."

"Only two years."

"I've read the file. The police found the killer. And the murders stopped."

"The police identified a suspect who died in a car chase," Kevin blurted out, raising his voice. His sudden anger made the reporter wary—Ron Christopher's eyes flicked momentarily to the nearest door. Kevin lowered his voice. "The investigation two years ago was garbage. Lieutenant Patterson was convinced from the start that such a brutal killer had to come from outside the Yale community."

"Yale students and teachers don't seem likely types to go around strangling people, breaking their backs, and ripping their limbs from their sockets," Christopher pointed out in a reasonable voice. "One doesn't tend to associate brutal homicides with the intellectual elite."

Kevin was rocked by the sudden, graphic reference to the brutality of the killings. He had a momentary vision of Anne's body when he had gone down to the morgue to identify her; her snapped neck, her lacerated back, her right arm dangling from its socket . . . With a tremendous effort he willed the memory away. "Why should we assume that a Yalie isn't capable of murderous brutality?" he asked in a weak voice. "That was Patterson's first mistake."

"You seem obsessed by the old case."

Kevin held the edge of the coffee table for support as he whispered, "My wife was one of the victims."

A great change came over Ron Christopher as he digested this piece of information. His manner, which up to now had been abrupt, detached, and coolly professional, softened. "I'm sorry, I didn't know," he said. "I understand why you were so involved in the investigation two years ago."

Kevin nodded.

"I can see how such a thing could become an obsession."

"I'm not crazy."

The reporter sipped his apple juice and studied Kevin carefully. "I didn't say you were."

"The second mistake Patterson made was in calling off the investigation when his prime suspect died." Kevin plunged in again. "Sure, there was a bit of circumstantial evidence, but that's all there was. And now that second mistake has come back to haunt us, because whoever it was that killed Anne is killing again!"

Christopher put his empty juice glass down carefully, so that it barely made a sound. His notebook was open on his lap. "And do you have any ideas—any theories—that might relate the murders two years ago to the one yesterday?"

Kevin wished to God he had something to offer. "I don't have enough information yet. That's why I need to know how and when the girl died. I know the police always hold back information, and Yale is probably pressuring your paper to downplay the whole affair, but any details you have would help me. . . ."

Christopher exhaled, raised his eyebrows slightly, and then stood up. "I sort of resent you implying that I'm holding back information from my readers," he said with quiet dignity. "I've come here and heard you out politely, and frankly you haven't told me anything new. I've got at least fifteen other leads on this story to track down, and the general panic on campus is a story in itself, so I'll be going now."

Kevin followed him to the door. "I didn't mean to insult you. . . ."

The reporter turned back to face him and held out a business card. "Call me if you find out something. Maybe we'll be able to help each other more in the future."

Kevin took the card and nodded.

"I'm sorry for your troubles, Professor Randall," Ron Christopher said in parting. "I don't know if you're familiar with the Church of Latter Day Saints, but I know people who could help you."

"Thanks," Kevin told him. "I'll keep it in mind."

Christopher turned, scurried to the stairs, and descended in quick, mouselike steps.

Kevin put on his frayed Burberry trench coat and headed for the Old Heidelburg. He had lived in New Haven long enough to understand the significance of the gloomy gray rain clouds—the cold drizzle that had been falling all day was a harbinger of the long, bleak winter. As he walked out the main gate of Trumbull College into the chill mist, a shiver slithered down his spine and he pulled his collar tight around his neck.

Damn the New Haven weather. He turned onto York Street and glanced toward Saybrook College and the seam-faced granite and limestone façade of Davenport College. York Street was oddly empty. The cold and the wet striking together for the first time had cleared the usually busy thoroughfare.

A lone young man staggering under the weight of a knapsack made his way toward Sterling Library. Kevin felt for him—at Yale the academic pressure and the miserable winter weather settle over the university together.

The trees were already stripped skeletons, and the grass had lost all the healthy greenness of summer and lay pale and heavy with fallen rain. Room lights dotted the dark walls of Jonathan Edwards College as undergrads sat at their desks trying desperately to catch up with their reading assignments. Kevin reached the stark art and architecture building, a corrugated concrete colossus thrusting up seven stories into the murk.

He stood for a second at the corner of York and Chapel, looking back at the long and empty street that seemed permeated with gloom and foreboding. A glance at his watch told him he was five minutes early for his meeting with Hobbs. He was struck by the change that had transformed the campus in little more than a month. Walking down this same street in September, the grass had gleamed emerald green and there was still a sweet touch of summer honey in the air. Incoming freshmen and their proud families had formed a huge, engaging stampede as they laughed and lugged suitcases and stereos up newly swept slate steps and through arches and gates and narrow stairways. In every college courtyard Frisbees circled through the air while soccer balls bounced off two-hundred-year-old walls.

The change had been in the air for about a week. Kevin had felt it. Every year it was the same—every year, one night in early October the ivy, which seems all summer to be basking and sunning itself on the stone walls of Bingham and Davenport, suddenly clings to those stones for dear life. A bitter wind blows down from East Rock, lashing the old trees. And then the darkness takes hold.

Kevin was sure no campus in America was as gloomy, as fortresslike, as shadowed, and as haunted as the Yale campus. He drew the collar of his trench coat tighter around his neck, denying the cruel wind and dampness the slightest opening. Looking back down York Street, Kevin shivered again at the murk and the old buildings that seemed somehow to be brimming with evil. The Gothic towers, the crenelated escarpments poking their massive shadows out of long-dead and forgotten generations, the trees bent over as if bearing heavy weights, and the never-ending drizzle whose continuous hiss seemed to spawn echoes and flickering shadows, all combined to give the October night a dank, dark power.

October. Kevin knew why the lights in Saybrook and Davenport Colleges burned so late. On these first bitter nights of winter, the canker worm of a thought that he may not be able to pass no matter how hard he studies first occurs to a freshman. Late at night, his eyes aching, the fear of failing rises up in his body like the juices of nausea. He looks down at his incomprehensible books. His eyes flick to his watch. Outside his window, darkness, dampness.

And it is in October when those first happy romances of September are split by the academic pressure: the pretty girl from a happy home who had lived a perfect life, the daughter of a mayor or a doctor, who came to Yale and was swept off her feet by a poised upperclassman to whom she yielded up her carefully preserved virginity like an admission ticket. Now, suddenly, she is alone. She feels used and lonely, and behind in her studies. She comes down with a cold, the winds strip her of her voice. She lies in bed peering out her window at the shadowy darkness.

These students staggered into Kevin's classes every October, fearful, pale, and pained like suffering phantoms. He knew there was no remedy for them except a long Christmas spent at home—if they survived that long.

The bells of Harkness Tower sounded the hour. Seven o'clock, Hobbs would already be there. Kevin turned toward the stores and shops of Chapel Street. The echoing gongs of the bell pursued him as he hurried toward the Old Heidelburg—they seemed to fit the dreary chill of the evening, and in their long metallic cries he heard a prophecy that whatever evil was loose on the campus would strike again and again until it was uncovered and destroyed.

Kevin found Jack Hobbs in the restaurant's main dining room, already half finished with a huge stein of beer. After Ron Christopher, Jack Hobbs's heartiness was a pleasure to encounter. He was big, bluff, and burly, with a thick head of flaxen hair and slow, bull-like black eyes that made him look stubborn and even slightly dumb. Foam from his beer coated his untrimmed mustache like shaving cream lather. Kevin held out his hand. Hobbs hesitated and then shook it with a grip that was painfully tight. The Yale police sergeant sometimes amused his friends at parties by crushing walnuts in the palms of his hands.

Kevin studied Hobbs. "Hello, Jack. . . . Been a long time."

"Nearly two years," Hobbs muttered and took a long drink. "Frankly, not long enough to suit me." His gaze flicked up from his drink to Kevin. "You look like shit. What'd you put on—twenty?"

"Twenty-five," Kevin acknowledged, breathing hard after the short walk. "I've tried to hold it together. . . ."

"You've aged ten years in the last two."

"I've been through a rough time."

"Yeah, well, I wish I could feel more sympathetic," Hobbs said, and drained his beer.

There followed nearly a full minute of silence. Hobbs wasn't a talker, and Kevin was content to use the silence to ease into a reconciliation with this unpredictable man.

A pretty waitress with curly blond hair walked over and asked if they were ready to order. She looked at Hobbs with interest, but he did not respond and her smile soon faded. Hobbs ordered the biggest steak on the menu, a green salad, a side order of onion rings, and another Budweiser. "And make the steak so rare it's still flopping around on the plate when you bring it."

Kevin ordered a steak too, a salad, and a large mug of Becks. The waitress brought the beers almost immediately, and then hurried away to the next table. The walls of the Old Heidelberg were covered with Yale memorabilia: oars from long-forgotten races against Harvard and Princeton were crossed above pictures of Yale athletic heroes of the past several decades. This old beer hall was the poor man's Mory's—supposedly Nathan Hale had carved his initials into one of the tables.

"I should have hung up on you today," Jack Hobbs muttered. "Lucy wouldn't have liked it, but I should have hung up."

Kevin's memory conjured up a picture of a large and striking woman with a head of long, bright-red hair and a fiery temper. "How is Lucy?"

"She's taken a part-time job that she hates," Hobbs said. "Otherwise she's fine. The boys eat like horses."

"Four, isn't it?"

"Yup." The pride glowed in Hobbs's eyes. "Danny, Eric, Tim, and Scott. Danny just won a football scholarship to Eastern Connecticut, and I think the other three will be even better. Scott may make pro someday." He stopped and looked at Kevin, "That is, if they don't starve at their own dinner table."

His bitterness lay between them for a while, as tangible as the two place settings on the table. "Tell me, Jack," Kevin asked finally, "what is this injury that you think I've done to you?"

Hobbs answered quickly and angrily. "I'm not a professor," he snapped, "I don't give lectures, I don't write books. I'm a cop."

"A good one," Kevin interjected.

"Shut up and listen. Not even a cop. Just a better than average campus security officer. I handle complaints. I set patrols. I break up parties. I train new guys. And all I ever wanted was to sit in the big office and run things myself. And I would've had that job if you hadn't come along with your theories and your petitions asking me to call so and so and help you complain about such and such. So I became the troublemaker and somebody else got the job, and now I'm still pulling home just about the same lousy paycheck I was five years ago."

The salads arrived, and Hobbs attacked his savagely. The dinner crowd was large and enthusiastic—casually dressed students, professors, and businesspeople in suits filled the restaurant's two large dining rooms and created a constant buzz of conversation. The waitresses, all plump and vaguely Teutonic, bustled about distributing beer and food at high speed.

"But we were right," Kevin said.

"Maybe you were right. But I was wrong, and I've damn well paid for it."

When the waitress came back to take their salad plates, Kevin ordered another round of beers. The tip of Hobbs's nose was already starting to glow faintly red. While Hobbs continued to avoid a conversation, Kevin could feel the big man's anger slowly melt into displeasure and then reshape itself into reluctant camaraderie as they drank. Jack Hobbs was not the sort of man who could remain angry when another man was paying for his drinks.

The steaks arrived. They were large and rare and Hobbs ripped into his like a hungry jaguar. He polished off half his steak and more than two-thirds of his heaping portion of onion rings before he looked up at Kevin with a resigned smile. "Well, you're buying me a damn fine meal, anyway."

"Good stuff," Kevin agreed.

"And I needed a drink."

Kevin raised his own mug.

"So what is it, Kevin?" Having reached this point and called Kevin by his first name, Hobbs put down his fork and stared across the table with a mixture of amusement, wariness, and curiosity. "You know I can't fight the battle with you again."

"I'm not asking you to."

"Maybe we were right and Patterson did go after the wrong man. I'm not saying that's true, but maybe it is. The point is that all that was in the past. Whatever we thought then has no pull on me now. Think of me as a different man if it'll help."

Kevin looked at him for a long time. There was raw power in the cop's bulky arms and the knotted cords of muscles that ran down his stomach just beneath a small layer of fat. Kevin glimpsed the keen quickness that sparked around the edges of Hobbs's black eyes. "You look like the same man to me, Jack," he said.

Hobbs's fists clenched. "Maybe you've got no one else to think of. I've got a family to take care of. I'm not dumb enough to make the same mistake twice."

"Even to protect people?"

Hobbs's fists slammed down on the table. "So that's my job? To save the world? I should sacrifice myself again? And for what?—for some half-baked theory that even two years ago seemed a little bit absurd." He took a few breaths and calmed down. "No, let Lieutenant Romano handle this. He's good, Kevin—a hell of a lot sharper than Patterson. Take my word for it."

"I don't have to," Kevin said. "I know what Romano is like. I went to see him today. He told me I should work with you—"

"Bullshit. He threw you out of his office, is what he did," Hobbs interrupted. "I called Romano. He said you started shouting at him and he booted you the hell out. Look, I really have to be going. Lucy's probably already getting worried."

Kevin grabbed the big man's hand and held Hobbs down in a sitting position. "Jack, I want only one favor. That's all I'm asking."

Hobbs didn't say anything, but he transferred his weight back to his chair and Kevin let go of his hand. Hobbs mopped his face with a red cloth napkin.

"When I talked to Romano he said something that made me

think. He asked me if I thought the killer might have taken a two-year vacation. He was making fun of me. But suppose for a second he was actually close to the truth."

Hobbs's face betrayed no emotion. His eyes, however, were alive with thought.

"Suppose our original assumption two years ago was correct. These murders were all committed in libraries. The Yale libraries require IDs to get into the stacks, and everyone who enters and leaves is looked at closely. A crazed townie murderer would have a hard time getting in. And why choose a library? The dorms are much easier to break into, and the students are more vulnerable there. There are other spots on campus where the students are isolated. Why would a killer from outside the university choose the single place where traffic in and out is closely controlled, observed, and even searched for books? Besides, I think there's something about a university library that scares off ordinary people. It's an unknown place—an off-limits place—and the last place your average murderer would want to wander around in." Kevin broke off to look at Hobbs, who was waiting for more. "Those were our thoughts two years ago, and it seems to me they still hold up pretty well."

The waitress came with the check, and Kevin handed her a credit card.

"Now let's say we were right," Kevin continued without breaking stride. "Let's say there's a crazy member of the Yale community out there who has access to the libraries and knows the campus backward and forward. Then the most logical explanation for the murders stopping two years ago and the fact that they've started up again is that the killer has been away and has just returned."

"Away where?" Hobbs asked. He looked curious despite himself.

Kevin shook his head. "I don't know where. It depends on the person. Professors get sabbaticals and take time off for research. Grad students take years off to finish dissertations. Undergrads who flunk out are readmitted after a certain time away. And who knows . . . it might be an administrator or a janitor."

"Patterson was right, it's a wacky theory," Hobbs said after a minute's thought. "The demands on professors and students and administrators are just too great for one of them to be a homicidal lunatic and continue functioning. Tell me honestly, do you really believe a Yale professor could go nuts and not be noticed?"

Kevin whispered his answer. "Jack, I'm a Yale professor. And there've been times during the past two years when I've almost lost control."

"There are probably dozens of students and teachers who've been away for two years and returned," Hobbs objected again.

"But not violent ones," Kevin countered. "Or ones with a past history of getting into trouble. I bet there are just a few of those."

Hobbs looked as if he would object further, but then he choked back his words. "So what are you asking me to do?"

Kevin leaned across the table, his voice quick with urgency. "I know the university police force has access to the registrar's records and the New Haven Police Department's computer files. Run through it for me, Jack. Find out who's been away for two years and now come back, or at least tried to come back. Check on which of those people have any kind of police records."

Hobbs was shaking his head before Kevin even finished. "You're asking me to aid a private investigation with Yale police files? Those records are private. If you kicked up some kind of fuss again and they traced this stuff back to me, it'll be my neck on the block."

"I won't kick up a fuss. I'll work quietly," Kevin promised. "If you don't do it, we'll both go crazy wondering. You'll end up pulling the information anyway, just to see for yourself. I know the kind of man you are."

"Maybe, but you don't know how much trouble you've already caused me. No."

"I almost killed myself today," Kevin confessed then, surprising himself. "I had a pistol in my ear and my hand was on the trigger. I could have ended it in less than a second."

Hobbs's face drew taut in worry. "You should be seeing a shrink. Jesus, Randall, I know what you've gone through. I can see it in your face and in what's happened to your pride in the last two years. I feel for you—I really do. Talk to a doctor."

"I've talked to the best doctors. They didn't help. Jack, imagine if it had been your Lucy. And your sons too—Anne and I always meant to have children, but that dream died with her."

The waitress came back with the card and the charge form. Kevin signed it, leaving her a generous tip. She picked up on his tension, thanked him, and ducked away quickly.

"Listen," Hobbs said, "I have a relative—no, Kevin, listen. She's Lucy's cousin, a real sweetheart. And she's kind of artsy so I think the two of you might hit it off. You know, she's always bugging Lucy and me to come with her to plays or to the ballet or God knows what. Whaddya say? She teaches junior high school. Her apartment's full of books." Hobbs saw the anguish in Kevin's face and misread it as hesitancy, so he took a different tack. "Listen, she's a looker too. Terrific figure, great breasts. And not to divulge family secrets or anything, but the women of that family are hot-blooded. C'mon, whaddya say, I'll fix you up."

"I'm not looking," Kevin whispered. "But thanks all the same. There's only one thing you can do for me, Jack."

Hobbs stood up and pulled on his coat. Kevin followed him out the door. Chapel Street was awash with puddles as a hard, driving rain beat down with increasing fury. "C'mon, I'll give you a ride," Hobbs offered, and they were soon in his big Chevy.

Hobbs didn't head directly for Trumbull College. He followed Chapel to Howe and then turned right toward Broadway. The usually pulsing corner of Chapel and Howe was completely empty—the rain had swept the sidewalks clean of pedestrians.

"You really almost killed yourself today?" Hobbs finally asked.

"It wasn't the first time."

"If I got you that list of names, it might come back to haunt me later on. There are a lot of people on the New Haven force who were friends of Patterson and don't like you much."

"I'll never tell anyone. If I say I won't, you know I won't."

"Yeah," Hobbs said, stopping at a red light, "I guess I do." When they reached Trumbull College, Hobbs pulled up at the correct gate, and Kevin couldn't help being impressed that Hobbs remembered exactly where he lived after two years.

"Listen," Hobbs said, "I'd like to help you but I can't. It just doesn't feel right—I have to think about myself. I'm sorry."

As Kevin opened the car door, the cold rain was gushing off the curb and slicking down the pavement. He closed the door again, unwilling to accept defeat but unsure how to continue the dialog. Hobbs looked over at him and the only sound was the *swish-swish* of the windshield wipers. "Don't say no," Kevin requested. "That's all I'll ask you. Just let it sit for a while."

"Let me help you another way," Hobbs said. "Meet Lucy's cousin. You'll like her."

"I couldn't like her. No matter how great she is."

"Don't shoot yourself," Hobbs said unexpectedly. "I wouldn't want to think of you as having taken the coward's way out."

"I hope we can both come through for each other," Kevin replied, and then he left the car and hurried toward the shadowy iron portcullis that closed off Trumbull Gate from the dangers of the New Haven night.

Rainwater all around, flowing through pipes, trickling through cracks, frightening the vermin that scurry for their lives . . . roaches . . . silverfish . . . rats that hiss like snakes and snakes that dig like rats . . .

Her footsteps, faintly . . .

Feeling the demon come on and whirling away through darkness, her steps descending through time, her face, her yellow eyes turning to blood red, and all the pain she had caused and would cause, surely there must be a way to escape, to end the chase, to stop the footsteps that were starting to get loud again, starting to swell till they filled all space and time, as she came on and on . . .

How can the darkness move? asked the voice.

No time for questions or answers. Hush. It's just the creatures that crawl on the edge of darkness and feast on corpses. The maggots of time.

No, it's more than that.

Darkness can move from night to night, jumping over day. Or from death to death, stepping over life and crushing it.

I can hear her.

I'll quiet it.

Chapter 4

Kevin woke up and, bleary with sleep, reached for the bottle that always stood on his night table. His hand swept through the air but came up empty. The morning sunlight filtered through the curtains of his bedroom with enough force so that when he opened his eyes, he had to squint in order to see. The roar of the jackhammer vibrated in from the street and, with the sudden shock of the loud sound, Kevin remembered. His head dropped back into the cool pillow seeking relief, but the queasy feeling soon sprouted into a light-headed nervousness that made lying down unbearable. He sat up in bed and took several long, deep breaths. The previous night he had gone to bed sober for the first time in months, and he knew that what he was feeling would get worse before it got better.

He got out of bed, threw on an old robe, and moved slowly to the kitchen. The jackhammer seemed to get louder. A bottle of Glenlivet sat in the cabinet above the stove, and it was only with the greatest effort that he turned his body toward the refrigerator and took out the quart of orange juice he had purchased the previous evening. He poured himself a tall glass, amazed at how his hands shook. At the first taste of the juice his throat tightened in protest. It took him five minutes of tiny sips to finish the glass, and he wondered if he was drinking slowly out of sickness and distaste, or to put off what was about to happen.

After fifteen minutes of rooting around in the cavernous bedroom closet, Kevin found a jockstrap and a pair of sweatpants. The first sweatshirt he picked up had the crossed swords over an American flag emblem from a United States Fencing Championship of years past. Remembering, he held it up for a second and the white fabric rippled as his hands trembled. Kevin put the shirt aside, disgusted with his present self, and chose instead a plain gray sweatshirt with holes in both elbows.

He stretched for a full half hour. In his glory days his body had been remarkably limber, and he noticed with a mixture of dismay and interest that he could not even touch his toes. His calves and thighs had absolutely no give to them, and even his arms were stiff as he pivoted his torso from side to side. When he rolled his head around to loosen his neck, he became so dizzy that he had to sit down with his head between his knees and wait for the room to stop spinning.

A few students stared at him as he ambled through the Trumbull College courtyard toward the street. Not so many years ago he was generally acknowledged to be one of the finest all-around athletes at Yale, and now they stared at his jerky half walk, half run with amused smiles.

He began to jog west on Chapel Street, trying to find old rhythms, to force his arms and legs into remembered patterns. When he had trained for the Pan-American games he had run fifteen miles a day. His loping strides had eaten up hills with the same appetite as long flat stretches. Today, for the first couple of blocks, Kevin felt pretty good. His arms swung high, pulling his knees up and down in a steady rhythm. He tried to breathe through his nose and to forget about the running and lose himself in the cold clear New Haven morning. The sky overhead was a whitish gray and seemed to sag down, as if pregnant with rain.

After about three blocks he suddenly had to slow. The cramp hit his left side first, but within seconds another cramp was tying a knot into his right side. Less than three blocks! Disgusted with himself, he forced his legs to keep moving, even though his pace had slowed to little more than a fast walk. Then his right Achilles' tendon began to throb. He was breathing through his mouth now, sucking in a gasping breath with every pained stride.

The nausea overcame him just as he passed St. Raphael's Hospital. As he crouched in the gutter vomiting toward a sewer drain, a kind woman with white hair—perhaps she was a nurse—stepped close and asked if he needed medical help. He looked up and shook his head, and then a fresh wave washed over him, and he could feel the sickly sweetness of the orange juice as it slid up his throat and back through his nostrils.

He ended by walking. He tried to walk quickly, but every quarter mile or so he had to sit down on a bench or lean against a tree and rest. When he reached the Yale Bowl and the emerald flats of the Yale athletic fields, he sat with his back to a grassy rise and watched the women's soccer team practice. They were sturdy-looking girls with muscular legs who shouted to each other as they plowed through the winter grass, and with each second that Kevin watched them he felt his legs tighten up.

The girls brought back a memory. When he had first come to teach at Yale, he and Anne had played on Trumbull's coed intramural soccer team. Anne had loved soccer, or football as she called it, and she had been absolutely appalled at the rough and unskilled American version of the game. They had put her at right wing and him at right inside. Watching the girls' varsity push and shove each other on this bleak practice field now, Kevin could still remember her style. Anne had moved around the field in long, graceful strides—whatever she had done, she had always done it with more grace than seemed humanly possible—and while she shied away from the awkward collisions that are so much a part of American soccer, she had won the team over with her courageous runs and short, accurate passes. Trumbull had coasted to the championship that year, and he remembered the party in their apartment: Anne pouring cider for the student athletes and kidding everyone with her gentle humor that at times was playful whimsy and at times delightfully soft and clever sarcasm. At one point during that party Kevin had looked over at her as she sat trading good-natured barbs with two freshmen, and the thought came to him that she would make a wonderful mother and that they should start a family fairly soon.

The soccer ball rolled near him, but when Kevin got up to retrieve it, he found he could not run, and had to walk after the ball in painful, jerky steps. He tried to kick it back to a girl who was waiting at the edge of the field, but the ball squirted clumsily off the side of his foot. As she ran after it, the girl threw him an impatient look that was part pity and part pure disgust.

The walk back into town was long and agonizing. He broke it up with many short rests, but by the time he limped up the stairs of his Trumbull entryway every joint in his body ached. Once inside he moved instinctively toward the liquor cabinet where a half-finished bottle of Glen Morangie sat waiting to ease his pains, but with a final act of will he went to the kitchen and set a kettle on to boil for a cup of tea.

He drew a bath so hot that when he slid his aching body beneath the water his skin turned bright red. It felt scalding when he moved about, but when he lay still with the waterline up around the top of his shoulders and sipped his Darjeeling tea with milk, a pleasant, dreamy feeling enveloped the outside of his body. The tea warmed his stomach, and soon the outside warmth seemed to merge with the inside warmth, and Kevin leaned his head back against the rim of the tub, closed his eyes, and for the first time all day managed to relax.

The relaxed glow stayed with him after his bath, as he limped to the front door to fetch the mail that had just been deposited through the slot. At the sight of the top letter his rehabilitation suffered a serious setback. Staring down at the envelope with the English Department letterhead and the chairman's initials, he sighed. He ripped it open and read the brief note. By the time he had finished it, he was standing at the liquor cabinet with a glass of scotch in his right hand. Even in his best years, Kevin had hesitated to face Charles W. Lansbury without a drink or two beforehand. And in those days, the news had always been good. Staring down at the note that was really a summons, Kevin felt a certainty that this time the news was likely to be bad, and even a large swallow of Glen Morangie could not quiet his fears.

Charles Whitney Lansbury did not make a move or utter a sound as Kevin entered his office and limped painfully toward the empty chair. He merely watched. Kevin eased himself into the wooden armchair and looked across the large desk at the famous professor. Lansbury was dressed formally as ever, in a dark three-piece pinstripe suit and vest. His shiny blue eyes did not betray anything, but they seemed to notice everything. Without warning he leaned forward and extended his right hand. Because Kevin's body was stiff from his morning's exercise, he moved awkwardly when he grasped the chairman's palm.

"Are you ill?" Lansbury asked.

"No, just sore," Kevin replied.

Lansbury allowed a long interval of silence. Kevin felt his probing glance and returned it with a careful scrutiny of his own. Lansbury was large and ungainly, yet there was something so formal and correct about the man that he always seemed perfectly suited to his environment. He had a complex and fascinating face full of crags and valleys—a face as inscrutable, distant, and variegated as the lunar surface. The thinning, longish white hair was untrained and uncombed; it fell where it wanted like a vine on a particularly fertile hill. The nose slid down to a sharp point. The eyes were brilliant blue baubles, glowing in their own wet, wise world.

"I suppose you know why I asked you to come," Lansbury said. It was a statement rather than a question.

The thing Kevin found most unnerving was that, despite their great differences, he knew Professor Lansbury liked him. He felt it even now. They were as different as two men and two scholars could be. Kevin had made his reputation on the basis of three short, highly controversial books of criticism. His brilliance, while widely acknowledged, was erratic, sporadic, and limited to a fairly narrow area. Though he had done tolerably well as an undergraduate, the depth and force of his thesis had caught nearly everyone by surprise and had been in large part responsible for his Rhodes scholarship. Some members of the faculty, including Lansbury, had hailed it as one of the most impressive undergraduate theses of the past few decades.

Lansbury, on the other hand, had no flashes of brilliance. Watching him, Kevin was always reminded of the chairman of his high school's English department, Mr. Brewster. Mr. Brewster had been teaching high school English for more than thirty years and his knowledge of the finer points of English grammar and of the more obscure allusions in Chaucer and Milton and Shakespeare had been immense. Kevin imagined all the learned and capable Mr. Brewsters with their hard-won pedantic expertise arranged in a chain of competence from least to most, and he felt Charles Whitney Lansbury would most definitely be the final link on the high end of the chain.

Of course, that wasn't entirely fair. At a certain level, pedantry blossoms into omniscience, and Lansbury in his writings gave evidence of having passed that barrier. None of his many books and articles contained revolutionary theories or strikingly controversial assertions. Rather they built brick by brick, literary atom by literary atom, slowly forming impressively complex organisms of sophisticated thought. Kevin had heard Lansbury's Italian and his French in lectures, he had glimpsed the man entertaining visiting scholars from Germany and Russia in their native languages, and he knew from the notes in Lansbury's books and articles that the man was able to quote directly from original sources in Spanish, Portuguese, Greek, Latin, Sanskrit, and Japanese.

Now the full force of that amorphous yet vital intelligence was trained on Kevin. Lansbury's thick palms came together on his desk and his fingers intertwined as he opened his mouth to speak. "I was instrumental in bringing you here, Kevin," he said. "A number of my colleagues tend to be—shall we say conservative—in their recognition of younger scholars. But I say, if a man writes a brilliant book then he writes a brilliant book, be he twenty or seventy. And you have written several remarkable books." The hands separated and moved apart, and reformed into two large and stonelike fists. "Remarkable," Lansbury repeated as if sorry to let this phase of the conversation go and move into the next phase.

Behind Lansbury rows of filled bookshelves climbed in uneven steps toward the high ceiling. Kevin spotted one of his book, *Byron's Muses,* and at the very second he saw it Lansbury leaned forward and said, "But, Kevin, I'm afraid things can't continue the way they've been going."

"I won't fall back on personal tragedy so you don't have to be tactful on that account—" Kevin began, but Lansbury cut him off.

"Please," Lansbury said, and he was at his most formal while at the same time Kevin sensed an undercurrent of strong sympathy, "I want you to consider me as a friend. If not as a personal friend then as a . . . professional friend. As an ally against those who are perhaps not as understanding and empathic as one might wish."

"There've been a lot of complaints?"

"Yes, I'm afraid there have," Lansbury admitted. His heavy brows rose slightly so that his piercing blue eyes suddenly blazed out with frank directness. "Accusations of missed classes, missed committee meetings, a complete cessation of all scholarly research, ill-preparedness for lectures, moodiness, disrespect for colleagues, and public drunkenness."

Kevin suddenly found himself smiling. He simply could not stop the grin from spreading across his face. The corners of Lansbury's own mouth twitched up slightly in a faint but unmistakable answering grin.

"I suppose it wouldn't do much good to promise that I'll behave from now on?"

"No, it would not. We received several complaints yesterday. Apparently you were so hung over that some of your students feared you'd be physically sick in class."

With the grin still riding bravely on his face, Kevin asked: "So then are you going to sack me?"

"Please understand me here," Lansbury answered quickly. "My influence and my friendship extend only so far." The voice became hard for a second. "So far, and not an inch beyond. If I felt you were taking advantage of me, of my department, or of this institution, I would do everything possible to replace you as quickly as possible. And I would feel no guilt." Lansbury's bulk shifted backward on his chair and his eyes softened a tiny bit. "I do not feel, however, that that is now the case."

Again there was a brief silence, and Kevin thought to himself that Lansbury used silences as subtly as Chinese painters use empty spaces. "I lost my two brothers in World War II," he began in a totally different voice. "One was a Ranger at Omaha Beach. That was Arthur. He fell with so many other good men on June 6, 1944. The second, Winthrop, perished nine days later halfway around the world when the marines landed at Saipan. I was a high school sophomore then, and I idolized both Arthur and Winthrop. I didn't go back to school for a long while. . . ." Lansbury was far away, and it took him a second or two to fly back over the intervening decades. "What is it that your man Byron wrote? 'Man, being rational, must sometimes get drunk.' Well, I agree with him, and I remember that when I lost my brothers I tried several ways of dealing with it. So I do understand, Kevin Randall, and I would like very much to help. Very much. I have a suggestion."

Kevin waited. The afternoon sunlight glinted in patches off Lansbury's balding head.

"Go away," Lansbury whispered persuasively. "Far away for a little while. I happen to have heard of an immediate opening for someone in your area at the University of Edinburgh. I took the liberty of making some inquiries and the people there were very, very receptive. Take it, Kevin. Spend a year there, or two. Then, when you're ready, we'll talk."

"And what about my classes?"

"Already taken care of," Lansbury said. "This is not a unique situation. In cases where a professor cannot continue a lecture class in midsemester the department pitches in jointly to share the responsibilities."

For a moment, but only a moment, Kevin played with the idea. He thought of a light teaching schedule, of scotch single-malt whiskeys without end, of trout fishing in secluded lochs, and golfing at

St. Andrews. Anne and he had taken two such vacations and had gloried in the austere beauty of the Scottish countryside. . . .

He looked back at Lansbury and shook his head. "I'm sorry, but it's out of the question. I must remain in New Haven."

"Why?" Lansbury pressed.

"Because I must."

"Some memories can be self-destructive."

"It's not that," Kevin told him. "There's something I must do here."

Lansbury studied him for one moment only, and then, seeing his resolution, said, "Then there appears to be only one solution. I suggest that you take a medical leave of absence for the rest of this semester, next semester, and the summer. You will remain on full salary, and your leave will in no way be construed as a disciplinary action. Let us hope that by next September you will be ready to resume your duties in full. If not, I'm afraid I will not be able to help you any further. Is such a proposal acceptable?"

Kevin nodded and held out his hand. "Thank you."

Lansbury did not release his grip right away. "Why won't you take that job in Edinburgh?" he whispered, and there was real curiosity in his voice. "We both know it would be better for you. Why stay here?"

"I have no choice," Kevin said, and there was suddenly something in his voice that made Lansbury scrutinize him very closely indeed.

"I don't know what you're up to," Lansbury said in a low, even tone. "But if you're in trouble I'd like to help. Do you owe money? Is it your health? Have you done something you shouldn't have?"

Kevin shook his head three times. "It's a matter of revenge," he said very quietly, yet there was savagery wrapped around every syllable.

"That sounds rather personal," Charles Whitney Lansbury replied with equal gravity. "If I can help you in any way, please don't hesitate."

"I won't," Kevin promised, and though he did not voice it aloud he realized as he exited the office how much Lansbury had already helped him. He was now on medical leave—relieved of all teaching responsibilities—and therefore free to pick up the bloody trail and follow the chase wherever it might lead him.

Evelyn chose the most isolated desk she could find, on the fifth-floor stacks. It was off in its own shadowy alcove, separated from the other desks on the floor by shelves and shelves of French and German literature. A bare hundred-watt bulb hung straight down toward the desk, and when she pulled the chain to turn it on the shadows seemed to retreat in every direction.

Sterling Library was strangely empty. The murder three nights ago had scared a lot of students into studying in their rooms. The fear and panic on campus hadn't surprised Evelyn—she considered most of her Yale peers to be sheltered and overprotected children who didn't really know the first thing about taking care of themselves. Anyway, with them in their rooms, she had this whole part of the fifth floor to herself.

It certainly was unnaturally quiet. There were no nearby students engaged in whispered conversations, no nervous pre-meds pacing back and forth between their books and the water fountain, and no distant laughter from sophomoric underclassmen exchanging dirty jokes. The only sound was a distant shuffling, or perhaps it was a scraping, that soon faded away leaving the place in complete silence.

Although she didn't really enjoy writing research papers, when the time came to work Evelyn liked to get right down to it. She preferred to write in silence and isolation, and when things were going well she could turn out four or five pages of clean copy every hour. She composed grammatically perfect, fluid sentences without effort, could structure an essay as she went along, and never bothered to proofread.

Her arms still throbbed from the afternoon's grueling crew practice. It would be good to finish this paper, take a very hot shower, and relax. There was a party at Ezra Styles's later on, and a lot of her teammates were going. . . .

An unpleasant, musty smell made her sniff several times. She wondered if the recent rain could have leaked down and rotted some of the books. Or perhaps her wet down jacket was responsible for the doggish odor. She sniffed it—it smelled fine.

She set to work on her comparison of *The Seven Samurai* with *The Magnificent Seven*. Many American film critics argued that Kurosawa was the most Western of the great Japanese film directors, and even accused him of borrowing too much from Hollywood. It was said that in his admiration of John Ford, and with his love for Western and Russian literature, he forsook Japan's unique artistic traditions and native narrative styles.

Evelyn intended her comparison to be a skillful refutation of that criticism. She began by showing how in its visual style, narrative structure, and story content *The Seven Samurai* was really a distinctively Japanese film. She talked about how Kurosawa used his own Kendo training to achieve such absolutely true-to-the-art swordfighting scenes, how the structure of the film conformed to the requirements of classical Noh drama, and how contrasting the groveling peasants with courageous samurai pointed up the urban-rural distinction in the socioeconomic system that exists in Japan even today.

The shuffling sounds came again, closer now. Evelyn glanced up—maybe some pre-med was dragging his tired body back and forth between his biology textbook and the men's room.

Four pages done in one hour. Three more to go. Evelyn thought for a second about the party. Most of the rugby team would be there. Patrick of the hairy chest and the great beer-drinking capacity—Patrick of the blue-collar Boston background whose every third word was a profanity, yet who could quote large sections of Aristotle while squashing beer cans against his forehead—would be there. He seemed so much more real to her than his preppy teammates, no doubt because he had learned about life in the same tough neighborhoods that she had lived in.

Perhaps tonight Patrick would take her in his arms and carry her up to what she imagined was an unmade bed with unwashed sheets, and would rip her clothes off and grunt and groan while she panted and purred. Or perhaps she would take him by his long black hair and tug him back to her neat little single room, and dance naked with him while her stereo played fast jazz. . . .

Evelyn heard the breathing and stood up quickly. Someone was kidding around, trying to spook her, and she didn't think it was funny. The narrow aisles between the steel shelves were very dark. She walked to the perimeter of the circle of light and peered toward where she had heard the sound, but all was empty and still. Then she backed up to her desk and stood for a second, thinking.

If someone had really been there, he or she was gone now. Nothing moved and there were no sounds.

She felt an urge to pick up her books and leave, and slowly fought it down. She only had two more pages to go, and she was already all set up here. In less than an hour she could be done for the evening.

Evelyn sat back down, but turned her body so that she was facing the direction she thought the sound had come from. She forced herself to concentrate on the paper. Having proved that *The Seven Samurai* was a distinctively Japanese film, she next began arguing that *The Magnificent Seven* failed as a Western specifically because it tried to copy too many features of Kurosawa's movie.

Were they footsteps? She peered into the murk. No, there was nothing there. She listened. Nothing. Nothing.

It had been an interesting cultural transposition to set *The Magnificent Seven* in a small Mexican village so that the old Mexican wiseman could correspond to the Japanese village elder, but it just wasn't the same. The motivations for the gunfighters didn't make sense because there was no tradition in the Wild West that corresponded to the code of honor and brotherhood of the samurai, and—

Suddenly Evelyn found herself standing and running—not just running but sprinting madly. She had always been one to make instant decisions, and when that breathing and scraping had begun again they hadn't been just creepy but downright threatening.

She was in superb shape from crew, and she flew down the narrow aisles, past the dark metal shelves.

Whoever it was, was gaining on her, and he knew the layout of the stacks far better than she did because he was hemming her in, just the way a boxer cuts off an opponent.

"HEEEEELLPPP!" she screamed, but no one answered her. He had cut her off from the stairs and the fire alarm, and apparently there wasn't anyone on this floor who could hear her. The elevator was in the other direction. Then Evelyn surprised herself by turning around and taking off toward the elevator. Her unexpected move seemed to put a tiny gap between herself and the as-yet unseen presence that chased her.

She reached the elevator, jammed in the button, and hammered on the doors. "HEEEELLLP!" she bellowed, hoping it would carry down the elevator shaft.

Clear, heavy footsteps approached through the shadows.

Evelyn turned and put her back to the elevator door. She raised the ballpoint pen she had carried during her flight and prepared to defend herself with it as if it were a knife. The footsteps and scraping drew yet nearer, the animal smell came, and more heavy breathing. Then the elevator door opened and two members of the hockey team stepped out.

"What's up, Ev? You look crazed—" Tim Jeffers, the starting right wing, began. He shut up when he saw how badly frightened Evelyn was.

As she fell into Tim's arms, Evelyn knew that by a fluke of time and the most provident chance, she had just escaped a horribly painful death.

So near, she is so near, when she screams the blood dances through her jugular, the fear cracks the lines of her face, as she stares . . .

She knows I'm coming, she's screaming, a pen in her hand . . .

So close, so very close . . .

Back, back, back into the shadows, not making a sound, where did those two come from? Holding it back, keeping it all in until all is black and quiet before it explodes out against the shelves and the books . . .

Ripping. Damn her.

Rending. Kill her for the pain she gave . . .

Cracking spines. Glorious . . .

Is it over? the voice asks.

No. I'm burning with it. When she turned to fight, I caught fire—I still feel it, she ran, she looked, she hated, she hurt, she vanished, she is gone, she will return.

Soon?

Or not.

Chapter 5

In a police car parked a hundred feet down from Trumbull gate, Jack Hobbs was waiting for him, and Kevin barely had time to get into the car before Hobbs roared away up Elm Street. "I don't have much time and I'd rather we're not seen together," he told Kevin without looking at him. "Please don't call me at work anymore, or at home. Everyone at the station's jumpy, and I don't want anyone putting the two of our names together."

When they were far enough away from the Yale campus, Hobbs slowed the car down a bit. "What is it?" Kevin asked.

Hobbs pulled into the parking lot of a truck stop and let the motor idle. As he turned and looked at Kevin for the first time, there was tension in his face and wariness edging at the corners of his eyes. "I'm running that list through the computer for you. I'll have it later today." He paused to examine Kevin carefully, as if still unsure that he was doing the right thing. "If it comes out that I turned over New Haven police records to a private citizen engaged in an independent investigation, I could catch serious shit. Like I said, everyone's jumpy. If your name comes up, it would be even worse."

"Why are you doing it then?"

"There was an attack last night. Not an attack really, but an . . . incident. A girl was studying late in the library. By herself. She heard scuffling footsteps, heavy breathing, smelled something rotten. She bolted and the footsteps chased her. She didn't see a thing. Ran to an elevator and got lucky—just as she reached it the doors opened and a couple of guys on the hockey team got out. They brought her into the station, still half hysterical. They didn't hear, see, or smell a thing, by the way."

A huge sixteen-wheeler pulled into the parking lot and coasted to a stop. The truck driver walked by them on his way to the diner. He was a big man and the stiff way that he moved indicated that he had been driving for a long time. Kevin envied him. How peaceful it would be to just take a big rig on the highway, turn on some soppy country music, and leave everything else far behind.

"They don't know what to make of her story," Hobbs concluded. "Romano thinks it was a prank. Those scuffling footsteps and the smell and the breathing all sound like they come from a bad late-night TV movie."

"But you believe her?"

"I wish I didn't." Hobbs was quiet for a long minute. "She seemed like a pretty tough girl, and something had scared her half to death. Yes, on a gut level, I believed her. So I'm gonna get you the list you wanted. But whatever you do after that, I want you to leave me completely out of it. I've got enough on my hands right now to worry about. We've got to train three new guards, plus organize student patrols. The press is sure to get hold of the story, and then I'll have parents calling me from all over the world again to make sure their little girls are okay. The last thing I need right now is more hassle. Okay?"

"You have my word," Kevin replied. Hobbs shifted the car into drive and headed out of the parking lot.

"Where is Romano starting?" Kevin asked as they reentered New Haven.

"Known sex offenders and men with any kind of past history of violence toward women. He's got about twenty or so names already—" Hobbs broke off suddenly as they were almost sideswiped by a tan station wagon with an old woman at the wheel. When she saw that she had just missed hitting a police car, she gave Hobbs a sheepish look of apology. He waved her on.

"One other thing I forgot to tell you," Hobbs continued. "We don't have a definite connection yet, but this morning a librarian found dozens of books torn apart and pages completely shredded near where the attack occurred last night. A couple of shelves were overturned, a metal brace was ripped clean out of a wall—somebody threw a hell of a violent fit. They're still checking for prints, but I hear they haven't found anything."

"How do you want me to pick up the list?" Kevin asked as they neared Trumbull College. "Should we arrange a drop point?"

"I'll leave it with Laura Donovan. That's my wife's cousin. I already told her you're taking her out tomorrow night."

The car came to a quick stop. "I really can't," Kevin said.

"She expects you about six," Hobbs continued. "She said she'll make dinner. I think there's a show afterward at the Yale Rep she'd like to see."

"I'm still too close to Anne. It would just be painful for me— for both of us. Thanks for thinking of me but . . ."

"I'm not thinking of you, I'm thinking of her," Hobbs said. "Anyway, she'll have the list, so it's up to you if you want it or not. A lot more names popped up than we figured, so I trimmed it down to five or six based on what I could figure out from the Yale police and the New Haven Police records."

"Jack—"

"It's up to you, Randall. Here's her address."

He produced a small piece of paper. Kevin hesitated and then took the paper.

"Now get out and remember that you're on your own," Hobbs commanded.

"Bye, Jack," Kevin said, and held out his hand. Hobbs took it with the grip that crushed walnuts, and for a moment the two men studied each other's face deeply.

"One last thing," Hobbs said. "If by some miracle you do ever catch the guy, make the bastard suffer."

Kevin didn't answer with words, but his eyes sharpened to two saber points.

On the first snowy night of winter, Midori finally got up the nerve to show Jennifer her collection. The snow had begun to stick at dusk, and now the grounds of Cheltenham Castle were covered with several inches of white powder, which, through the castle windows, glinted magically in the moonlight.

"At least give me a hint?" Jennifer demanded playfully.

"It was my mother's collection before me, and her mother's before her. It's the kind of collection you want to keep increasing in size." Midori grinned mysteriously, as if she had just made a little private witticism.

"China?" Jennifer guessed. "Jade? Painted screens? Oh, you're a perfect sphinx!" She pouted, pretending frustration.

Midori gave herself a lot of credit for Jennifer's newly regained ability to play and tease. For the first few days they had been together, Jennifer had barely shown a fleeting smile. Now they had great fun together, and if Jennifer's bad dreams hadn't completely stopped, at least they were less frequent and far less virulent.

Midori offered her hand and, giggling like two schoolgirls, they hurried down the corridor to Midori's room. She was wearing one of her young and innocent outfits, a plaid skirt and white blouse that made her look all of fifteen. Jennifer had gone out to see the snow earlier in the evening so she was wearing jeans and a green sweater. Holding hands and walking down the corridor together, they could easily have passed for two school girls strolling home from lessons.

Midori's room was furnished in the classic Japanese minimalist tradition. A seventeenth-century Jibei print of two courtesans untying each other's kimonos while a young girl looks on hung above an antique mahogany bureau. A small writing desk faced the large window where the moon and stars were half hidden by a gauzy veil of snowflakes. Midori had dispensed with a traditional futon in favor of a Western-style bed. On the bed's thick coverlet, dragons embroidered in silver and gold chased each other across an expanse of brilliant scarlet silk.

"I've never shown this collection to anyone before," Midori whispered. "I've never trusted anyone enough to keep the secret."

She kissed Jennifer lightly on the lips.

Midori disappeared into her walk-in closet and reemerged with a large and richly inlaid lacquer box. She set it down on her desk, pressed three gilt panels in careful order, and then twisted the top off. Looking up at Jennifer who was waiting expectantly, she shook her head. "It'll be better if I just dump them out on the bed."

Midori carried the box to her bed, looked at Jennifer a final time, and upended it so that the box's contents spilled out onto the coverlet.

Jennifer stared down for several seconds and then looked up at Midori for confirmation. "Your family has a dildo collection?"

Midori burst out laughing and nodded. "As I said, it's best if the collection keeps increasing in size. Some of them are more than a hundred years old."

Jennifer looked back down and her eyes widened in amused fascination. There were dozens of them. Some were carved from soft woods, some cast in bronze, some were ivory, and a couple were modern rubbery plastics. Several were carved to exactly resemble the penis, while others preserved the useful shape but had faces or wings or even flowery patterns etched on them. Some were short, some long, some two-pronged, they were yellow, black, white, and several of the modern ones could be plugged into wall outlets.

"But I thought you hated men?" Jennifer asked.

Midori shrugged.

"Which is your favorite?"

The Japanese girl sorted through the pile and with becoming modesty hesitated just a beat. Then she picked up a black rubber dildo that was about seven inches long and whose length was made up of four distinct sections.

Jennifer took the dildo in her hand and felt the smooth rubber shaft of the end joint that widened out into a thick head. Without saying a word, she undid the cord from the back and plugged it into a socket near the bed. Immediately the black dildo came to life. The four sections began to move independently, so that the total effect was of a short black snake wriggling rhythmically.

Jennifer gave Midori a firm push onto her bed. Her short plaid skirt hiked up her thighs, revealing a triangle of white panty. Kneeling on the floor in front of her, Jennifer pushed Midori's legs wide apart. Her right hand caressed Midori's hair, while her left hand squeezed inside Midori's panties.

Midori moaned and tore open her white blouse. The nipples of her small breasts were already distended. She reached over to the pile on the coverlet and selected two silver clasps designed to resemble butterflies. She positioned the butterflies so that the clasps lightly pinched her areolas, and then let her head settle back onto the coverlet.

Jennifer moved the vibrating head of the black dildo over the cottony surface of Midori's panties in slow circles, pressing just a bit harder each time, and soon the Japanese girl clutched the posts of the bed and moaned more loudly.

Jennifer slid Midori's panties down and off. She probed the triangle of black pubic hair with her index finger, and was surprised at how quickly and easily her finger completely disappeared. Soon the head of the dildo replaced Jennifer's finger, and when the shaft vanished, Midori began to writhe on the bed.

As Jennifer gently thrust the full seven inches of the dildo in and out, Midori's gasps came quicker and quicker. The butterflies on her breasts tossed back and forth with her uneven breathing as if they were caught in a strong wind. She slid to the very end of the bed, and Jennifer understood her silent request and altered the angle. Then Midori came and came again, and her bucking hips rode out her wild orgasm.

Closing her legs, Midori purred softly and curled up like a kitten. Jennifer lay down next to her. For a while neither girl spoke. Midori's breathing was still unnaturally loud, and Jennifer found that she also was breathing a bit hard. Then Midori rolled over to face Jennifer and gave her a thank-you kiss on the forehead. "You choose one," she whispered. "Let me do it for you."

Jennifer shook her head.

"Please, I want to."

"No, really. But thanks."

So the moment had come, and Midori asked the question that had been bothering her for days. As a lover Jennifer was very giving and very responsive, but she steadfastly refused to be penetrated. Whenever Midori's finger began to explore too deeply, Jennifer would reach down and firmly withdraw Midori's hand. "What is it that happened in America?" Midori whispered in the lightest possible voice, "that frightened you so much?"

Jennifer searched her eyes with her own.

"Were you raped?"

Jennifer shook her head.

"Some physical thing? A disease? An injury?"

Jennifer shook her head again.

"But it was something that happened with a man? And even as close as we are now, you can't tell me about it?"

Jennifer opened her mouth to speak but then shut it again as if she didn't trust herself. She nuzzled against Midori's breast, taking her nipple in her mouth in a tender and infantlike way, as if she would escape the evils of the world by returning to a time when sleeping and suckling were all life required.

"Where did it happen?" Midori probed ever so lightly. "New York? At your home? Something with your father?"

Jennifer looked up at her again, and this time her hazel brown eyes flashed with a determination to tell as much as she could. "At college."

Midori waited, holding her breath, but in the end all she got was a question.

"If you knew something about someone you once loved that would destroy that person if you told it, but if you didn't speak up other people might suffer—and if you were terribly afraid of that person because they were powerful and you had betrayed them and hurt them—would you still have an obligation to speak up or . . . is it okay to just hide away?"

Jennifer's face was taut with tension. Her eyes implored an answer even as her tight lips showed that she knew none could be forthcoming.

Midori put her arms around Jennifer and held her close to let the warmth from her body answer for her. When they were both naked and lying breast to breast listening to the wind howl, Midori finally answered. "Has the world been so good to you that you feel you owe it so much? Stay here with me."

Jennifer nodded and snuggled yet closer.

Laura Donovan opened the door as soon as Kevin rang the bell. He was immediately attracted by her strikingly feminine beauty, but felt guilty for noticing it. He had hoped for a date he could easily dismiss. She wore a long dark-blue dress and her full white breasts rose above its décolletage.

"Professor Randall, please come in," she said, and ushered him into her spotless apartment.

He advanced, and every step seemed like an incursion into dangerous territory. He handed her the flowers and said, "Please call me Kevin."

She took the flowers from him with a grateful smile. "They're lovely. Let me put them in water and get you a drink. Jack said you're a whiskey man so I bought a bottle of Wild Turkey. Do you drink it straight up?"

The temptation was tremendous, but Kevin dug down deep and found the courage to say "Sorry, but I'm on the wagon these days. A glass of juice or a Coke would be fine."

She nodded and produced an envelope. "Jack said to give you this. He said it was about a case you're interested in." Then she turned and walked toward the kitchen, as Kevin tucked the envelope carefully into the breast pocket of his jacket.

The apartment was full of soft things. Fluffy white and pink cushions were arranged invitingly on the living-room couch. Spider plants in tiny red and blue pots hung suspended from the ceiling in macramé slings so that their thin green and white leaves dangled down in a cascade of coils and tendrils. A large bookcase contained sets of books arranged in careful order according to color and size. Stepping closer, he saw that the volumes were indeed all new and alphabetically arranged so that the complete Hemingway followed the complete Hawthorne, which followed the complete Hardy.

"They're from my book club," Laura said, hurrying into the living room with a drink in either hand. "I started reading very late and I'm still making up for lost time, so I buy them in sets. It must seem foolish to you, but I had to find my way to literature. No one in my family reads at all. I bet Jack hasn't read a book in five years, and for Lucy it's probably ten. Cheers."

He sipped and couldn't quite identify the taste. "Apple juice with a splash of cranberry," she helped him. "Mine's a little stronger. I need the rum to relax me."

"Are you nervous?"

"Yes," she admitted. "Yes, I am. Jack's told me about you. I would like you to like me."

During dinner, Kevin struggled not to like her. After a tasty cold cucumber soup and a tart Oriental salad, she brought in a magnificent duck, which had been roasted in a glaze of honey, coriander seeds, cumin seeds, saffron, and white pepper. She served it with wild rice and lightly steamed asparagus. Halfway through the main course he complimented her on the superb meal.

She rewarded him with a smile that kindled merry, gratified fires in her large brown eyes. "I also started cooking very late and I'm trying to make up for lost time," she said, and Kevin smiled at the repetition of the phrase. "So I'm taking a cooking class through the mail. The recipes are terrific, but it's hard to force yourself to cook when you live alone."

The reference to living alone was thrown out innocently enough, but she interpreted his ensuing silence as a tactful inquiry and said, "I was divorced eight months ago. I'm still getting used to being on my own."

Kevin thought of Anne and put down his fork, and Laura must have glimpsed the pain in his eyes because she quickly said, "Jack told me a little bit about what you've been through. I'm sorry to bring up the past. Let's just enjoy tonight."

Later they saw Ibsen's *Ghosts* at the Yale Rep, and even though the house was half empty, Kevin was aware that several faculty couples watched him and Laura with interest. She was totally enthralled by the play and sat on the edge of her seat watching the actors in fascination.

During the third act, as Osvald's sickness began to destroy him and the audience sat gripped by the final twists of the tragedy, Kevin tried to stop thinking about Anne and concentrate on the drama. He failed. Laura's knee and thigh occasionally brushed his leg as she shifted around on her seat, and though her concentration was focused on the stage she flicked her eyes toward him every few minutes to see if he was enjoying the play. He wondered if she sensed how much pain he was in.

His fingers found the envelope from Jack Hobbs that he had tucked into his breast pocket. He ran his index finger over the square outline of the envelope. Somewhere in this New Haven night, perhaps even only a few blocks away, the person responsible for all his grief might be stalking new victims.

On the walk back to Laura's apartment, they skirted the edge of the campus and the feeling of a malignant nearby presence continued to haunt Kevin. Shadows jumped backward into darkness as they walked by, and the leafless trees huddled together as if sharing lonely secrets. Sensing his mood, Laura was mostly silent, except for a few assurances that she had enjoyed the play tremendously. A block from her apartment she surprised him by putting her hand in his own, and he surprised himself by closing his fingers around it. Her palm was small and warm, and they walked hand in hand to her building like two teenagers coming home from a first date.

"Come up for a cup of coffee," she invited.

"I really can't," he protested, but she was already leading him inside and toward the elevator. They rode up in such a complete silence that he could hear the elevator motor pulling the cable up the shaft.

They drank their coffee on the couch, and Anne's specter sat next to Laura, shaking out her long black hair and following Kevin's every move with jealous eyes.

"You started thinking about her during the play. I felt it," Laura said after a particularly long silence.

"I tried not to."

"You don't want to talk about it?"

"I'm sorry."

"I understand," she said a bit sadly. "I had a wonderful time anyway, Kevin. I don't know how to say this but I respect your silences." When she moved a tiny bit closer to him on the couch, he felt her warm breath against his cheek.

Kevin drained his coffee and stood up. "I should be going." Grabbing his coat, he hurried to the door, but she was already there. "Good night," he said, offering a handshake.

She took his hand and looked into his eyes. "Jack told me her name was Anne, and that she's been dead for two years," she whispered. "It's a shame we both have to be so lonely."

"I wish I could let her go," Kevin replied in a very strange voice. As he realized how much of the truth he had let slip out, suddenly the tears came. He hadn't cried in two years, not when he had found out about Anne's death or when he had gone to identify her, nor even at her funeral, but now two tracks of hot tears burned down his cheeks.

Again Laura took him by the hand and looked into his eyes, and when they kissed he wasn't at all sure who initiated it and who tried to pull away. They kissed for a long time. Then, without a word, Laura led him down the corridor into her small bedroom, and he followed her while his tears continued to fall.

They undressed each other in an instant. When they embraced he realized that she had also begun to cry, that she was fighting her own specter. She was breathing quickly, and each time she exhaled her hot breath snaked against his throat.

Then he took her by the hand and pulled her to the bed. They both tried and tried, but when Laura finally did moan it was mostly from the pressure because the harder they tried, the softer he remained.

Finally she reached up and took him by the elbows and pivoted him around so that he lay on his back. She crouched over him and began at his eyes, licking the salty tears away and sealing his lids shut with her tongue so that he would no longer see Anne's specter. Then she moved to his lips, then on down across his chest, skidding across his stomach, her tongue traveling more and more slowly . . .

She hesitated for a second and then took him in her mouth and rolled him and caressed him, but the flaccid question mark never became an exclamation point.

Gently but firmly he pulled her up and then sat up himself so that they were facing each other.

"You didn't want to," she whispered. "I shouldn't have pushed. Please stay."

"I did want to, but . . ." he told her. "I'm sorry."

He kissed her on the forehead before he turned away to dress. "Thank you for the dinner, Laura, good-bye," he mumbled as he pulled on his clothes. After leaving the bedroom, he hurried down the stairs.

The cold New Haven night revived him somewhat, but as he walked back toward Trumbull College he felt miserably empty and terribly alone.

In his room he took a glass of scotch and paced his apartment from wall to wall, as if he were searching for something. The glinting fencing trophies laughed at him and the rows of books were lifeless and useless. He felt he could drink ten bottles and still not find the numbing escape he craved.

Suddenly his fingers touched the envelope in his breast pocket. He took it out and ripped it open, and read the five names in the dull lamplight:

Roger Van Dorn
Peter Pusecki
Amy Strong

Karl Reinschreiber
Ali Shahrzad

And as he stood there by the lamp, all of Kevin's frustration, embarrassment, rage, and hunger for revenge became concentrated more and more narrowly on the five names that Jack Hobbs had culled from the New Haven Police Department's computer and the Yale registrar's records and scrawled in pencil on a small, yellowing square of paper.

Chapter 6

At the *Yale Daily News* office, the young woman in the swivel chair behind the desk was two-thirds of the way through a paperback edition of *The Divine Comedy*. She had the look of someone who has been through hell: her eyes were bleary, her hair was oily, and she slumped forward over her desk. Kevin decided she had just pulled one all-nighter and was contemplating another one. She made several false starts as she tried to find a polite way to refuse his request. "It's late. I'm new here. Our record room is for *Daily News* staff use only. Couldn't you come back tomorrow and check with one of our editors?"

Kevin glanced at his watch, feigning great impatience. "The thing is, the English department needs this information right away," he told her. "It's absolutely urgent—for the disciplinary review committee." He paused, to let the severe name of the committee he had just invented pierce her tired mind. He made his voice ring with authority. "The chairman himself suggested that I come over here tonight and cross check our information with the *Yale Daily*'s records." She flinched at that. Kevin guessed she was an English major and that his passing reference to Lansbury had hit home.

"Well," she admitted, "I don't suppose it could do any harm." She opened the desk drawer and took out a huge ring of keys. Her movements were slow and imprecise from lack of sleep.

A moment later they were walking up the steep stairs to the record rooms on the third floor. She tried several of the keys before she found the right one. The door creaked open, and she led the way into the windowless room and flicked on a light. The record rooms were a little library of Yale memorabilia. Back issues of the *Yale Daily,* arranged chronologically, endlessly whispered the secrets of a century of campus life to the stone walls and steel shelves. In the next room, Yale Banner yearbooks stood in stacks, and, on shelves on the far wall, Kevin saw hundreds of copies of *The Old Campus,* a guidebook that listed and provided pictures of each year's crop of incoming freshmen.

He turned to the young woman with a grateful smile. "Thank you. Sorry I can't tell you what this is about—it's absolutely confidential. But you've been a great help."

She was reluctant to leave him alone in this room that was supposed to be off limits. "I'll wait, so if you need any help . . ." She rubbed at her red eyes with her knuckles.

"Thanks, but I'll be just fine."

She hesitated a minute and then was gone. Kevin closed the door behind her. The record rooms had the eerie feel of an old royal family crypt—the tomb of the Yale clan where generations of the secrets and hopes and ambitions of powerful men and women were now preserved from the prying fingers of the sunlight and the cruel touch of time and change. There was no dust—everything was clean and freshly swept out—but the feeling of age and death and the inexorable passage of time permeated the rooms from the high ceilings to the unpolished wooden floors.

After taking a legal-size pad of yellow lined paper out of his briefcase, Kevin looked over the five names he had copied onto the top sheet. According to Jack Hobbs, more than a dozen names had initially popped up on both the New Haven Police's computer and the Yale registrar's files. Hobbs, using university police records and other sources available to him, had been able to trim that list down to five names. Kevin began with Van Dorn, the only one of the names he recognized. Roger Van Dorn was a tenured anthropology professor with something of a reputation as an adventurer. In a *Guide to the Yale Faculty,* Kevin found a capsule biography. He read it through twice, taking notes on the salient facts.

Van Dorn had been born in 1950 in Rotterdam to an aristocratic Dutch family. After studying at Cologne and Oxford, he had come to Yale as a lecturer in 1977. He was a cultural anthropologist specializing in the tribes of New Guinea, and his list of publications was impressive. Scanning the list, Kevin saw that most of the anthropologist's books and articles seemed to be about initiation, warfare, and other manifestations of violence in savage societies. There was absolutely no mention of any outside interests or personal life— no marriages or divorces or children. From a campus phone directory Kevin learned that Van Dorn was a resident fellow of Timothy Dwight College, one of Yale's twelve residential colleges.

Peter Pusecki was not listed in any of the current Yale directories or New Haven phone books. Kevin found Peter's picture in *The Old Campus* from two years before, when the young man had been a freshman. Next to the picture was the name of his freshman roommate and the information that Peter had come to Yale from Edgewater High School in New Jersey. In the tiny snapshot, Peter stared directly back into the camera. He looked big and powerful—even though it was only a head shot, it was possible to see the way his thick neck swelled out to broad shoulders. His residential college affiliation had been Trumbull, Kevin's own, which was a bit of a break because Kevin would have an easier time inquiring about him. Kevin stuck the booklet in his briefcase and moved on to the next name.

Amy Strong was elusive. Kevin checked all of the student directories and several faculty lists before finding a recent announcement of her appointment to a junior deanship. The item contained a summary of her educational background and professional experience. After earning a B.A. and an M.A. at Berkeley, Amy Strong had come to Yale for a Ph.D. in social psychology. Upon graduation she had accepted a midlevel administrative job at Mount Holyoke for two years. This past September, Yale had brought her back as an associate dean and the new assistant director of the campus Women's Center. Her office was in the Hall of Graduate Studies, two floors above Kevin's own.

He glanced at his watch—an hour and a half had passed and he still had two names to go.

Karl Reinschreiber's Yale career had been so notorious that Kevin quickly located several *Yale Daily News* articles about him. As a freshman Reinschreiber had attempted to found a neo-Nazi group, and when the JDL had heard about it they had come to the campus. A violent confrontation had ensued. In his sophomore year, Reinschreiber had been arrested for writing obscene racial epithets outside the Afro-American Students' Building. And near the end of his junior year, two years ago, Reinschreiber had been thrown out of Yale for threatening his roommate with a loaded pistol. Kevin noted the affiliation with Saybrook College—it would be fairly easy to learn if Reinschreiber had really applied for readmission.

Kevin drew a blank on Ali Shahrzad. His name appeared in the *Old Campus* freshman guide of two years before, affiliated with Calhoun College, but where a snapshot should have been there was only a blank square. There was no information about where he had lived as a freshman or who his roommates were.

"Find what you were looking for?" the tired girl at the front desk asked him. She was underlining whole passages with a yellow marker, apparently at random. Her eyes looked as if they were about to fold shut of their own accord.

"Yes, thank you, you can lock up now. You should really go to bed," Kevin told her. For a second she contemplated his suggestion with longing in her eyes. Then she returned to hell, and Kevin walked out onto York Street.

"You'll have to forgive the clutter," Roger Van Dorn said as he led Kevin into his living room, stepping around several wooden crates. "As you can see, each time I return from the field, I like to bring a small bit of New Guinea with me." The walls of Van Dorn's apartment were covered with exotic masks and weapons. The oblong wooden masks were several feet long and were painted in simple but unusual geometric patterns. Several had cowrie shells swelling from their eye sockets, and the most unnerving of them had teeth stitched into its gaping mouth.

"Human teeth," Van Dorn explained, noting the direction of Kevin's gaze. "And this too." He took a long bone dagger from its wall mount and handed it to Kevin, who ran his fingers along its smooth surface and then felt its sharp point. "A human femur. They make them from pigs too, but there's something more dramatic about human bones, don't you think?" After Van Dorn replaced the dagger, he motioned for Kevin to sit in an old leather armchair.

Van Dorn sat down in a matching chair a few feet away, and for several seconds the two young professors studied each other in silence. Kevin knew that Van Dorn was about thirty-eight, and he was impressed with the Dutch anthropologist's youthful appearance, tanned face, and muscular body. In fact, except for his blue eyes and reddish-blond beard, Van Dorn could easily have passed for a South Seas native. His face was a dark bronze color from long and continuous exposure to the sun, and his cheeks and the corners of his eyes had many tiny lines as if the heat had cracked the sunburned glaze of his skin. Kevin had seen Van Dorn at faculty meetings, but in those genteel surroundings he had not appreciated the power of the man. Van Dorn exuded a raw animal energy that, while contained and controlled as he sat in his armchair, seemed a natural complement to the ferocious masks on the walls.

"So," Van Dorn said after giving Kevin a chance to get settled in his chair, "you are thinking of heading off to my part of the world?"

Kevin nodded and fought down the panic. He knew his pretext was weak, but it was the best he had been able to come up with on short notice. "Yes, to the University of New South Wales. And I thought that while I was there I might detour to Port Moresby and perhaps even see a few outlying villages. I talked to Curson—my only close friend in the anthropology department—and he said you'd be the man to see."

Van Dorn smiled and the lines around his eyes fanned out into tiny creases. "I do know New Guinea quite well. But I wonder what there is at the University of New South Wales to interest an English poetry professor?"

Kevin hesitated. Van Dorn noticed and immediately filled the silence. "But I've been remiss as a host," he said, rising out of his chair. "No questions without drinks. Can I get you a drop of scotch?"

Kevin had to swallow a few times before he could bring himself to mumble "Sorry, but I'm on the wagon. If you could manage a glass of ginger ale. . . ?"

"I'm afraid cold water will have to do," Van Dorn replied with slightly contemptuous distaste, and walked out of the room. Kevin watched him go. Van Dorn wasn't tall and his shoulders weren't particularly broad, but he was obviously in superb shape. Certainly he looked strong enough to kill young women quickly and brutally. Could Van Dorn be mad? Enough to have actually murdered Anne and the other girls? Kevin looked around at the masks and daggers and felt the anger and desire for revenge welling up dangerously inside him.

Van Dorn came back into the room with two glasses, and as he took his ice water, Kevin inhaled the sweet aroma of a costly single malt from Van Dorn's glass. "Confusion to the enemy," Van Dorn said, raised his glass in a toast, and then took a large sip. He rolled the scotch around once quickly in his mouth, swallowed, and sat back. "Now then," he said, "you were explaining about the University of New South Wales."

"Trelawny," Kevin responded, this time with no hesitation. "A British explorer of the early nineteenth century. We don't know much about his early life except that he was thrown out of school for thrashing his master and then spent several years sailing the seas. He was tall, strikingly handsome, mostly self-educated, well spoken, and he fancied himself a gentleman. In 1822 Trelawny suddenly arrived in Switzerland and thereafter played a role in one of the most important series of events in the history of Western poetry."

"I assume," Van Dorn said, cutting in, "that you refer to the time Byron, and Mary and Percy Shelley, and later Leigh Hunt spent together?"

Kevin sipped his water. He would have to tread carefully. Van Dorn had a degree from Oxford—he might know far more about the period than Kevin realized. "Exactly. Shelley introduced Trelawny to Byron who first spurned him as too common, but soon dubbed him 'the pirate' and spent a great deal of time with him. It was Trelawny who taught Shelley to sail his new little boat, the *Ariel,* and it was Trelawny who helped Byron hatch his mad schemes from Genoa. And, most important of all, Trelawny was the only man who gave us firsthand accounts of Shelley's funeral, when they cremated his body on the shores of Lake Geneva, and of Byron's death on Missolonghi. His *Recollections of the Last Days of Byron and Shelley* is the best source description we have."

Van Dorn was intrigued. "This Trelawny seems more than a mere footnote to literary history."

"And yet," Kevin finished bravely, making this part up as he went along, "Trelawny's early career remains lost in shadow. Where did he sail to, and what did he do there, and how did it influence his later dealings with the great poets? We don't know, or at least we didn't know until recently. But apparently at the University of New South Wales they've uncovered and are in the process of editing a large collection of correspondence and diaries from British whaling captains and gentlemen adventurers of the nineteenth century. Not only do they have several letters by Trelawny, but they also have his diary. They won't copy it and they won't let it out of the country, so if I want to see it I have to go there." And if that doesn't do as an excuse, Kevin thought to himself, I might as well give up right now.

"Just like those provincial academics," Van Dorn said with an elitist snort. "When they get onto something, however small, they guard it like a bloody gold mine. When do you leave?"

"As soon as I can," Kevin told him. "And I thought that while I was over there I might do a bit of sightseeing. I think I could allow myself two weeks in New Guinea, perhaps even three."

Van Dorn bridled at Kevin's use of the word sightseeing. "New Guinea isn't exactly famed for its picturesque boulevards," he noted sarcastically. "Travel there is often more hardship than pleasure. Perhaps you should go somewhere else."

"No, ever since I read Margaret Mead I've been fascinated by New Guinea," Kevin responded gently but firmly.

"Come, then," Van Dorn said. Kevin followed him into his small study. A number of carved wooden figures of varying heights stood on the floor or perched menacingly from the ends of crowded bookshelves. All of the statuettes were vaguely human in shape but had grotesquely enlarged facial features and sexual organs. One of the largest had a nose like an enormous beak that hung down between two ponderous breasts. A collection of artfully decorated short pieces of bamboo caught Kevin's attention. "Penis sheathes," Van Dorn explained as if it was perfectly obvious. "And now about your trip."

A large map with elevations and annual rainfall hung above Van Dorn's desk. "Here is Port Moresby, where you'll want to book transport and guides." Van Dorn traced a finger down the spine of mountains that divide the island. "This is the central range—the Owen Stanleys, the Kubor, the Kratke, the Bismarck, the Hagen, the Hindenburg, the Victor Emanuel, and the Star Mountains, which extend into West Irian. Those Star Mountains, my friend"— Van Dorn raised his eyebrows for dramatic emphasis—"are very wild country, indeed. These colored dots mark mountain valleys where I've done fieldwork—no other anthropologist has dared to penetrate so far into West Irian. Now where were you thinking of going?"

Kevin eyed the map. "It'll be my first visit, and I'd like to play it safe. I'd like to see a few villages where the insects and reptiles aren't too dangerous . . ."

"Then don't go at all."

"Why?"

"Because when you go swimming around New Guinea who knows whether you'll tangle with a vicious moray eel, meet a shark face to face, or step on a deadly poisonous stonefish? And when it comes to insects"—Van Dorn smiled—"you can choose between centipedes, millipedes, malaria-carrying mosquitoes, stinging green and red tree ants, scorpions, and spiders so big they actually eat birds! I could move on to reptiles and mention skinks, agamid lizards, which run erect on their hind legs, monitor lizards that grow up to fifteen feet, poisonous taipan snakes, and aptly named death adders. But"—Van Dorn grinned—"why go on? You get the picture. If you want to play it safe, then stay out of New Guinea. Try Bali or Tahiti."

"But why," Kevin ventured, at last finding a way to turn the conversation in the direction he wanted, "did you decide to devote your life to studying such a place?"

Van Dorn stroked his beard and did not answer immediately; Kevin felt he had struck a nerve. The carved statuettes surrounding them seemed to lean forward, eager to hear their master's answer. "Do you realize," Van Dorn finally asked seriously, "that there are now only two areas in the entire world where cultures still exist that have not been touched by so-called civilized man? One, the Amazon basin, is shrinking day by day, and there may in fact be no more uncontaminated peoples left there. The second area is the steep mountain ravines of New Guinea and the swamps around the Sepik River. There are hundreds of little societies there, each with its own language and customs. So I say thank God for the stonefish and the death adders and the bird-eating spiders and whatever else serves to slow the incursion of the known into the unspoiled."

"Your sympathies, then, lie with the savages?" Kevin asked. "And the brutality of those peoples doesn't repel you?" He watched Van Dorn carefully, observing how his eyes glittered in the dimly lighted study.

"Savages?" Van Dorn repeated with a mocking undertone. "Brutality? Primitive? Barbaric? That's just semantics—for me words like 'savage' and 'primitive' have absolutely no meaning." Van Dorn paused and looked at Kevin, and his lips twitched just a bit as if he were suppressing a strong emotion. "Consider the Murngin of Australia. Technologically they're one of the most backward societies we know of. But instead of violent warfare, they settle disputes by playing at war and dancing around each other in a complex but often harmless simulation of real fighting. While we civilized men, on the other hand, aim real nuclear warheads at each other's capital cities."

"Is that what you like about these so-called savages? That they are often more peaceful and humane than technologically advanced civilizations?"

Van Dorn took down a two-headed carved stone ax and showed Kevin the faint but unmistakable bloodstains. "A parting gift from a Mount Hagen headhunter friend of mine," he said. "No, Professor Randall, you mistake me. I detest self-serving generalizations about the goodness of civilized man. To me the great evil of technological progress is that it breeds conformity. It distances men from the natural elements and his natural urges—territoriality, hunting, and food gathering, the struggle to mate with the optimum partner. Technology anesthetizes him and robs him of his unique identity." Van Dorn's voice had grown louder, and now it actually quivered with fervor. "I prefer variety, and if I have to witness cruelty—and make no mistake, every society has its own pet tortures and torturers—I like that brutality to at least be original and fresh!" And, as if to drive home his point, Van Dorn swung the stone ax down on the desktop, where it made a noticeable dent in the wood.

Kevin stared at the bloodstains on that stone axehead.

Van Dorn looked down at the dent he had put in his desk and then frowned oddly at Kevin. Suddenly he turned and led Kevin back into the living room. They halted by the mask with the human teeth, and Van Dorn smiled apologetically.

"Forgive me if I got a bit carried away," he muttered, "but we were discussing something I care a great deal about. I wish there were some way I could explain to you the fascination . . ." He looked up at the mask as if it were an old friend. "The Gussii of East Africa, for instance, believe that relations between men and women are necessarily adversarial and violent. When a Gussii man decides to take a wife, he kidnaps her and has his friends hold her down while he rapes her. But the women get their own back. The young men are circumcized at twelve or thirteen years. As the boys lie in their tents recovering, the young women come in, shed their clothes, and dance around them, naked, until the boys become aroused. Though they can't stop themselves from growing erect, their pain is said to be unbelievably excruciating." Van Dorn paused for a breath and looked right at Kevin. "Such cruelty doesn't shock or disgust me, it intrigues me. I've seen some relationships in the so-called civilized world that are just as cruel, but the torture is veiled and skillfully subtle. I prefer it when it bubbles close to the surface."

Van Dorn moved a step closer. Kevin didn't want his inquiry to seem too direct, too confrontational, but he was powerless to stop himself from asking the next question. "And when cruelty bubbles close to the surface? Boils up, in fact. How do you feel then?"

Van Dorn's shoulders tensed. "For example?"

"Well, street crime right here in New Haven. The muggings, the rapes, the murders. Surely you don't condone them and find them fascinating?"

"We are two very different men, Professor Randall," Van Dorn said in such a low tone it was almost a whisper. "You see something evil in violence, while I see aggression as indispensible to human competition for survival. To tell you the truth, I'm as little upset by a drug addict committing robbery and murder in an alley in New Haven as I am by a headhunter dispatching an enemy in West Irian. I wish you had been in Calcutta four days ago. I delivered a paper at an international anthropology convention there on initiation and warfare among the Ga'e-Wanake, the people I've been living among for the past two years. You might have found my paper revolting, but you would have enjoyed the discussion that followed. There were many who agree with you—it's hard to shock anthropologists, but my paper met with a very mixed reaction."

Kevin immediately spotted the fleck of gold that had unexpectedly been uncovered, and he headed straight for it. "Then I should apologize. Here I've been taking up your time and you've only just gotten back, and haven't even had time to unpack."

"I got back to lovely New Haven two days ago, but don't worry, I unpack in bursts."

Kevin dared one more question. "I gather you're not teaching this semester?"

Van Dorn nodded modestly. "I was lucky enough to get a large

grant. It paid for my two years in the field, and it will allow me to
spend this semester turning my results into a book. But I've bored
you enough about headhunters and philosophy, when you really only
came here for traveler's advice." Van Dorn wrote down a few sug-
gestions: villages Kevin might want to visit and places he might
want to call. He escorted Kevin to the door, and Kevin's last view of
Van Dorn was of him smiling good-bye amid the angry faces of the
oblong masks hanging behind him.

The streets of New Haven seemed broad and comfortingly civilized after Van Dorn's cramped apartment and crazed conversation.
Still, if Van Dorn had been at a convention in Calcutta when the
recent library murder had taken place, then despite all of his suspicious opinions and mannerisms, Kevin would have to count him
out as a suspect.

Chapter 7

"Ali Who?" the secretary in the Calhoun College dean's office asked in an unusually loud voice. She was a woman in her sixties, with a mottled complexion and shoulders that sagged tiredly.

"Shahrzad," Kevin told her. When she craned her neck toward him, he realized that she was slightly hard of hearing. "Shahrzad. Ali Shahrzad."

"One moment." She disappeared into a small file room and returned with a gray manila folder. "Yes, we do have that student. He just returned from a two-year leave of absence."

"I teach in the English department and I need to get in touch with him. Does he live on campus?" Kevin enunciated clearly.

"No," she said. "He lives off campus." She screwed up her nose. "That's odd. We should have a street address for him, but all we have is a post office box number."

"How about a phone number?"

She nodded. "I'm afraid I can't give it to you, though. It's unlisted, and there's a note that we shouldn't release it to anyone."

"Why all the secrecy?" Kevin asked, trying to sound offhand

and loud at the same time. "I just want to get in touch with him about a term paper."

The secretary shrugged. "If you want to leave him a message, I can see that he gets it."

She offered him a note pad, but Kevin declined. If Ali Shahrzad went to such great lengths to protect his privacy, Kevin decided that it might be wiser to find out a bit more about him before he tried to meet him. "That's all right," he told her, "I'll try to get in touch with him through my department. If not I'll come back and leave a note."

Kevin hurried up Elm Street to Saybrook College. He knocked several times before the door to the Saybrook dean's office was opened by a nervous-looking and very thin young man. "I'm sorry, but Dean Ellis went home sick so the office closed early today. We'll be open tomorrow morning at nine," he said apologetically.

Kevin smiled at him. "I don't think I really need to see Dean Ellis. I teach in the English department, and I just need to get in touch with one of your students. Karl Reinschreiber."

The thin young man cringed slightly at the name. "Karl hasn't been a student here in two years," he said. "I know—he was in my class."

"Didn't he come back this year?"

"I'm sure they would never let him back in. He's visited the campus several times and told people that he's applying for readmission, but there's no way they'd ever let him back. He even threatened to sue the school over it, but I don't think anyone took him too seriously."

"Why not?" Kevin asked. "I don't really know him at all—I just need to get his address for a grade referral."

The assistant lowered his voice. "Karl's a nut, and he's dangerous. He goes around in fatigues and belongs to creepy ultra-right organizations. When he was a freshman, he was always doing something violent. He might have applied for readmission this year, but I guarantee you the Yale admissions office would never, never give itself a hundred headaches by letting him back in."

"I'm sure you're right." Kevin thanked him with a smile. "He doesn't sound like a safe fellow to have around. Well, good-bye then."

The assistant gave him a wave and quickly closed the door.

Kevin's own residential college, Trumbull, was just across Elm Street from Saybrook. William Tracey, the Trumbull dean, was a good friend of Kevin's. The portly assistant professor of Byzantine history ushered Kevin into his inner office with a warm handshake. "Jellybean?" the dean asked, pointing toward a large bowl that sat on a corner of his desk.

Kevin shook his head and explained that he was trying to track down a Trumbull student, Peter Pusecki.

"Peter Pusecki," the dean mused, his hands clasped together. "No, he's not a student here now. I remember him—he left two years ago in midsemester. Actually, he didn't just leave, he vanished. Didn't even bother to tell his family or friends where he was going."

"And he never resurfaced?"

Dean Tracey thought for a long second. "Well, Kevin, this is confidential, of course, but he did send us a letter of intent to re-enroll for this semester. It put me in a bit of a bind—because when students who've made mistakes try to come back I do whatever I can for them. So I set the first stages of the readmission process in motion, even though I could tell from that preliminary letter that nothing would come of it—"

"Why?"

"It just wasn't . . . lucid. I shouldn't talk about this, but I was sorry to see one of our own students so . . . off base. He didn't even attempt to explain why he had vanished in midsemester, or what he had done in the interim. He didn't furnish a return address. The writing meandered. As it turned out, he never followed up that letter, so we just scotched the whole thing."

"You wouldn't still have the letter lying around?"

"I'm sure we don't. You know how good Mildred is about keeping things neat. If I may ask, why are you so curious about Peter Pusecki?"

"He borrowed some books from Lansbury a long time ago—

departmental property—and I said since he was in Trumbull I'd try to track him down. We thought maybe he'd come back."

"No luck. Sorry, but I doubt you'll ever see those books again. Give Lansbury my condolences."

"I will," Kevin promised, standing up. "Have to run now. Thanks."

Dean Tracey leaned back and popped a yellow jellybean into his mouth. "Don't mention it."

An exterminator's truck pulled up under Kevin's window just as Kevin was dialing Sam Curson's phone number. The faded blue truck came to a stop as he heard the anthropology professor's office phone ring and ring again.

"Hello?" Curson, though an old friend, always managed to sound as if he had been doing important work and resented being disturbed. In reality, Kevin knew that Curson spent his afternoons in his office reading science fiction.

"Sam, this is Kevin. I wonder if I could ask a strange favor of you. It's about Roger Van Dorn."

"Then I'd rather not get involved," Curson said warily. "He strikes me as a bit of a nut."

"Oh, he'll never know," Kevin assured him. "I just need you to check and see if he was really at an anthropology convention in Calcutta last week, and if so, what day he delivered his paper there."

"Why don't you just ask him yourself?"

"Sam, play this one my way and I'll owe you a big one."

There was a pause while Curson hesitated. Then he said, "I must know someone who was at that convention. I'll call you when I find out." Then he rang off.

In the street below, the exterminator, a tall, thin man, got out of his truck with a large equipment bag and disappeared into the pizzeria.

Kevin dreaded his next call. Of all the silly things he had ever been party to, he considered his membership in a Yale secret society during his college years to be the most ridiculous. More specifically, he had always considered Dan Roberts to be an ass, and he now felt strange asking the man for help. When he got CIA headquarters in Langley, Virginia, he had to go through three different secretaries before Roberts's flat, midwestern voice said, "Dan Roberts speaking."

Kevin gritted his teeth. *"Forsan et haec olim meminisse iuvabit,"* he said into the receiver.

There was a momentary pause. Then Roberts supplied the proper response: *"Nunc est bibendum*—a Harvard man's brain is no better than his bum. Which brother is it?"

"Brother Randall. I hope they don't bug your phone, Dan. They'll think you're out of your mind."

"Not to worry," Dan Roberts replied. "The head of internal security is a Bonesman, and you should hear some of his mumbo-jumbo. How's English poetry? Still parsing away?"

"Still parsing away," Kevin admitted. Then: "Dan, I need a favor."

"Want me to spy on your wife?"

Kevin knew that Roberts meant it as a joke and had no idea what had happened to Anne, but that didn't stop it from hurting. He forced a little laugh. "Nothing that messy. I just need you to run five names for me, no questions asked. I'd be interested in whatever you have on them." Kevin gave him the five names, spelling each of them out carefully. Then he forced himself to say "It's a great service you render, brother."

"What is pledged in youth must live on to the grave, brother," Roberts responded by the book. "I'll have these in a day or two for you. Bye."

Kevin was grateful to hang up the phone. In the street below, the exterminator came out of the pizzeria and walked into the neighboring bookshop. Does he do the whole street? Kevin wondered absently. No one ever questions an exterminator. Perhaps he was going from shop to shop handing out cards and trying to drum up new business? Or maybe, Kevin thought with a rare smile, he's just buying himself a book.

It was four-fifty. The receptionist at the *New Haven Register* had said that Ron Christopher usually came in at five o'clock. Kevin took out Christopher's business card and dialed. He got the same receptionist, and asked to be put through to Christopher's extension. The reporter picked up the phone on the first ring with a loud "Christopher here."

"This is Kevin Randall calling. The English professor."

"I remember."

"How's the story unfolding?"

"They're thinking of restricting use of the libraries to certain floors at certain times. And the football players may organize student patrols. That girl who was killed—her roommate's transferring to Stanford and gave me a very good interview." Ron Christopher sounded busy but very pleased. "Now, what do you want?"

"Another favor," Kevin said. "And this time I have something to give you in return."

"What?"

"I've got five names of people from the Yale community who have returned after two-year absences. They've all tangled with police in the past. I'm sure at least some of them have made it into your paper. Get me anything you can on them."

"And in return?"

"You probably already know that a second girl was chased through the library stacks. She ran for her life, and two hockey players saved her at the last minute—"

"Old news," Ron Christopher broke in. "The police think her imagination may have been working overtime. The number of calls to campus security to report suspicious activity has gone way up—a lot of the students are a little edgy."

"I bet you don't know what they found in the library when they checked it out," Kevin said.

"What?"

"Someone threw a violent fit in a far corner of the same floor where the girl was almost attacked. Books were ripped apart, shelves were overturned, and a steel bolt was ripped from a wall, which would have required great strength."

"How did you find out about this?"

"I can't tell you."

"How can I confirm it?"

"I promise you it's true."

"Maybe . . . it's interesting, but of no real use to me."

"It's just the beginning," Kevin promised. "I'll have more very soon. Now will you check on those names for me?"

"I suppose it can't hurt," Christopher agreed reluctantly. "Do you think any of them are involved in this case?"

"As soon as I know that, you will too," Kevin promised, and spelled out the five names for the reporter.

Ron Christopher copied them down. "Would you be interested in attending a Sunday Sacrament Meeting?" he asked Kevin. "I've been thinking about you, and I really think you would find it healing."

"I'm sure I would. I just don't feel ready."

"Well, think about it. There's no solace in dwelling on revenge."

"I will," Kevin promised. "Bye."

Perhaps Ron Christopher was right, perhaps healing was what he needed and not vengeance. But deep in his heart, Kevin knew that for him, the former was not possible without the latter.

———————————————

The yells and whistles penetrated the corridor of the Payne Whitney Gym. Standing just outside the door of the fencing room, Kevin listened to the clang of foil on foil and Duroc's encouraging profanity. He knew he shouldn't be there; he still had a very long way to go before he could permit himself to walk back into that room where he had once reigned supreme. But he had just jogged four miles without a cramp, and the last two of them had been respectably paced, so he felt he deserved a little reward. He would permit himself to stand here a few seconds more and listen, and remember.

When Duroc came through the door suddenly, Kevin turned his face away and began to hurry down the corridor. But Gaspar

Duroc's voice was insistent. "Kevin, don't run away. It took you long enough to come back."

Ashamed of himself for running, yet positive that if anyone would understand it would be Duroc, Kevin turned to face him. "The Lion," they had called Duroc in his youth. His long blond hair had been his trademark then—Kevin had seen pictures of the young Duroc looking like a seventeenth-century musketeer with a dashing mustache and carefully trimmed long blond locks. Now Duroc's white hair was cropped close to his head, and his wrinkled face and rigid bearing gave him the air of an old army sergeant. He was still light on his feet, though. After gliding up to Kevin, he shook his hand and he pounded him on the back with gusto. "We've become strangers, old friend," Duroc complained, affection lighting up his gray eyes.

"I'm sorry I never called to explain . . ."

"I read about Anne in the papers," Duroc said. "I tried to call you, and to come by to see you, but you were never home."

Kevin stepped close to his former coach and sparring partner to offer an explanation, but he saw that the old man already understood, so he merely whispered, "Part of me died with her."

"But part of you is coming back to life, I see," Duroc observed cheerfully, noting Kevin's sweat-soaked running outfit. "Come, meet my team. They need inspiration."

"I can't yet," Kevin protested, but Duroc had taken him firmly by the arm and was leading him through the double doors and into the little fencing gym.

A dozen young fencers, in jackets and masks, were either engaged in couple drills or stood watching the couples lunge and parry back and forth along the fencing strips. It all came back to Kevin in a rush as he watched: the pairs momentarily frozen in the on-guard position, weight evenly distributed, right feet forward, right elbows six inches from right hips, so that the foils and forearms formed straight lines, and then the sudden dance of movement forward and back across the strip, the awkward lunges and parries and cutovers and repostes as the student fencers put their drills to use.

Duroc clapped his hands twice and everyone stopped. The fencers on the strips lowered their foils and raised their masks. "Our visitor is one of your professors and a great fencer," Duroc said. "A national champion, my own equal with the saber. Salute!" At his command the fencers turned sideways to the attention position and then saluted Kevin with their swords in the centuries-old gesture of respect. Duroc clapped twice more, and they resumed their practice.

"You didn't have to do that," Kevin told him.

"Some are talented but most are just . . . aggressive," Duroc muttered, one eye on his fencers. "For two years I've had no one to test my own saber with. I want you back, my friend, if only to fight with you."

"Look at me," Kevin told him. "I couldn't push you now."

"And look at me, I'm an old man." Duroc grinned. "I say you could get it back quickly if you tried."

"But I couldn't work out with your team in this condition. Not after two years."

"Come any Tuesday after practice is over," Duroc said, leading Kevin toward the door. "We'll spar after everyone else goes home. You can be as awkward as you like."

They reached the door. "I'm sorry I didn't return your phone calls or answer your letters," Kevin told the old fencer. "I was in a deep depression—"

"Please, don't say another word," Duroc cut him off. "I've waited for you to come back and now you have and that's an end to it."

They shook hands quickly and firmly, and then Duroc moved back into the fencing gym with steps so quick and balanced that his feet never seemed to leave the floor.

When he reached his apartment, Kevin took his saber out of the closet and for the first time in two years dared to grip it with his right hand. He looked into the mirror and saw a thirty-three-year-old man with a face lined by suffering standing where a handsome young man had once stood, holding the same saber, and peering into the mirror with eyes no longer innocent.

Chapter 8

Kevin knew it was ridiculous, but as he walked up the path toward the Women's Center, he had the distinct feeling that he was entering enemy territory. The small building had once been a church from which all traces of religion had been removed. A sign reading YALE WOMEN'S CENTER hung over the front door. As he passed under that sign he could hear yells echoing from the main room of the center. He walked down a a short hallway and through a double set of doors to find their source.

The women were standing in two lines, and every few seconds they would shout out in unison and thrust their right knees up and forward as if to crush the testicles of an imaginary attacker.

Hanging back in the shadows, Kevin involuntarily moved his right hand down across his body as if to protect his groin.

A short, stocky, energetic woman dressed in a white cotton karate *gi* stood in front of the two lines, counting off the drill in Japanese. *"Ichi,"* she yelled.

The knees went up as the women shouted, *"Tskeeai!"*

"Ni."

Again the knees crushed the air.

"*San, shi,* go!" At "go" the women in the two lines followed up their knee thrusts with right elbow strikes.

Then the women stopped and listened attentively as the instructor spoke. "He will expect you to freeze up, to go into shock, to wilt," she told them in a strident voice. "If you do, even for a few seconds, he'll have you. The moment you are attacked is the moment to fight back. Women who fight off rapists do so in the first ten seconds of the assault. First, scream. Then fight back with anything you have in your hands. A pen is a great weapon, or a nail file. Go for the eyes, the jugular, the instep. Nine out of ten times, if you keep your wits about you, attack and make noise, he will pull back."

Sunlight streamed into the small auditorium through three high stained-glass windows. The large room was spotlessly clean, yet it had the dank musty smell of damp fur. Kevin wondered if the women shared the center with pets, or if the rain and sleet that had been falling off and on for days had dripped through the roof and was rotting something. Hadn't Jack said the girl who had been chased through the library stacks described smelling a musty odor?

A young Oriental woman dressed entirely in black came out of a side door and hurried over to Kevin. "Can I help you?"

"I'd like to speak to Dean Strong."

"Is she expecting you?"

"No," Kevin admitted. "I called her office for an appointment, and they said she'd be here all day. So I walked over to see if I could catch her. Is she still here?"

The woman nodded toward the stocky woman who was leading the self-defense drill. "That's Amy Strong. She should finish in five minutes. Please follow me."

Kevin followed her into a narrow hallway and through a door marked AMY STRONG in simple black lettering. "Are you sure she won't mind my waiting in her office?" Kevin asked.

"Why should she mind? As soon as she finishes I'll tell her you're here."

Amy Strong's office was small and windowless, and the musty odor was stronger in the confined space. A poster of Corazon Aquino hung above the desk. On another wall was a poster with the words "Want it done right? —Hire a woman!"

A copy of a periodical called *Lesbian Ethics* sat on a corner of Amy Strong's desk, next to an early edition of Gertrude Stein's *Ida*.

Kevin inspected the bookcase. Some of the writers' names— Andrea Dworkin, for instance—he recognized as radical feminist theorists, but he was unfamiliar with most of the books.

The door opened and the short stocky woman he had seen leading the self-defense class entered. A white towel hung around her neck, and she was using a corner of it to rub the sweat off her forehead. Two dogs, a mangy collie and an old and sad-looking cocker spaniel, poked their heads in and then retreated. The woman gave Kevin a polite smile. "I'm Amy Strong. Forgive my pets for not being more gracious."

"Kevin Randall. I don't believe we've met before. I'm in the English department."

"What do you teach?"

"Romance poetry."

The Oriental woman came in with two glasses of iced tea. She handed one to Dean Strong and the other to Kevin. The tea was strong and slightly lemony.

"So, Professor Kevin Randall," Dean Strong said as she walked to the window, and opened it a crack, "what can I do for you?"

Kevin pulled out the copy of the literary magazine he had brought with him. "I read this month's issue of *Thermadon*."

"What did you think of our magazine?"

"Very impressive," Kevin said truthfully.

"Thank you. Coming from a Yale poetry professor, that's a nice compliment. It's been quite a challenge to try to start up a new literary magazine here."

They were both still standing. She hadn't invited him to sit down and hadn't taken a seat herself—while she was perfectly polite, Kevin got the feeling that she didn't want the interview to drag on. Beyond that, he had very little feeling for her as a person. Her administrator's cool served to keep him at arm's length. He decided to push her a little.

"But I thought that *Thermadon* might do better to reach out to a wider audience. So I've come to make a suggestion. May I sit down?"

She nodded, and Kevin sat. She remained standing, so that she looked down at him. "Perhaps if you knew where we got the name for our magazine from, you would understand our choice of subject matter."

"If I'm not mistaken," Kevin replied, "Thermadon was the river that flowed through Themiscyra, the capital city of the Amazons in Greek mythology."

She rewarded him with a grudging look of respect. "Score one for the Yale English department. But if you know what Thermadon was, then you must understand its significance. The Amazons were a community of women who had cut themselves off from men and founded their own society. Thermadon was the river that nourished them, and provided commerce and communication and the exchange of ideas."

"And your literary magazine is supposed to nourish the feminist community here at Yale, and provide communication and help the exchange of ideas," Kevin finished for her.

"Exactly. And it seems to be fulfilling that role fairly well. It is a magazine by women, for women. With all due respect, Professor Randall, if the subject matter doesn't seem broad enough for you that may be because it's not intended to be."

Amy Strong reached down and pulled tight the black belt of her karate *gi*. Her movements were quick and decisive.

"You misunderstand me," Kevin said. "I like the activist tone. Most of the new literary journals at Yale are so stiff and overwritten they're stillborn. *Thermadon* is refreshingly political. That's why I wanted to make my suggestion."

"Which is?"

"Two of my graduate students write angry, politically charged poetry. I know they've had trouble publishing in the *Yale Review* and other magazines. I wondered if you'd consider publishing them. They're both quite good poets, original thinkers, and men."

Dean Strong studied Kevin carefully. She seemed to be searching for an answer to a question that she wasn't exactly sure of. "You walked all the way over here to see if I would accept poems from your graduate students? You're an unusually dedicated teacher."

And you're an unusually suspicious editor, Kevin thought to himself. "I also wanted to tell you how much I admired your first issue," he reminded her a bit lamely.

"Which you've already done. No, Professor Randall, I don't think we're the right place for you to take your talented male graduate students' work. We're a women's magazine."

Kevin pretended to get angry. He let his voice rise. "If there were a men's center on campus that published poems about men's problems exclusively, and wouldn't consider submissions by women, wouldn't you consider that to be sexist descrimination?"

She didn't even have to think—an answer crackled off her lips. "The situations are not at all analogous. Women have always been discriminated against. Men have always had more opportunities. We're trying to provide an outlet, a vehicle of expression for a group that has previously been silenced."

"But why can't you also set up a constructive dialog with the other half of the species?" Kevin pressed. He could see her administrator's cool slipping away as she got angry. He wondered how far he could push her. "Do you think you provide a service by polarizing the community? Most of the material in your magazine about men isn't just negative, it's hateful."

She took a step toward him, and her fists were clenched. Her eyes blazed with anger. "What the hell do you want here?" she demanded almost threateningly, and then suddenly caught herself and fought for control. It was fascinating to watch. Her burning eyes widened slightly and softened, the tension went out of her arms and back, and her fingers folded flat as she clapped her hands lightly against her sides.

In a more subdued tone, she said, "You should read some separatist theory. A number of brilliant theorists have advocated women living with women in small, supportive communities . . ."

"And how would such communities reproduce themselves? Wouldn't they be giving up their posterity?"

"I see you're trying to provoke me," Strong said through tight lips. "I don't know what you're after. . . . You succeeded once, but you won't find me such an easy target again. As for your question, it's the typical male reaction— 'Hey, you can't do without me and my penis.' But the simple fact is that a penis isn't necessary for human reproduction. Sperm is what is necessary, and given that sperm, a turkey baster will work just as well as a penis."

Kevin stood up. "Surely you wouldn't want children to grow up thinking their father was a turkey baster?"

"I've seen some families where the children would have been far better off with turkey basters than with their fathers." She stepped toward the door, ushering him out.

"And women who feel differently?" Kevin asked, fishing. "Women who prefer husbands and who see your little enclave here as an oddity and maybe even an embarrassment. Is there anger toward them?"

"This is a center for all women, and I am a dean for all women, and every woman has an absolute right to make her own decisions for herself," Dean Strong said with deep conviction. "I feel that we should end our discussion. I'm sorry I can't help your graduate students, but it's out of the question." She paused and then added as if in afterthought, "And I don't know why you came here and tried to provoke me, but no doubt you had your reasons."

"Thank you for your time," Kevin responded, heading out. At the door he turned and said, "I wish you good luck with your magazine."

"If you're sincere, I thank you."

The two dogs Kevin had seen before, and a surly-looking German shepherd, followed Kevin to the front door.

On the way back up Elm Street, Kevin veered off across the rectangle of the New Haven Green. It was four-thirty and the green was thronged with men and women hurrying home after work.

Kevin sat down on a bench facing the old campus to watch the parade of townspeople. The cold, clear afternoon was slowly giving way to an absolutely freezing evening. Perhaps that was why everyone seemed to be moving unusually quickly—they were trying to keep warm and to get home before night fell. A poodle pulled an old woman from tree to tree, yanking her along by its red leather leash. A teenage couple passed, holding hands and swinging their joined fingers high in the air with each step as if to proclaim their love.

Beyond the green, the Gothic brownstone gargantua of Phelps Gate separated the bustling New England city from Yale's old campus. The city and the university existed side by side but now, in the twilight, it was possible to see very clearly how they were really two completely different worlds—a flat, open world of workdays and a towering, shadowy world of academic mysteries.

An old couple hobbled by, the man walking very slowly with a cane and the woman adjusting her speed to his unsteady footsteps. Kevin found himself thinking that the simple things in life really were the best and that nonreflective people were truly blessed. He remembered when Jack Hobbs had asked him if he really believed that a member of the Yale community could be mad enough to commit murders and still be able to function in the highly pressurized intellectual world.

The question had bothered him, but after meeting with Van Dorn, and Amy Strong, and hearing about Karl Reinschreiber, Kevin was tempted to think that no one could successfully compete in the higher intellectual circles of a place like Yale without being a bit crazy—there had to be a fire of painful self-doubt or suppressed rage burning beneath the surface. And if such a fire got suddenly out of control . . .

Kevin got up and set off for the *New Haven Register*. If one of his five suspects did have a fire burning out of control, then it might have flared up in the past and been noticed. Amy Strong with her fighting skills and quick temper and Roger Van Dorn with his collection of deadly weapons and affinity for the savage side of humanity might have a secret rage they kept hidden from the world.

Most of the staff of the *Register* had gone home for the night, but Ron Christopher was still at his cluttered desk. He was reviewing the proofs of an article for the next morning's edition, making occasional marks in the margin with a blue pen and clicking his tongue as he read.

His desk was filled with all manner of office junk: stapler, tape dispenser, pen and pencil holder, in-and-out baskets, a Roladex for phone numbers, two dictionaries, a thesaurus, a map of New Haven and surrounding towns, and a stack of old newspapers that had apparently piled up over the past few days. Watching him in his cluttered space, Kevin was once again reminded of a ferret—nestled in his narrow tunnel.

Christopher looked up at Kevin's approach and smiled.

Kevin smiled back.

"You look better," the reporter said. "Happier."

"I don't know about happier, but at least I've been sleeping better," Kevin admitted. "And yourself?"

"I was able to confirm that story you told me about the mess they found in the library the morning after the girl thought she was being chased." His nose twitched. "Still can't tell me your source?"

Kevin shook his head.

Ron Christopher pulled over a chair from the next desk and motioned Kevin to sit down. "I can't really use the story," he said, "but I appreciate the tip. Maybe you can help me out down the road."

"Maybe I can."

"So I ran a check on those five names for you." Christopher pulled a packet of clippings out from a drawer and dumped them on his desktop. "Reinschreiber was the big winner—he was in and out the news as often as he was in and out of jail." He thumped a thick wad of clippings that had been paperclipped together, and Kevin saw the headline on the top article: "Yale Student Arrested for Keeping Firearms in Room."

"This Van Dorn thing started off interestingly," Ron Christopher continued, drawing Kevin's attention to another article whose headline proclaimed: "Student Sues Yale, Professor for Beating." Kevin skimmed the article quickly. Apparently, a few years ago, there had been a sit-in rally in the Hall of Graduate Studies by a handful of students who wanted the school to divest its holdings in any companies doing business with South Africa. During the rally, Van Dorn had tried to get through to his office and the students had blocked his path. The confrontation had escalated into a shoving match and finally a fistfight, and one of the students had gotten his nose broken and been punched in the eye. The student had tried to press charges of assault and battery, but Kevin saw in a small follow-up article that he had dropped those charges a week later.

There were two clippings about Amy Strong. The first from when she had been a graduate student. She had been one of the organizers of a rally for the Equal Rights Amendment and had been arrested when she led a small group of demonstrators to the Yale president's house and refused repeated requests to leave. As the police were carrying her away, one of them had apparently gotten a bit rough with her, and she had kneed him in the groin. Charges and countercharges had been filed and then dropped.

The second clipping was barely a month old. Amy Strong had served on a panel sponsored by the New Haven Police Department on campus security for women. According to the article, she not only taught the self-defense classes at the Women's Center, but also taught a class for New Haven policewomen on how to fight against much heavier opponents.

"Nothing on Pusecki or Shahrzad?" Kevin asked.

Ron Christopher pointed to a tiny clipping from an events column. Two years ago the son of the former Shah of Iran had come to Yale to rally support for his proposal that Iran hold free and open democratic elections. The article mentioned that the Shah's son was introduced by Ali Shahrzad, an Iranian student who was a Yale freshman.

"I drew a blank on Pusecki," Ron Christopher admitted.

"Can I have these?" Kevin asked.

The reporter packed them back into the envelope and handed it to him. "So tell me," he said, "do you think any of them are involved? Reinschreiber sounds like a good candidate for a homicidal lunatic."

"I don't have anything yet," Kevin told him, getting up. "But when I do, I promise you'll be the first to hear about it."

"Thanks." Ron Christopher lowered his voice. "I was talking to one of my colleagues about you. He said he once interviewed your wife about something she was doing for the New Haven Big Sister Fund. He said she was one of the nicest women he's ever met."

"Thank him for me," Kevin said, turning his face away.

"If I can help . . ."

"You have helped."

"I mean help *you*. Won't you please come to a Sunday meeting with me? No pressure—just see what it's like. What do you say?"

"I'm sorry, but no," Kevin told him. "I'm really not interested."

"I won't stop trying . . ."

Kevin shook his hand and headed away, into the cold New Haven night.

. . . And as soon as he got outside he felt her presence . . .

He walked home quickly. The freezing night had fallen over the city. A layer of smog and clouds made the sky moonless and starless, and even the regularly spaced streetlights were unable to pierce the inky black shroud.

. . . And Anne was following him. . . .

Kevin sped up, till he was nearly running. He forced his mind to go over the day's investigations, thinking about Amy Strong, thinking about Ron Christopher, thinking about anything that would keep her specter away.

. . . But Anne was just behind him, step by step she was overtaking him, arms spread wide, eyes glistening. . . .

Why had she chosen tonight? Was it Ron Christopher's innocent comment about her that had roused her spirit? Was she angry that he had gotten so wrapped up in the investigation that he hadn't been mourning? Was it this chilling night that had brought her memory out?

He stopped running and let her spirit throw her arms around him. By giving in, he gained a little time, but he already recognized the onset of an agonizing night. He had suffered enough of them over the past few years to know the warning signs very well. And there was absolutely no way of escaping.

The knowledge of what lay in store for him moved Kevin to

stop off at the Chapel Liquor Store and buy a bottle of Glenlivet. He hadn't had a drink in more than a week, but tonight he knew he had no choice.

. . . She didn't come for him right away. She let him think it might have been a false alarm and that he might get a good night's sleep. She stayed away for so long that he actually put the bottle of scotch away untouched.

Kevin tried fixing a steak for himself but when it began to cook, his hunger turned to nausea. So he wrapped it in tin foil and stuck it back in the fridge.

He took down a volume of Byron's letters, hoping to lose himself in Byron's spirited defense of Alexander Pope and his scathing attacks on Wordsworth, but after about five minutes he had only read a half a page.

A romantic comedy was on TV. He forced himself to sit and watch a few minutes of the sop, and then his revulsion literally catapulted him out of the chair to switch off the set.

. . . She came for him at ten, and he was almost grateful for the chance to surrender. . . .

Kevin put one of Anne's favorite records on the turntable, poured himself a scotch, and stretched out in an armchair. The scotch went down smoothly.

. . . She came to him through one of her favorite doorways—his memory of their honeymoon in Asia. It had been one of those few, perfect times in life when everything seems viewed from a magical height so that all the day-to-day cares recede and only the great romantic sweep of hills and rivers and fields are visible far below. In Japan they had climbed Mount Fuji and shared a cup of sake at the top at sunrise as the dawn broke across the Kanto Plain. In Bangkok they had waltzed in the garden of the Oriental Hotel to live string music, looking down at the Chao Phraya River aglow with millions of small boat lights. And in Hong Kong they had taken the Star Ferry across from Kowloon and then ridden the tram up to the very top of Victoria Peak. It was near closing time, and all the other couples had left, so that for several long moments they had had the most spectacular view in the world to themselves. They had stood on the farthest lookout embracing each other, savoring the galaxy of lights far below, an embrace above an embrace of lights, a dream of love above a lovely dream . . .

Kevin drank down his scotch. He understood what he had to do on this night, and though the knowledge made him shudder there was no fighting it. He had received the same summons before, and he had struggled against it, but in the end he had always complied. So he tugged on an old woolen sweater and then his trench coat, and set off.

It was a night worthy of a Poe poem. The wind howled ghoulishly and the bare tree branches seem to rap out "Nevermore, Nevermore," and it was easy to see New Haven as a dark tarn of Auber in a misty midregion of Weir.

Soon the main gate of the Grove Street cemetery reared up before him weighty and primeval as a neolithic dolmen. Carved into the giant cross slab was the stark promise "And the dead shall be raised!"

Almost as soon as Kevin stepped inside the old cemetery, a cold rain began to fall. At first it was just a whisper among the gravestones, but it soon became a hissing of the spirits, and then the sky burst open with lightning and the demons began their thunderous dancing.

Kevin found Anne's grave. It was by itself in a lonely corner of the cemetery, by a high stone wall. Her father, nearly overcome with grief, had wanted to take her body back to England and bury her in the family crypt, but Kevin had refused to let her go. He had wanted her near him, only a block from Trumbull College, so that he could walk over and talk to her on nights like this. Lord Barrington-Mayfield hadn't liked the arrangement and for the first time they had argued, but in the end it had been Kevin's right to decide.

The stone was white marble and the inscription was short and simple: her full name, Anne Elizabeth Barrington-Mayfield Randall, and the dates of her short life, with an engraving of a wild rose branch beneath them. Finally, there was the verse that he had selected, from Ben Jonson:

> *Underneath this stone doth lie*
> *As much beauty as could die;*
> *Which in life did harbor give*
> *To more virtue than doth live.*

The rain built to a cold cascading crescendo. His forehead and cheeks were numbed by the icy torrent that also soaked his trench coat and sweater. The bells from Harkness tolled midnight.

Anne's body was six feet below where his shoes indented the muddy sod. Kevin could not keep back the morbid thought that the seams of her coffin must be slowly loosening under the constant weight of earth and that the coffin worms might be well into their gruesome feast. How evanescent it all seemed—the rain lashing the gravel paths of the churchyard; his living body an interloper in this dark necropolis; warmth above cold, momentary life above infinite death . . .

The vast host of bards that he had loved and studied in his life visited him in the graveyard as he stood alone. Their great dirges descended upon him with the rain, and their most mournful lines wailed out with the wild wind.

There had been the moments following tender lovemaking when he had rested his head on Anne's stomach, and they had fantasized together about the family they would soon begin. Anne had wanted three children, and when she talked about them her voice had softened with a maternal warmth that seemed to light the dark bedroom. Kevin had savored the idea of introducing his children to the world of literature that he so loved. He even had a list of books in his mind that he planned to read to them on long winter evenings. Now he could not stand to read even a page from any of those children's classics.

At two in the morning the cold rain turned to hail. The pellets of ice stung the exposed skin of his face.

He had planned to teach his children soccer and baseball and, of course, tennis, which Anne had loved and battled him at in set after set. All through the New Haven summers they had played tennis every day, sometimes opposing one another and sometimes playing as a mixed doubles team. She had a hard serve for a woman, and she could return anything when the points were crucial enough. After a game, they usually picked up some ice cream and went home to cook an exotic meal and make love—often right in the dining room—then they ate the ice cream.

Kevin ran his fingers through his hair, and found it damp and icy with melting hailstones.

By four the hail had stopped, and the night wind moved the cloudbank aside to that the morning star found a peephole through the gloom. That lone star hanging in the darkness conjured up the spirit of Wordsworth, lover of nature, mourning his beloved Lucy by first trying to capture her gentle essence:

> *A violet by a mossy stone Half hidden from the eye!*
> *—Fair as a star, when only one Is shining in the sky.*

> *She lived unknown, and few could know When Lucy ceased to be;*
> *But she is in her grave, and, oh, The difference to me!*

That was exactly the phrase; Anne's death had made such a difference to him that the very world itself seemed changed. He knew he was still the same man living in the same city wearing the same clothes and behaving in many ways as he had before Anne's death. But the trees and the summer grass and the winter sky now seemed merely a shallow imitation of what they had once been.

The lovemaking of Anne's soft hands in his own had sometimes been as rich as the lovemaking of their bodies. Their fingers would softly intertwine, palm to palm, back to palm, back to back, and he would slowly draw his index finger across her warm palm till she had tightened her fingers around it as if to feel the blood pulse.

There had been the mornings when she had watched him shave, and he had watched her comb out her long black hair. On such mornings, they found exquisite joy in each other's simplest gestures. For breakfast they would eat wild apples and fresh honey and kiss with the sugary taste thick on their lips.

Dawn broke, a pale white-yellowish puncture in the eastern sky. Kevin stood lone and immobile, all his extremities numb with the cold. Tennyson came then to end the procession of shades, came with his own special and tender grief:

> *Dear as remembered kisses after death,*
> *And sweet as those by hopeless fancy feigned*
> *On lips that are for others; deep as love,*
> *Deep as first love, and wild with all regret;*
> *O Death in Life, the days that are no more!*

Kevin hurried through the still streets that gleamed with a bluish drabness in the early-morning light. Once home, he drew a hot bath and soaked in it, and his hands and feet thawed slowly and agonizingly. After his bath he sipped two cups of strong black coffee, and he was just pouring his third cup when his telephone rang.

"Brother Randall? This is your favorite CIA operative calling you back."

Kevin winced as Roberts's stupid chatter cut through the delicate mood of mourning that he had built all night and was still immersed in. "Good morning, Dan," he muttered.

"Got a good one for you. Know why Henry Wadsworth got laid so often? Because he was a Longfellow. Get it? A long fellow . . ."

Kevin attempted a laugh, but it came out sounding as if he were choking on something deep in his throat.

"Well, I thought it was pretty funny," Roberts said defensively. Then: "I ran those names for you."

"Any results?"

"Pusecki was listed as a missing person a year and a half ago. The New Haven police looked into it, and the police in his hometown of . . . Edgewater, New Jersey, also investigated. There were apparently no leads. He just vanished."

"People don't just vanish," Kevin said.

"Of course they do. Thousands of them vanish every year. The children get the publicity, but there are lots of teenagers too, and students, and even old people. And Pusecki vanished."

"What about Reinschreiber?"

Dan Roberts sounded more enthusiastic. "Now there we had a real red-blooded American boy. His file begins at Yale—you probably know about some of his undergrad stunts. He tried to join our company—passed the CIA written test, but he was found to be too unstable. He trained as a mercenary in a camp in New Mexico that's run by an international munitions dealer, and then he disappeared for a while. We think he went to Nicaragua as a military advisor but we aren't sure. Anyway, he was shot in a firefight about two months ago."

"Shot how?"

"Shot dead. The government identified him by his dental records and sent back some teeth and bone fragments."

"And that's a pretty positive identification? A few teeth and bone fragments?"

"These days, yes," Roberts said. "The docs have turned it into a science. I've also got the goods for you on that Iranian."

"Shahrzad?"

"Yeah, he's another real cutie. His father was one of the heads of SAVAK—the old Shah of Iran's brutal secret police force. When the revolution came, his father got the whole family safely out of the country along with their personal fortune, which CIA sources estimate at four hundred million dollars. They resettled in Beverly Hills, where the old man still lives in one of the most carefully guarded private homes in America."

"Why the security?"

"The new government of Iran put a price on his head, or at least that's the rumor. Ali is the old man's youngest son. We've got a little bit on him because he joined several pro-Shah organizations that we monitor. Kid's supposed to be nutso."

"How do you mean?"

"He's been in and out of mental institutions for uncontrollable violent behavior. Once got into a fight with two U.S. marshals at an airport and put them both in the hospital. His father somehow kept him from going to jail. Also, a couple of years ago, a Robert J. Lawrence—a Wall Street bigwig—got a court order restraining Ali from harassing his daughter. Apparently Ali kept after the girl and was arrested, but all charges were later dropped."

"Anything on him in the past two years?" Kevin asked.

"Nothing. But I'd stay away from him if I were you. He sounds rich, mean, dangerous, and crazy."

"What about Amy Strong?"

"Nothing at all. Whoever she is, she's kept her nose clean, as far as the Agency's concerned."

"And Van Dorn?"

"Van Dorn was once arrested on flight from Port Moresby to Kuala Lumpur when a passenger noticed that he had a spear in his flight bag. It turned out to be an anthropological curio, and the American consul in Malaysia got him off the hook. Helpful?"

"Extremely."

"I won't ask why you wanted the info—probably ties into poetry somewhere down the line, I figure."

"It does, and thanks, brother," Kevin said, and hung up.

As he sipped his third cup of coffee, he thought about the information. The teeth and bone fragments might not be 100 percent satisfying, but if they were good enough for the CIA they should probably be good enough for him to eliminate Karl Reinschreiber as a suspect.

That left four: Shahrzad, Pusecki, Strong, and Van Dorn. He had no idea where to look next, or even if he was merely wasting his time on a crazy revenge fantasy.

That job at the University of Edinburgh was probably still open. He could leave this city of gloom far behind. Or, even better, he could swallow a few pills and be rid of the pain forever. They would bury him next to Anne, and it would be as close to her as he could ever come.

Kevin closed his eyes, tilted back his chair, and flirted with the sweet image of his own death.

She who chases must be chased, and she who inflicts pain must be made to suffer for it, and if this is not true then truly nothing matters.

In the beginning there was darkness, and darkness was upon the face of the deep, and when she first came she brought pain in her right hand and blood in her left hand, and all of what came after was her fault and no one else's, not mine, not the other's, but hers . . .

The first time?

Grab her by the neck and wring the life out. That worked for a while, but the demon had come back.

The next time?

Back to the place of the books, back to laugh and torment.

Snap her neck and gouge her back through to the spine, and rip her arm till it turns in its socket, and the blood is over the deep, and all is quiet . . .

That had worked each time.

And then the long jump . . .

And now the jump back . . .

She would not stop, she had come again two weeks ago and with her footsteps the ringing singing stinging pressure had built till freshly spilled blood finally quieted everything again, and the books alone watched and knew, just as they always know.

The last time?

Had been the escape, which still burned.

It's going to happen more often now?

Yes, I can feel her coming again, much stronger now—her footsteps, chasing through time, louder and harsher.

I am afraid.

Now is when the pain begins.

Part Two

All My Madness

All my faults perchance thou knowest,
All my madness—none can know!

—George Gordon, Lord Byron
from "Fare Thee Well"

Chapter 9

Midori did not know whether she disliked the man or if she was jealous of him—she knew herself to be prone to the latter, but she suspected that in this case she really did not like him.

Jennifer's father had come to Cheltenham two days ago, unannounced, unexpected, and at least as far as Midori knew, unsummoned.

He had arrived in the morning, during breakfast. His tall, stiff body cast a long shadow over the table where Midori and Jennifer sat sipping tea and nibbling on toast. Jennifer jumped up at the sight of him—actually jumped out of her chair to throw her arms around him. Only after a very long hug did she remember to introduce Midori.

"Dad, this is my best friend, Midori Kawabata. This is my father, Robert J. Lawrence."

The man the tabloids had nicknamed the King of Wall Street looked down at Midori, examining her hair, skin, posture, and clothing with that peculiar stare that very, very rich American men use, as if he wanted to put a price tag on her. "Charmed," he said, and his mouth full of capped teeth flashed a smile at her that would have done honor to a TV evangelist.

For two days he had stayed in a special temporary guest suite at Cheltenham, taking long walks with Jennifer. Midori politely declined to go on those walks, saying that no doubt father and daughter wanted to be alone together. But she knew what the father's message must be, she sensed what had brought him across the Atlantic to Cheltenham. He wanted Jennifer to come home.

"Come home, my only child." Midori had seen it in his face the first day he had appeared.

"Come home, you've healed enough." She had heard the echo of it as she had watched the two of them stroll away from Cheltenham, bundled up against the cold and matching each other step for step.

"Come home, and whatever it was that hurt you in the past won't get at you again." She felt his promise as he sat at tea with them, exchanging conversational pleasantries while, at the same time, communicating with his daughter in a much deeper language of subtle, imploring glances.

Midori admitted to herself that the second reason why she disliked the King of Wall Street was that he knew what it was that had hurt Jennifer so badly. He knew, and he had allowed it to happen. And Midori didn't know, but she was not going to allow it to happen again.

On the afternoon of Lawrence's second day at Cheltenham, Midori joined Jennifer when she took her father through the portrait gallery. The portraits were off in their own wing of the castle. A guard walked constantly from room to room, and several of the most valuable paintings were encased in airtight glass.

Jennifer started with the Gainsboroughs, her favorites. "Cheltenham has the finest collection of seventeenth-century English portraits in the world, except maybe for the National Gallery in London," she told her father.

"It better have the best, for the amount it costs to stay here," he replied.

Midori, who had tagged along, noticed that the King of Wall Street watched his daughter and only occasionally glanced around at the paintings.

"These are the Gainsboroughs. Do you see how lyrical and unpretentious the landscapes are behind the figures? Thomas Gainsborough started off as a landscape painter, and only later began painting portraits because he needed the money from rich society patrons."

"Smart fellow," the King of Wall Street observed.

"Dad, at least try to see what I see in them." She waited while he stopped and studied a portrait intently. "Do you see how relaxed and unforced the pose is? It's as if he took Van Dyck's techniques after a century and a half and brought them up to date. And the lighting is so effortlessly translucent, it just has to remind you of Rubens."

"It smacks of Rubens, all right," he agreed.

She punched her father on the shoulder, and he lightly punched her back. The father-daughter interplay was so cute it actually made Midori feel a bit sick.

Jennifer led her father over to the Reynoldses. "Sir Joshua Reynolds, Gainsborough's rival, was the first president of the Royal Academy. He felt that painters should follow set rules and procedures, and even wrote them down in a book. Do you see how fake, how forced, how absurdly allegorical his paintings are compared to Gainsborough's?"

"Absolutely." The King of Wall Street nodded. "When I have my portrait painted, I'm going the Gainsborough route."

"Dad, he's not a highway."

"And what do you think? Gainsborough or Reynolds?" He had asked Midori.

I think you know that I love your daughter and want to keep her here. "I don't like either of them," she had answered honestly.

"Midori only likes a painting if half the canvas is blank," Jennifer told her father.

Don't speak for me, or defend me to him, or criticize me in front of him, Midori had pleaded silently. Just make your decision and don't keep us waiting.

That night, just after midnight, Midori was surprised to hear her bedroom door open and close and Jennifer's light footsteps approach her bed. In a moment, Jennifer slipped underneath the covers, trying to kiss her.

"Why do you keep turning away?"

"I don't want your good-bye kisses," Midori told her.

"You think I would leave you?"

"You already have."

"He's my father. Aren't I allowed to spend a little time with him?"

No, Midori thought, no, you're not allowed. You're not allowed because you love him, and I want your undivided love. You're not allowed because my own father would never, never come from Japan to visit me here. When he pays for me to stay here, it's not really because he hopes that I'll get better and come home—he pays so that I'll stay away. He feels that his crazy daughter who has breakdowns and fits and frenzies in public places is a disgrace. Deep down we hate each other . . .

Midori rolled over and summoned her courage and demanded, "Are you going home or not?"

The silence had been thick and complex. "No," Jennifer finally said. "I'm not ready yet."

"But he wants you to go back?"

Jennifer nodded, and Midori felt her nod in the darkness.

"And you will go back, sometime?"

"We can't hide here forever, can we?"

Midori put her arms around Jennifer then, clutching her tightly, holding on as if for dear life. "Yes, we can," she whispered. "That's the one advantage of being so rich. We can hide out forever and ever and ever."

"Did I know Peter Pusecki?" The young man on the couch played to his girlfriend for dramatic effect. "Sharon, he wants to know if I knew Peter Pusecki! You tell him."

"They were freshman roommates," the girl in the armchair told Kevin. "Bradley has ever so many wonderful stories about him."

"I'd like to hear some of your stories," Kevin said. "Anything you can tell me." He didn't like the girl at all. She was wearing an expensive black tapered-leg silk jumpsuit that made her look like the Catwoman. A light-blue shawl was thrown over one shoulder. She had on huge earrings and lucite bracelets and enough perfume to embarrass a flower garden. Her eyes never strayed far from Bradley Sutton. Everything she did or said seemed calculated to please him.

Bradley Sutton looked as if he was used to being treated well. His thin, pinched face widened out at the neck into a body as soft and poorly defined as a pillow. He was dressed in pleated slacks, a white shirt, a black Basco blazer, and a thin pink tie. Together, Kevin estimated, the couple were probably wearing close to two thousand dollars worth of clothes.

Bradley's upperclassman's suite in Yale's newly renovated Mc-Clellan Annex was very spacious, perfectly neat, and filled with expensive gadgets and toys for grown-up children: a thirty-six-inch Sony video monitor, a German stereo system with three-way speakers, a black Italian leather sofa and matching chairs that could be tilted or reclined by remote control, and four whole shelves of compact discs and videotapes. Bradley's Phillips-Exeter Academy diploma hung on one wall, across from a picture of Oscar Wilde looking fat and ghastly pale.

"Peter Pusecki was a boor," Bradley said, delighted with the word he had chosen. "A through-and-through boor. Not a bore, mind you."

"And not a Boer," his girlfriend contributed cryptically.

"It was naive of Yale to think that two eighteen-year-olds from such different backgrounds and . . . pedigrees . . . could find enough in common to become friends. I should have gone to the dean's office the very first day, when he occupied the bigger bedroom. Instead, I politely suggested that since he had fewer possessions, it was logical for him to take the smaller room."

"What did he say to that?" Kevin asked.

"Nothing. He just moved in as if I wasn't there, locked the

bedroom door when he was done, and went out without saying so much as a word to me!"

"I didn't think the bedroom doors locked," Kevin said. "I thought only the outside suite doors locked."

Bradley Sutton nodded in agreement. "You're absolutely right—the bedroom doors don't lock. But Peter had a lock on his within about ten minutes. Imagine, he walks in, takes a good look at me, moves his one trunk into the bigger bedroom without saying a word, and then installs a lock and leaves."

"Didn't you tell me his father was a locksmith?" the girlfriend asked.

"An unemployed locksmith. I don't think anyone in that family ever had a steady job."

"Why else do you call him a boor?" Kevin tried to nudge the conversation back on track.

"He was a slob," Bradley answered quickly. "I wasn't sure about his bedroom, because he kept it locked, but when it came to the living room, he never picked anything up. I mean, he would clip his toenails while I was entertaining company and leave the parings wherever they fell on the rug. I once found one of his old socks in my alabaster Exeter drinking mug. And, please forgive the vulgarity, Sharon, he would make the most grotesque bodily sounds with complete strangers in the room. I think he enjoyed driving us away with his noxious noises and odors."

"Was he happy at Yale?" Kevin asked.

"He was . . . incapable of understanding the rules and rhythms of an Ivy League university," Bradley asserted. "As far as I could gather, he came from a miserable hole of a high school. It seems to me that no matter how smart a person is—and in his own way Peter was about as clever as they come, I'll give him that much—it's grossly unfair of Yale to assume they can make the jump all at once. In fact, while he was here, Yale kept its hands off and let him falter and finally fall. So why have you come around trying to find out about him now?"

"It's part of an effort by the university to look into the cases of students who matriculated in the past three years but didn't graduate," Kevin said glibly. "As you probably know, one of the percentages Yale and Harvard bat back and forth is the number of freshmen who enroll compared to the number of seniors who eventually graduate. In order to bring up our numbers just a bit, we're looking into the cases of students who matriculated and then for one reason or another didn't finish."

"Well, you can forget Peter Pusecki," Bradley said smugly. "The director of admissions must have been snorting cocaine when he admitted him. Shar, honey, get me a Perrier, would you?"

"You take a lot for granted, you know," Sharon said, even as she hurried over to the fridge.

"She loves to do things for me," Bradley told Kevin, actually raising his voice slightly to make sure that she heard him. "Can you explain that? All my father has is a lousy five million dollars or so."

"Brad, I don't think that's funny," she said from the other side of the room. "Professor, would you like a drink too?"

"No, thank you," Kevin said. "Why do you say that Peter was an admissions mistake, when you admit that he was very smart?"

"Oh, he was smart, but he had no focus, no foundation to build on, and God knows no study habits. Listen, do you want to hear a story about him?"

Kevin nodded.

Sharon came back with the Perrier, handed it to Bradley, and then sat down next to him on the couch to complete his audience.

"A month or two into freshman year, a water balloon war broke out in our entryway," Bradley began. "It was room against room, and as the hostilities escalated, so did the weaponry. It wasn't long before guys were taking the fire extinguishers off the walls and spraying them at enemies. There were a few people like Pusecki who didn't join in, and of course no one wanted to antagonize him because of his size, but it got so bad that people began lowering ropes out of their windows and crawling down them to go to class."

"What do you mean, that no one wanted to anger Peter because of his size?" Kevin cut in.

"You haven't seen a picture of him?"

"Just from the neck up."

"Well, he was a giant. Six four or six five easy, and believe me, it was solid muscle. You would swear that he had spent his whole life in a gym. Anyway, at a certain point in our little fire extinguisher war, the master of Trumbull College stepped in. He fancied himself a disciplinarian and he felt that we were creating a fire hazard by shooting off fire extinguishers. So he sent out a stern warning that the halls of our dorm would be patrolled at irregular intervals. And he changed the fire extinguishers from the type you can just pull off the wall to the type enclosed in a glass case. And the cases were wired so that if anyone broke the glass or tried to take an extinguisher, all the dorm's fire alarms would go off."

"And Peter wasn't involved with this?"

"Not at all. He was too busy with his girlfriend to care about water fights," Bradley said, and a shadow passed across his face. He sipped his iced tea. "Those new fire extinguishers really stymied the rest of us. We were sitting around in my living room, trying to figure out what to do, when Peter walked in. He listened to our frustrated conversation for just a few minutes and then he offered us a deal. If we would make sure that no students came out of their rooms that night, he would take care of the fire extinguishers for us.

"No one knew quite what to make of it, but everyone was intrigued. So that night, we stayed out of the halls. The next morning every single fire extinguisher was gone. None of the glass cases had been broken, and none of the alarms had been set off—it was like the fire extinguishers had just disappeared. And later that day the news came that they had reappeared. All ten of them had been found inside the master's locked inner office. They had been discharged all over his office, causing at least a thousand dollars worth of damage. And there were no clues. The master investigated, the Yale police investigated, and the New Haven police were finally brought in. No clues were ever found, and no explanations were ever put forward for how the extinguishers were swiped or how whoever swiped them got into the master's office. But we had a pretty good idea who did it, and Pusecki became a bit of a legend after that. Everyone admired him for his ingenuity, but there was also a feeling that he had gone a bit too far. It would have been enough to just steal the extinguishers. To break into the master's office and do so much damage was criminal and . . . not quite in the sporting spirit, if you see what I mean."

"How did he do it?" Kevin asked. "You were his roommate, didn't you ever ask?"

"I never asked because he would never have told me," Bradley said. "As you've probably gathered, we weren't the best of friends. But he had tremendous technical cleverness—he could pick locks, wire stereos, repair refrigerators, fix cars . . . all that sort of thing." Bradley stopped talking and glanced at his watch and then at his girlfriend. "I'm afraid we've got a Rockingham Club luncheon to go to," he told Kevin. "Time does fly when you begin reminiscing . . ."

"You've been very kind," Kevin told him. "Just two more questions. We're trying to track Peter down, and when you mentioned that he had a girlfriend, the thought came to me that maybe she might know where he is. Were they close?"

"Were they close?" Bradley repeated back, as if the question was absurd. "They were so close they were disgusting. The thought that a girl like that, wealthy, polished in every way, gentle, graceful, finely finished, could spend twenty-four hours a day with the likes of Peter Pusecki . . ."

"If you think I'm going to sit here, listening to this, you're crazy," Bradley's girlfriend exploded in sudden anger. She got up and without a backward glance stormed to the door. "I'll be waiting at the club," she called back, and left, slamming the door behind her.

"Sharon gets a bit jealous when I talk about Jennifer Lawrence," Bradley confided to Kevin. "And well she should. I don't mind saying I developed quite a crush on her when we were at Exeter. Half the men in our class did too. And the ones who didn't had something wrong, if you know what I mean."

"What was it about her?"

Bradley Sutton hesitated, and then smiled. "It was like . . . there are so many millionaire fathers who lavish money on their daughters and waste it. Believe me, I've dated my share of them. They've had dancing lessons but they can't dance, singing lessons but they can't sing, and they've been to finishing schools but they're about as finished as the three stooges. Well, Jennifer was the one girl who made it all work for her. She'd had art lessons and not only could she sketch wonderfully but I think she knew more about some areas of art than some of the professors here. She'd had music lessons, and when she played the cello it was pure magic. Her manners were perfect but they were also natural, and somehow she had managed not to turn into a little bitch. And she was so lovely, so innocently, playfully charming, it could take your breath away."

Bradley stopped for breath. "She sounds perfect," Kevin prompted him.

"She was. Except that there was one tiny screw loose somewhere. She didn't go out with many guys, but the ones she did choose were real oddballs. How else do you explain Peter Pusecki?"

"Seems like an unlikely match."

"I've never seen two people like that," Bradley said, his hands knotting together. "They were like animals in heat. I couldn't get to sleep at night because of the moans that would come from his bedroom." Bradley paused, and his voice took on a thoughtful tone that Kevin hadn't expected to hear from him. "And I'm not even being fair. It was physical, but it was more than physical. He completed her, and I guess she completed him, and for a while, much as I hated him for it, I began to believe that the beast could make beauty happy."

"And then the fairy tale ended?"

"I don't know what happened," Bradley admitted. "We weren't friends, but toward the end of the second semester I couldn't help noticing that Peter started sliding downhill. He would be gone for days at a time, and sometimes when he was around he would be so lost in himself that he wouldn't respond to anyone around him. He stopped doing his classwork. I always thought he was a slob, but it got worse and worse. Frankly, I don't know how Jennifer could stand to be around him. And then he just disappeared." Bradley jumped up. "Listen, I've got to disappear now too, or I'm going to lose a girlfriend."

"I'm headed out myself," Kevin said, standing up with him. "I'll walk out with you."

Bradley Sutton carefully double-locked the door behind them and they started down the wide stairs side by side. A young woman who passed them purposefully ignored Bradley, who purposefully ignored her right back. The old campus was crowded with freshmen coming home from their last classes of the day.

"Did Peter ever get in trouble with the police that you can remember?" Kevin asked, hurrying to keep up with Bradley Sutton's surprisingly fast pace.

"Just over the fight."

"What fight?"

Bradley grinned at the memory. "It's nice when two guys you don't care for square off." He slowed down a bit to tell the story. They passed through the High Street gate. "A couple of weeks before Peter disappeared he got into an incredible brawl with one of Jennifer's old prep school boyfriends in the Calhoun dining hall. They damn near killed each other. The cops finally broke it up and took them both away. A lot of property was damaged, but I guess the university decided not to press charges."

"The prep school boyfriend must have had his hands full."

"You never saw Ali Shahrzad," Bradley Sutton answered.

Kevin struggled to keep the sudden rush of excitement at the connection of names out of his voice. "Big?" he managed to ask.

"Wide. Talk about Jennifer's penchant for crazy boyfriends, there was a real candidate for the nut house. He was at Exeter for one year, until they threw him out. Guy was rich as Midas and good-looking to boot, in an exotic sort of way. All the girls were chasing him, and he let quite a few of them catch him, but he only had the real hots for Jennifer."

"With that much money, he must've been *very* crazy for them to kick him out of prep school."

"He talked to himself," Bradley Sutton answered. "Some people said it was because he was observing Islamic holy fasts. He raved about angels and demons. I always thought it was because he was on drugs."

Bradley Sutton crossed Elm Street against the traffic, forcing cars to swerve around him as if he had the right of way. Kevin followed, darting ahead of a taxi.

"Shahrzad got a real bad rep for mistreating women," Bradley continued. "Rumors, maybe, or maybe they were true."

"What kind of rumors?"

"The rumors were that he enjoyed hurting them. That's why they kicked him out. After Jennifer dumped him, a freshman girl accused him of tying her up and beating her. Maybe he was into that stuff. Why are you so curious about him?"

"It's just an interesting story—these two guys sound so different," Kevin said.

They turned onto York Street and Bradley took a small comb out of his breast pocket, ran it through his hair twice, and replaced it. "Our club meets at Mory's," he said. " 'Fraid this interview has to stop."

"You've been very helpful," Kevin told him. "Say, who won that fight in the Calhoun dining hall?"

"It was a toss-up. I really think they would have killed each other if the cops hadn't come."

Bradley crossed the street toward the old Yale eating club, and Kevin still followed him. "Just one more thing and I'll let you go eat," he promised. "Where did the Lawrence girl go?"

"Transferred to Penn," Bradley told him. "And what a loss it was for all of us."

"And Peter? If you absolutely had to take a guess, where do you think he might have gone?"

"To the devil," Kevin told him with no hesitation. "Or back to northern New Jersey. And in my opinion, they may well be one and the same thing. Good-bye." He turned and walked up the steps, and in a second Mory's heavy wooden door swung shut behind him.

Chapter 10

A black Jaguar rolled to a stop in front of Trumbull gate and a middle-age man in a dark suit pivoted in the driver's seat to wave Kevin into the car. "I hope you haven't been waiting long," he said with a slight Middle Eastern accent.

"Only ten minutes."

"Good. Ali is anxious to see you."

He pulled the sports car back out into traffic and guided it skillfully from lane to lane. The car was immaculately clean and completely lacking in personal touches save for a small plastic Playboy bunny hanging from the rearview mirror. The driver, who was well built and balding, sported a thick black mustache. He wove through New Haven traffic with only his left hand on the steering wheel, and used his right hand to feed himself some sort of food out of a small brown paper bag.

"Cashew nuts, unsalted," he explained, feeling Kevin's glance. "Would you like some?"

"No thanks. Do you work for Ali?"

The driver glanced at Kevin, and his eyes held neither warmth nor hostility. Then he looked back at the road. "My name is Fahmi," he said. "Shall we have music? I have developed a taste for country and western."

He popped a tape into the car's stereo and Hank Williams's crooning began. Kevin understood that the loud music was meant to discourage further attempts at conversation so he leaned back and tried to follow the car's route. They headed north toward Hartford and then east toward Manchester. Kevin was soon completely lost as the Jaguar left highways and large roads behind and began streaking through the Connecticut countryside. Darkness was falling, and by the time the Jaguar purred to a stop at a large, low-built ranch house, the sun had sunk below the horizon.

Fahmi led Kevin to the front door, rang the bell twice, and then unlocked the door with his own key. The interior of the house smelled strongly of unfamiliar spices. Fahmi led Kevin down a plushly carpeted hallway and knocked lightly on a closed door. A guttural command in a language Kevin couldn't identify sounded from inside the room. Fahmi opened the door and stepped in, and Kevin followed him.

"The Yale professor is here," Fahmi said, and left, closing the door behind him.

At one time the room had probably been the house's master bedroom, but it had been transformed into a small gym complete with a chinning bar, free weights, a bench press, a heavy bag, and wall mirrors. A magnificently muscled young man was doing rapid-fire chin-ups on the far side of the room. He wore only black sweat-pants, leaving his upper body and arms bare, and his massive biceps and deltoids jumped out several inches with every movement. His short, compact body had remarkably broad shoulders. His neck, like the rest of his body, was short and very thick. Long black hair hung down over his forehead above his dark eyes.

Kevin took another step into the room. The young man's body shot up and down like a piston, and his pace never altered or even slowed as he said, "The Calhoun master's office forwarded your note to me, Professor Randall."

Suddenly, and with great speed, the young man used the chin-ning bar to do a spinning dismount. He flew through the air and

planted both feet on the floor directly in front of Kevin. He smiled
and held out his hand. "Ali Shahrzad. I am sorry you had to come
so far just to find me."

They shook hands. Ali Shahrzad wasn't sweating at all.

"I take it you don't like New Haven," Kevin said.

"It's not that. For me, it is better to live in a place that is not so
crowded. I go in when I have classes, but I have managed to set up a
schedule that allows me to spend most of my time here. Would you
like some tea? I could have Fahmi make us some."

Kevin shook his head.

Shahrzad pulled a white towel off the bench press and draped
it over his shoulders. "Your note struck me as very curious," he said.
"You said that you needed to talk to me about a friend of mine at
Yale. I didn't think I had any friends here. I've made it a point not
to make any."

Shahrzad's voice was deep and musical. Now that they were
face to face, Kevin saw that the weightlifter's features were strikingly handsome in a boyish way.

"Not a friend from Yale," Kevin said. "A friend from Exeter
who also went to Yale. A girl by the name of Jennifer Lawrence. I
can't seem to locate her, and a number of people mentioned that you
were close to her . . ."

Shahrzad's smile quivered and he turned his back on Kevin.
"Jennifer Lawrence," he repeated to himself. For a long while he
was silent, until Kevin thought he might have gone into some sort of
trance or seizure. Not a single muscle moved on the massively developed back.

"Yes, Jennifer Lawrence," Kevin finally said. "A fellow named
Bradley Sutton whom I talked to suggested that you might know
where she's gone off to. She assisted me on a research project two
years ago, and we've just hit it lucky—a foundation has offered me
a large grant. Naturally I want to let her know and see if she wants
to continue working on the project, but it appears that she left New
Haven without leaving a forwarding address . . ."

Ali Shahrzad turned. His features had undergone a marked
change. His face no longer looked boyishly handsome—his eyes

were wide with near-maniacal fury. "Jennifer Lawrence has no heart or soul. Do not speak of her."

"Bradley Sutton said you and Jennifer were friends . . ."

"Do not mention her name to me," Ali Shahrzad commanded shrilly. "I don't know her anymore, I don't talk to her anymore, she is dead to me."

"Actually, though, I think she's still alive, and I must find her," Kevin said evenly.

For a long minute they stood in complete silence. Kevin noticed for the first time that the room smelled of incense.

Ali Shahrzad took a deep breath and let it out. Suddenly he glanced at a corner of the room, and Kevin followed his glance but saw nothing. "So she has come back," he said to the empty space, as if someone were there, listening. "She will always come back." The young man slowly returned his gaze to Kevin's face. "Sometimes you wish something were over but it cannot be," Shahrzad told Kevin in a low voice, "and sometimes you think you have buried some pain deeply but the memory and the pain refuse to stay buried. Do you understand?"

"Yes," Kevin answered truthfully. "I think I do." Ali Shahrzad looked at him, and for a moment they connected on a deep level.

"Well, that is the way it is with . . . the girl you spoke of," Shahrzad said, nodding. "I will speak of her no further. Her name will not sound in this house again."

"Okay," Kevin agreed. "I wouldn't have bothered you except that since you've been away for two years, and she's been away, it seemed possible that the two of you might have been in contact . . ."

"SILENCE!" Ali Shahrzad bellowed, and as he tensed the muscles of his shoulders and chest coiled like angry snakes. "You will not speak of her. You will not speak about the past two years . . ."

Shahrzad turned away and walked to the bench press. He put his white towel down on the bench, and when he turned back his voice was just barely under control. "This Bradley Sutton you talked to actually named me?"

"Well, yes, along with a number of other people . . ."

"I'm sorry you had to come all the way out here for nothing. Fahmi will drive you back to New Haven immediately. Do not ask questions about me or speak of me to anyone else."

Kevin didn't see how Fahmi could have been summoned, but at that moment the balding driver opened the door and said, "We can leave at once."

At the door, Kevin turned and said, "Thanks again. Sorry to disturb you."

But Ali Shahrzad gave no sign that he had even heard. He was back up on the bar, doing lightning-fast chin-ups and actually shaking the steel bar with his angry intensity.

Kevin called everyone he knew at Yale even remotely connected with Middle Eastern studies, but found out little more about Ali Shahrzad. Faculty members knew of him—they had heard about his political activism on campus and were familiar with his rich and powerful family—but few seemed to know him personally. The young man had apparently made a largely successful effort to attend Yale classes and at the same time keep his distance from teachers and fellow students.

Kevin was particularly struck by warnings he received from two of his faculty friends. They told him that he was poking around in a dangerous area and should stay far away from Ali Shahrzad and his infamous family.

So, for the time being, Kevin decided to take their advice. A question had occurred to him about Roger Van Dorn that he could answer very easily.

The secretary of the anthropology department was nice enough to check the two names Kevin gave her against past enrollment in Van Dorn's popular introductory anthropology class. She reported that Alyssa French, who had been murdered a short time ago in the stacks, and Irene Dunn, who had been killed two years ago, just before Anne's murder, had both taken Van Dorn's anthro survey class. Was it merely coincidence, or was Roger Van Dorn striking out at women he had met in his classes? Anne hadn't studied with

Van Dorn—had her death been a mistake? Since Dan Curson was checking whether Van Dorn had been at that conference in India, Kevin decided to turn his attention to Peter Pusecki until he had the answer.

Kevin stopped at the Yale Co-op and bought a manila folder like those he had seen used in the residential college deans' offices. Back in his rooms, he typed out a fake high school letter of recommendation for Peter Pusecki and put it in the folder. Then taking a copy of his own old college transcript, he whited out and retyped the names so that at first glance the transcript seemed to belong to Peter Pusecki. He wrote PETER PUSECKI across the tab of the manila folder in black Magic Marker, and headed down to the Trumbull dean's office.

Dean Tracey's secretary, Irma, still remembered Anne warmly, and all during Kevin's decline into chronic lateness and rule breaking in the past two years, Irma had helped him out by giving him second and even third chances to file forms and meet deadlines.

She was dour and fiftyish, with reddish-brown hair just starting to turn gray. "Dean Tracey's at a meeting. I really can't let you into the old students' files without his permission."

Kevin had looked up the administrators' meeting and purposely come by when the Dean would be absent. Now he tried to look desperate. "Irma, can you do this for me as a personal favor?"

"It's closing time."

"It will just take a few seconds. I have to write a recommendation for a student who wants to be readmitted, and I forgot some important details about him . . ."

"Ah, Kevin." She sighed. "Whatever are we going to do with you? This can't wait until tomorrow?"

"I'll miss the deadline. If you can just let me see his file for two seconds, while you're shutting this office up for the night, it would be a godsend."

After taking a key ring out of her purse, she unlocked a large gray metal file cabinet. "Under *P,*" Kevin told her. "Peter Pusecki. I can't tell you how grateful I am."

When she handed him Pusecki's file, he was horrified to see

that she had written Peter's name across the tab in green rather than the usual black Magic Marker. The one he had brought to switch would not match. Meanwhile, she was hovering over his shoulder.

"Go ahead and get ready to lock up. I'll be done in one minute."

She stepped to the window and slid the bolt down.

Kevin turned his body to the right, shielding what he was doing from her. Deftly he opened the top of his black briefcase, reached into the fake file he had prepared, and switched the contents of the manila folders.

"That's all I needed to know," he told her. "You really saved my neck. I'll be able to write him a decent letter now." He handed back the old folder with the faked contents and was relieved to see that she didn't bother to examine it. She just hurried over to her gray metal file cabinet, slid the folder back into place, and locked the drawer.

"Now go away, out, out, out," she said, shooing him away like a dog.

Kevin hurried back to his apartment, where he eagerly took out the Pusecki file. There were three letters recommending Peter to the Yale admissions committee. The first was from a biology teacher, a Mrs. Palmeri. It began with a disclaimer. She had only had Peter for one class, and even in that class hadn't gotten to know him very well.

"His grades on quizzes were extremely average," she wrote. "When I handed them back in class, he laughed with everyone else over his Cs and Ds that marked him as one of the guys. He almost never spoke up in class—he spent the whole time joking with friends. But before both the midterm and the final exam he came to see me and asked me if the results would be posted or announced in any way, or if they would be mailed directly home. Both were only mailed home. And on both those tests, Peter broke the curve by scoring one hundred percent."

"I would have suspected him of some kind of cheating," she wrote, "but for a strange thing that happened in October. We were studying one-celled animals, and the whole class for once was very interested. Peter seemed especially fascinated. One of our best and most complicated electric microscopes had broken and we didn't have the money in our budget to fix it, so we were sharing and making do with the few we had. One afternoon, when everyone had gone home, I passed the lab and noticed that a light was on. I had personally double-locked the lab a few hours earlier. My first thought was to call the police, but curiosity got the better of me. I let myself in a neighboring lab and peeked through a side window.

"Peter sat all alone in the lab, with the broken microscope disassembled in pieces in front of him. As I watched, he slowly put the microscope back together, piece by piece. He was working without a repair manual, and I could tell that he was doing this for the first time and relying mostly on intuition and trial and error. After about thirty minutes, he had reassembled the microscope. He put it back in its case and put the case back on the shelf where we store the microscopes. He was about to leave when I confronted him.

"He didn't seem at all nervous. He just smiled at me and said, 'The electric microscope'll work now.'

"'Where did you learn to do that?' I demanded.

"'Do what?' he asked, and then turned his back on me and walked out. He never mentioned the incident again, and after thinking about it, I never pressed him or talked about it with any of the other teachers. But I wasn't entirely surprised when he got a perfect score on my midterm and final exam, and for obvious reasons I didn't accuse him of cheating. I was a bit baffled when he asked me to write this letter of recommendation for him last week. I hadn't talked to him in more than a year. 'Please, I think you understand me pretty well,' he said with a slight smile. So I said I would do it.

"I can't speak about Peter's integrity or honesty or nobility of character. Nor can I even begin to estimate the sweep and limitations of his intelligence. But I would like to offer a final observation. When I was an undergraduate, although my major study was biology, my real love was acting. I was in the drama society and had big parts in all the college plays, and even considered becoming an actress. In my experience, the most difficult single thing for an actor or actress to do is to play dumb. It takes a very smart actor to play a very dumb role convincingly, and only a truly brilliant young man could turn such a role into his day-to-day high school persona."

Kevin reread the last paragraph and smiled. Peter had made a good choice—Mrs. Palmeri had understood him well.

The second letter was written by a Mr. Edward Hamilton, the principal of Edgewater High School. It was short and very much to the point.

I firmly believe that Peter Pusecki is the most brilliant young man I have encountered in my thirty-three years of high school teaching and administrating. Please disregard his poor grades—this is not a high school where grades mean very much anyhow. Please also disregard his lack of extracurricular activities. I believe that Peter's family is heavily in debt and that after school he works helping his father.

The fact that he scored so high on both the PSAT and the SAT without preparing for the tests at all, or taking a single advanced class in math or English, can be taken as an indication of his true ability. He is the first National Merit Scholar we have had at this school, and he may well be the last. His one request when I told him about his score was that I keep it an absolute secret from his fellow students.

I might add that Edgewater High School is a very tough, very unforgiving place. There are gangs, there is much violence, and the need to find a niche and fit in is not merely a question of teenagers conforming to peer pressure, but is really a matter of survival.

His personality is very deep, many-layered, and inchoate. I have gotten to know him only in the past year, and he has not really opened up to me. But I have seen flashes of gold— evidence of young genius. And I would be most curious to see what might grow if such a promising seed were planted and allowed to take root in a fertile Ivy League greenhouse. I know that Yale University looks for a certain well-rounded type and doesn't take many chances, but in this particular case

*I hope that you will be open-minded. It would be a shame for
this budding talent to bloom unseen and waste his talent on
the desert air.*

Once again Kevin smiled, at the paraphrasing of *Gray's Elegy.*
Hamilton's letter must have stirred up a certain amount of interest
in the admissions office.

The third letter was from a Mr. Hieronymus T. Marwick, vice
president of the Bergen County Yale Club, and the man who had
apparently given Peter his Yale interview.

The letter was really an injunction to the director of undergraduate admissions, whom Marwick addressed by name. It said,
simply:

Admit this young man.

Kevin put down the file, intrigued. He couldn't think of a place
at Yale to look for more about this brilliant young man who had
vanished. Edgewater, New Jersey, was only a two-hour ride, and a
brief trip away from gloomy New Haven seemed suddenly very
appealing.

Chapter 11

Kevin made his preparations quickly and thoroughly.

At a costume store he bought a plastic police shield, obviously a cheap fake if one looked closely but quite convincing when it was flashed.

"I need a car for a student movie," he told the salesman in Al's Used Car Rental. "It has to look like the kind of car a cop might drive or an FBI agent might pull up in."

The salesman immediately suggested an old black Plymouth Fury. Kevin rented it, and as he pulled out of the parking lot and pressed the accelerator he was surprised and pleased to feel how the car surged forward. He had forgotten the one good thing about those huge old American cars—they had terrific pickup.

He sat in the car outside Laura Donovan's apartment building for nearly an hour, until he saw her go in alone. Two minutes later, her living room light came on, and Kevin got out of his car. In his right hand he carried an envelope, and in his left hand he held a bouquet of one dozen long-stemmed red roses.

The sound of the elevator's motor pulling the cable up the shaft reminded him of how they had ridden up together in awkward silence when they came back from the theater. He forced himself to ring her bell.

Laura opened the door quickly, and her face froze in surprise. "May I come in?"

She stepped back a few steps and nodded that he should enter. "I . . . didn't expect to see you again," she mumbled.

"Would you like me to go? If you would, just say so."

"No," she said. "Don't be silly."

He sat on the couch, sinking down into the sea of fluffy cushions, while she sat on a loveseat a few feet away and studied him. "Why have you come?" she finally asked.

"To apologize for running away and not calling you back. It was cowardly."

"It wasn't," she said, lowering her eyes. "I understood."

"You deserved better. Here, please put these in water."

He handed her the roses, and as she inhaled their fragrance, she asked, "Why else have you come?"

"I'm going to New Jersey to investigate someone. I'm not exactly hot on the scent . . . but I've found some strange coincidences. Jack helped me out a lot at the beginning, and I know it sounds corny but if anything did happen to me I'd like him to know the progress I've made. He asked me not to contact him directly ever again, so I wrote down everything I've done so far, and I was wondering if you'd hold it for me for a while. I've irritated a number of strange people lately . . . and it sounds silly, but if you don't hear from me, please give it to Jack and tell him I said he should do whatever he thinks is best."

Kevin passed the typewritten pages to Laura who glanced at them and then put them facedown on the coffee table. "Okay," she agreed, "I'll do it."

"Thank you."

"And I won't read them."

"I know you won't."

"But you should take these back." She tried to hand him back the roses.

"Why?"

"Because people I do favors for don't have to bring me long-stemmed red roses," she said.

"I was going to give you the roses whether you agreed to help me or not."

She looked down at the roses and rearranged the blossoms with a deft movement. Then she looked back up at Kevin and whispered, "Maybe it's silly of me, but when a man brings me flowers I like it to mean something."

Kevin got up and sat next to her on the loveseat. Taking her right hand in his own, he said, "I can't be that man bringing you flowers the way you want them brought."

"I know."

He kissed her very gently on her cheek. "Please take them anyway."

She turned so their faces were only inches away. Her eyes were suddenly large and slightly sad. "You should go now," she said.

She walked him to the door and said, "Take care of yourself."

"Good-bye," he replied gently, "and be well."

Kevin drove out of New Haven at dusk.

The big black Plymouth Fury cut through the darkness as Connecticut gave way to New York state. The lights of the Bronx rose in the distance, and beyond them the night sky glowed above Manhattan. Soon he was shooting over the George Washington Bridge on the upper level, toward the jutting upper jaws of New Jersey's Palisades cliffs. The bridge was lighted up so that it seemed to extend the brilliance of the New York skyline across the mile-wide Hudson River to the dark gaping maw of suburbia.

Kevin headed straight for Edgewater. He drove down the main street of Fort Lee and seemed for a second to have entered another country as sign after neon sign flashed Korean and Japanese at him. Then he was through the Asian community and winding his way down the steep slope toward the water.

Even at night, Edgewater looked like a tough town. The bars and the liquor stores were the centers of activity, and small groups of teenage kids stood on street corners smoking and watching the traffic. From above, on the George Washington Bridge, the wide ribbon of the Hudson River had seemed to sparkle magically with the reflection of the skyline. From Edgewater, however, the Hudson was just a dirty river flushing the wastes of one of the most crowded areas on earth into the Atlantic Ocean.

Kevin parked for a second in the empty lot of a baseball field that faced out on the river. From his spot just behind the backstop he looked through the diamond-shaped wire openings at the lights of New York in the distance. It was odd to see that marvelous constellation of lights through the wire mesh—Kevin felt that all the wonder of the nearby city seemed somehow bound and fettered, and reduced in scale. And he wondered how anyone could grow up facing such a metropolitan gargantua and not feel dwarfed and stunted.

The Riverside Motel featured hourly rates and rooms with adult TV. "Just give me a regular room—I'll be staying a night or so," Kevin said to the toothless night clerk.

"You looking for company?" the clerk wanted to know. He was wearing a very old V-neck gray sweater over a T-shirt that was spotted with yellow stains. "I know a young lady could make you feel real good."

"No thanks. Only thing I'm looking for is Edgewater High School."

The toothless clerk wrinkled his nose as if he had just smelled a bad smell. "The school's a mile down on the right. But don't you be bringing any schoolgirls back here."

When he located number seventeen, Kevin was pleased to find that he had been given the last room on the row. The room had a bright-orange carpet, pictures of naked women hanging above the bed, and a condom dispenser next to the courtesy soap in the bathroom. To the right of the bed there was a coin slot, several control switches, and an explanation of how, for fifty cents, the bed would buck and wiggle for an hour.

At the Spotlight Liquor Store a few hundred yards away Kevin was surprised to find Pilsner Urquell. He took a six-pack back to his room, opened the window, letting in the stench from the Hudson River, and found an old episode of *The Honeymooners* on TV. Suspicious moans came through the wall from the next room—they sounded like a woman faking an orgasm without much enthusiasm. Kevin opened his first beer of the night and tilted it down. He had not spent time in New Jersey before and had not known what to expect; for some reason he found this seedy motel in this grungy town to be oddly palatable.

Sometimes, hidden in the forest of bookshelves, it almost seemed that she would not come and begin the pain all over again. Crouching in the shadows between the shelves or invisible beneath a grate, peering up at the legs walking past overhead, hoping that she would not come again . . .

But she always came, and she is coming now . . .

Why? The voice whispered the question.

To hurt, again.

And the pull of the pressure beginning to take control. There is so little light among the shelves, so much dark where the dead books stand.

She is coming. Step by step, returning to cause pain, and there must never be pain again because there has already been too much. Blood was in the air and death walked the stacks . . .

Mrs. Pastorelli paused by the picture of Babe Ruth.

Her full name was Anna Maria Pastorelli, but no one, not even the doctors at the Yale-New Haven Hospital, called her by her first name. They called her Mrs. Pastorelli or Head Nurse Pastorelli, and while the respect she was accorded was in part due to her age and extreme competence, it also owed a good deal to the recognition that she was a remarkably compassionate woman who had devoted more than forty years to serving the sick.

The picture of Babe Ruth always affected her strangely. It seemed to be on permanent display in the main hall of Yale's immense medical school library. Occasionally it would disappear for a month or so, and Mrs. Pastorelli would hope that some new curator had had the taste to banish it to a dark archive. But then it would reappear, grim as ever in its niche.

The caption under the photograph read: THE DOCTOR AND HIS FAMOUS PATIENT. There were two men in the picture. One was an old doctor clad in a white lab coat, his head as bald as his face was blank, a chart held almost threateningly in his right hand as if it contained some divination of inevitable decay; the other was Babe Ruth. The Sultan of Swat was seated in a chair with his hands on his knees. Despite the hospital gown it was possible to see the great barrel chest that was slowly rotting away. The index finger of the right hand that once predicted the most famous home run in the history of the game was pointed downward in a sadder prophecy. The Babe was looking at the doctor who was looking at the chart.

Mrs. Pastorelli shivered and felt her anger rise at the insensitive brutes who could hang such a picture here. In the photograph the Babe's child's eyes were transfixed in final pain: the unalterable pronouncement of doom had been rendered. To put such a picture in the entry hall of a famous medical school library—in a rotunda as antiseptic as a needle and as silent as a child's mausoleum—was to accent the darkest side of medicine. Mrs. Pastorelli's greatest virtue as a nurse throughout her long career had been a fierce determination to treat the ill as if they would one day be well and the dying as if they were still very much alive. Such a defeatist photograph was anathema to her, and she scowled at it for a second more before hurrying away toward the main reading room.

In the stillness, future doctors and medical scholars pored over abstruse texts with furious concentration. A heavy footstep would often provoke a reproving glance, and an innocent sneeze always drew several loud hissing shushes.

The book Mrs. Pastorelli wanted was not on the shelves, but she knew there was another copy down in the stacks. She descended to the first subterranean level, and then to the second. That far below ground level the flicker of the fluorescent lights was depressingly spectral, and the complete absence of other people made the silence seem menacing, feeding her growing sense of disquiet. But she was determined to find the book.

A young doctor, just out of medical school and impressed by the new letters after his name, had in her opinion misdiagnosed a seriously ill patient. She knew he was wrong from her long experience, but before she would challenge him she had to make absolutely certain that she was right.

A bell rang announcing the library closing was only fifteen minutes away. She would have to check the volume out and read it at home. As she scanned the shelves, looking for it, she felt the pricklings on her neck that always told her when someone was watching her.

Decades of making quick decisions had taught Mrs. Pastorelli to trust her intuition. When a mute patient wanted something, she usually sensed it within seconds, and when a shy patient was too embarrassed to ask a question, she usually guessed it and answered it for him. And now she sensed that someone was nearby, watching her.

There had been a burst of publicity about a murder in Sterling Library and another possible attack a few days later. But, Mrs. Pastorelli reminded herself, that had been in Sterling and this was the medical school library—more than a mile from Sterling—and security had been beefed up so that no one could possibly get in or out without showing a current university ID. She needed the book, and she wasn't about to let some prankster scare her away.

With her usual no-nonsense approach to danger, she walked in the direction she judged the person to be hiding and said in a loud voice, "You there, get out of here now or I'll alert security."

Footsteps padded away and then disappeared.

She hurried toward the footsteps, walking between tall, narrow shelves, moving deeper into the shadows.

All was still and silent.

Mrs. Pastorelli felt an urge to run back upstairs, but she suppressed it. For several decades she had taken care of the very hardest cases, endured the most disturbing sights and smells, and she wasn't about to be put to flight by some footsteps in a library.

She reached the wall at the end of the row of shelves but saw no one. Nothing was amiss, except for a peculiarly rancid odor that reminded her of the way the very worst of the New Haven street-people smelled when she cut away their clothes.

Though there was no one in this corner of the stacks, it occurred to her as she turned to walk back that perhaps the person she had heard hadn't bothered to scamper away, but had climbed up on the shelves, which reached nearly ten feet into the air. As she tilted her head up, someone fell on her with so much impact that she was knocked to the ground.

Though she was stunned, she managed to get to all fours, lifting the body that clung to her back with a tightening grip. Forty years of moving patients and heavy equipment day in and day out had given her surprising resources of strength and stamina. She twisted, trying to knock her assailant off balance, and bit down on the arm that wrapped around the lower half of her face.

And then she felt the vise begin to break her neck. One arm was under her nose, steadily pulling her head backward. Her attacker's other arm was behind her head. *No,* she thought, even as her consciousness began to fade, *No one has the strength to break a neck this way—it just can't be done.*

There was a rush of pain, like a sudden waterfall, red to black, and then the lights all went out.

Chapter 12

Edgewater High School was a square brown building with the musty plainness of an old cigar box. When Kevin approached the main entrance at ten the next morning, about twenty teenagers were hanging out listening to music and watching the traffic on River Road. Conversations died one by one as Kevin passed, and hostile eyes examined him.

He was wearing the oldest, shabbiest dark suit he owned. It had been stuck in the back of his closet in New Haven and looked about ten years out of date. His reflector sunglasses allowed him to look at the punks without their being able to see the direction of his gaze. Most of them wore blue jeans, and the boys had rolled their shirt sleeves up above their elbows to show off their biceps. They seemed curiously unaffected by the winter wind blowing off the river.

"You a cop?" a stocky, muscular boy yelled, moving out half a step as if to block Kevin's passage. A slight, crooked smile played on his face, making it difficult to tell whether the boy wanted to make trouble or was just having a bit of fun.

"Why?" Kevin asked, slowing but not stopping.

"Let him go, Mitch," one of the punk's friends advised.

"You here to solve our drug problem?" Mitch asked.

Pleased that his outfit made them think he was involved in law enforcement, he said "No," slowly.

"You lookin' for some young pussy?"

Kevin took off his sunglasses and looked Mitch right in the eyes. The teenager was nearly half a foot shorter than Kevin, but the bull-like compactness of his build made him seem oddly threatening. Kevin put his hand on Mitch's chest and pushed lightly. Mitch stepped backward and then to one side. The hint of a grin twisted into a smile as he gestured with his hand and said, "Go on in."

Kevin climbed the steps and entered the school. The usual glass cases, filled with sports trophies and plaques, flanked the door. The main hall's walls and high ceiling were a drab green color, and the floor a light gray. Spotting a faded sign indicating the main office, he headed for it.

An obese woman sat alone in the office's reception room, sipping a cup of coffee and looking at a cheesecake recipe in *Women's Day*. She seemed to be tasting the recipe as she read the ingredients, and it was a full ten seconds before she glanced up at Kevin. "Can I help you?"

Kevin took his wallet out of his pocket and flashed the police shield. "I'm with the Federal Bureau of Missing Persons."

"Who's missing?"

"Peter Pusecki. He used to be a student at this school."

She thought for a moment and then shook her head. "Haven't seen him around since he graduated. Haven't heard anyone talk about him either. He's long gone. What did he do?"

"We just want to find him."

"Sure you do."

"Is the principal around?" Kevin asked.

"He's not here today."

"What about the vice principal?"

"We don't have one of those."

"Well, who can I speak to?"

The woman smiled at him. "You can talk to me."

"I'm looking for two people who used to work at this school. One was a teacher, a Mrs. Palmeri."

"Gone," she said somberly.

"She died?"

"She cracked up right in her own classroom. The kids here can be pretty tough. Poor woman, she threw a fit and started crying and screaming. She left in an ambulance and never came back."

"Was she institutionalized?"

"No, she moved to Los Angeles and became an actress. Or at least that's what they say around the school. Some kids claimed they saw her on the soaps, but I don't know. . . ."

"What about Mr. Edward Hamilton?" Kevin followed up. "I believe he used to be the principal here."

"Gone," she intoned as before.

"Did he crack up too?"

"Not for me to say," she replied, and Kevin found himself liking her better, now that he was beginning to catch the pace of her humor.

"But he didn't go to Los Angeles?"

"No, he lives two blocks away, at the Rosewood Apartments. He turned seventy and was retired by the school system last year." She glanced at a wall clock and stood up. "I see the classes are about to change, and I need to run down the hall before the stampede starts. Come on, I'll walk you out."

"What was Peter Pusecki like?" Kevin asked as they walked through the empty hallway.

"Peter Pusecki," she repeated his name. "Nicest parents you could ever want. His mother is a saint. He was Hamilton's golden boy—he pushed him all the way to an Ivy League college. What's he done?"

"Just sunk without a trace."

"And you're looking for traces?" Kevin nodded. They were back in the main hallway now, and she pointed toward a squat man with close-cropped white hair who was hanging a plaque in one of the trophy cases. "That's Bill Tice, our gym teacher. He knows all the boys. He'll tell you about Peter, if you can get him to talk. And now I've got to go. It was nice meeting you." She turned and waddled away.

Bill Tice stood with his thick legs spread wide, while he finished adjusting the trophies. Kevin saw the muscles somersault across his back whenever he moved his arms. He closed and locked the trophy case without a sign that he knew Kevin was standing next to him.

"Excuse me," Kevin said. "Mr. Tice?" The gym teacher turned very quickly at the sound of Kevin's voice, but he still did not speak. "I'm trying to find out about a student who used to attend this school."

"Who?" Tice's one word was hard as a piece of gravel.

"Peter Pusecki. Do you remember him?"

"Sure."

"Did he play on any of the school teams?" Kevin asked, fishing.

"No."

"Was he a good athlete?"

"Didn't give a damn."

"About sports?"

"About anything."

A bell rang to signal the change of periods, and Bill Tice stiffened perceptibly, eager to get away and avoid the oncoming hordes.

"Was there anything unusual or different about him?" Kevin asked.

Bill Tice was about to start off down the corridor, but at Kevin's question he stopped and looked unexpectedly thoughtful. "Wouldn't shower after gym," he said. "And he wouldn't go swimming. I got the rec pool one September. All the kids loved it. That damned Pusecki refused to go in. Wore all his clothes and just stood by the side." The first wave of students, talking and joking, threatened to break over them. "See ya," Bill Tice rumbled to Kevin and, putting his head down, plowed off right into the center of the wave, which parted and reformed behind him.

The Rosewood Apartments were separate two-story units built around a central courtyard. Decades ago the complex might have been fashionable, but now the paint was peeling, the wooden fence along the lawn had fallen over in places, and the sidewalk was checkered with fallen roof shingles.

Kevin found Edward Hamilton's name on the mailbox of a particularly rundown apartment. He rang the bell and waited. The door finally opened a crack, and a grainy old man's voice asked, "Who is it?"

"Mr. Hamilton?"

"Yes?"

"I'm a federal agent." The door opened a bit wider. Kevin flashed his fake police shield through the crack and then pulled it back before it could be examined. "I'd like to talk to you about a former student of yours. I promise not to take up too much of your time."

The door opened. The man who looked up at Kevin was slender and stooped, as if long exposure to a strong wind had permanently bent his spine. He was dressed in a purple bathrobe that hung down to his bony ankles, and hornrimmed eyeglasses gave his scholarly face an intriguingly anachronistic quality. "Where did you get my address?"

"They gave it to me at the high school."

"Well, you're probably the only person who learned anything there today, then," he said bitterly. "Come on, if you're coming."

Kevin followed him up a steep and very narrow flight of stairs to an apartment that smelled of rotting linoleum and shoe polish. Hamilton led the way into his cluttered living room. Five pairs of shoes sat on the floor next to a rag and some black polish. A large blue sofa was piled high with paperback books, and two stacks of old *New York Times*es towered up from the ratty rug like stalagmites.

"Sit," Hamilton said, sweeping half a dozen paperbacks off an armchair onto the floor.

Kevin sat.

Hamilton perched on a low black stool and resumed polishing a shoe with the rag. On the wall near the armchair hung a number of framed testimonials to Edward Hamilton from the New Jersey Education Association, the National Association of High School Teachers, and a huge plaque from the United States Department of

Education announcing that Edward Hamilton had been chosen as the New Jersey teacher of the year. The teacher in Kevin felt a strong sense of shame that this man who had obviously given so much to his community's schools should end up in such an apartment leading such an empty and lonely life.

Hamilton put one shoe down and picked up another one. He tilted it this way and that, trying to judge which part of the shoe needed particular attention. "Well?" he demanded without looking up.

"Peter Pusecki," Kevin said.

Edward Hamilton dropped the shoe and looked very hard at Kevin. His wizened old face froze, and from deep within that icy exterior his brown eyes blazed with an angry question. "What about him?"

"He's disappeared, and I'm looking for him. No one's seen him in more than a year and a half. I know you were his mentor in high school and were instrumental in getting him into Yale, so I thought you might be able to tell me a little about him."

"Look at this sty," Edward Hamilton said, gesturing around at the cluttered apartment. "Even the roaches are disgusted. I was a good teacher and a good principal and I gave of myself and my life all that I could give. And this is my reward. And when I die maybe they'll name an auditorium after me, if I'm lucky."

He picked up the shoe and turned it over and over in his hands. "I have labored in the vineyards," he continued. "Thirty-seven years in a school system where the students don't want to learn and the teachers don't care about teaching and the community couldn't care less. *Thirty-seven years.* And every year we'd send a few students to junior colleges and community colleges, and once in a great while we'd send a particularly good student to a real four-year college. But never, never did we send a student to a really top-notch school."

Edward Hamilton broke off to cough several times into his palm, and a deep rattle sounded in his throat each time his body lurched forward. He regained control, cleared his throat several times, and then continued as if nothing had happened. "The goal of an old miner may be to find that one magical nugget of gold that he can take out of his poke and hold up to the light in crowded bars so that people will cluster around and marvel at it. My goal as an educator was similar, and similarly unrealistic. But just as they were getting ready to retire me and put me out to pasture, I uncovered my nugget."

"Peter was your find?"

"I recognized the luster beneath the mud, I glimpsed the gold in what everyone else dismissed as dross, and I scraped and polished and pushed until Yale University opened its doors to prove me right." Hamilton paused, losing himself in a memory, and a faint smile lighted his face. "His disguise was so carefully constructed, it had them all fooled. In grade school he got only average grades. He'd never taken a book out of our school library—he finally confessed to me that he'd walk up to Fort Lee and takes books out of that library and bring them home under his shirt to read late at night. To hear him talk, and to see him interact with his peers, you would have never suspected that he was really an intellectual double agent with a second life going on secretly behind his forehead."

"And he constructed the disguise to fit in?"

"Not just to fit in, but to survive." Hamilton rolled up his sleeve to show Kevin a huge scar that ran from his wrist to his elbow. "I got this from breaking up a knife fight. And did you hear about the umpire who was killed at the river ballpark this past August? He made a call the local boys didn't agree with, and he threw the manager out of the game for arguing, so after the game was over they stuffed him headfirst into a trash can and rolled him into the Hudson. The junior high kids in this town carry knives, and some of the high school kids pack guns. Take my word for it, if you grow up here and you're different, you don't last long."

Edward Hamilton got up and walked out of the room. In his absence, Kevin examined some of the paperbacks on the floor. They were an eclectic mixture—everything from romantic novels to science fiction to obscure books by moderately famous authors. Somewhere in the apartment a toilet flushed, and in a few seconds Hamilton returned to his perch on the stool.

"So Peter went off to Yale," Kevin said, picking up the story. "With your help and guidance. And he spent a few months there, and then he disappeared."

"They chewed him up," Hamilton said bitterly. "They threw him in and expected him to swim, and instead he drowned. It wasn't that he lacked intelligence—believe me, young man, his brain was as fine as anyone's."

"I believe you," Kevin said.

"But academics is a game, and in order to play you need to learn the rules and how the pieces move. Otherwise you flounder."

"A lot of people flounder and even drop out, but they don't just disappear," Kevin pointed out gently.

"You want to know where he's gone?" Hamilton asked.

"Yes."

"Forget it. You'll never find him. If he wanted to muddy his trail, he was smart enough and an experienced enough actor to do it so that not you nor I nor anyone could track him down."

"I take it you haven't heard from him, then?"

"Not a word in nearly two years," Hamilton admitted bitterly. "Not even a phone call." Resentment at having been betrayed by his young prodigy rang in his voice.

"And if you had to guess in which direction he headed?"

"In a direction you couldn't fathom," Hamilton replied with grim certainty. "He was a deep one, he lived a secret life for so long he developed all sorts of levels." Hamilton stood. "And you must be getting tired of this old man spouting bile and bitterness so I won't waste your time any longer."

Following the old man, Kevin made his way through the cluttered living room and back down the stairs. "Want some advice?" Hamilton asked Kevin on the landing as he opened the door.

Kevin nodded.

"Don't go into teaching, and if you have any children don't let them go into teaching. It's not worth it in this country. You'll just end up alone and bitter."

"I absolutely agree with you," Kevin said. As soon as Kevin was outside, Hamilton closed the door and drew the lock. Kevin waited on the porch, listening to the old man's footsteps climb the stairs, slowly and painfully, in a halting, tired struggle that finally ended in merciful silence.

The Palisades drop down rather steeply through the wooded towns of Fort Lee and Leonia until they level off into great marshy flats, which for more than two centuries have been used as a garbage dump. As Kevin drove toward the marsh on Fort Lee Road, he noticed the historical markers that pointed out where George Washington's army had passed through in its cat-and-mouse game with Cornwallis's troops. Cattails grew alongside the road, which rose up to bridge Overpeck Creek. A county park replete with a jogging track and hanging willow trees fronted the creek on the right and the swamp on the left.

Kevin's destination, Teaneck, seemed to be an affluent town. Following the local map he had picked up in a gas station, he soon found himself on a wide street where the houses were set back on deep lawns or professionally landscaped front yards. Branches of magnificent maple and oak trees formed leafless arches connecting estate to estate.

Kevin parked on the street outside number 777. A Mercedes XJL and a black Porsche sat in the driveway, and both had blue Yale University stickers on their rear bumpers. As he walked up the front path, Kevin found himself trying to guess how many rooms there were inside the gingerbread castle. Twenty? Thirty? He rang the bell, and chimes played the opening notes of Beethoven's Fifth Symphony.

A maid, dressed in a uniform, came to the door.

Kevin flashed his plastic shield and said, "I need to speak with Mr. Marwick."

"He's busy."

Kevin stuck his foot in the door so she couldn't shut it. "It's of the utmost importance. Tell him I'm a federal agent."

She debated with herself for a moment and then said, "Please wait."

The maid was gone for at least two minutes before the door was boldly drawn back to reveal a balding man in a smoking jacket. He stood completely at ease, hands on hips and pipe in mouth, the prototypical master of the house disturbed by an unexpected intrusion yet willing to be polite. "Yes?"

"Are you Mr. Marwick?"

"Indeed. Hieronymus T. Marwick." His smoking jacket had satin lapels.

"Vice president of the Bergen County Yale Club?"

"I continue to have the honor to serve in that capacity," Marwick said proudly as he puffed on his pipe.

"My name's Kevin Randall. I work for the federal government investigating missing persons. We're looking for someone you once had some contact with, and I was hoping that you might be able to help."

Marwick looked at Kevin with interest and mild skepticism. "Most of the people I associate with are too established to be missing," he observed. Then he smiled very slightly, and Kevin wasn't sure whether he was laughing at his own pompousness or whether he was merely following an inane comment with an idiotic grin. "Well, Mr. Randall, I suppose you'd better come in and tell me what I can do for you."

The interior of the house looked like a set for a movie satirizing the tasteless rich. At the end of the main hallway a five-foot miniature orange tree opened its fruit-laden branches beneath a gigantic Chagall painting of the burning bush. The main living room, vast and high-ceilinged, was furnished with a jumble of art objects collected from different countries and from different eras. Ming vases sat next to Etruscan statuary. Persian carpets gave way to Mexican serapes. Russian icons stared across at Andy Warhol photographs.

"What do you think?" Marwick asked.

"I think you've covered all the bases," Kevin told him guardedly.

"Yes, it's all here." Once again Marwick's smile could have been either moronic collector's pride or bemused self-sarcasm.

Marwick led Kevin to two chairs that sat in front of one of the living room's two fireplaces. Kevin perched carefully on an ornate straightbacked throne that looked at least two hundred years old. Marwick sat opposite him in an antique rocker, which he moved back and forth as he studied Kevin.

"Now then," he finally said, "you claim that someone I once knew has dropped out of sight?"

"A student you once interviewed for Yale," Kevin told him.

"I was hoping it would be one of my Harvard acquaintances."

"Peter Pusecki."

Marwick smiled sadly and his mouth turned down to mimic the droop of his pipe. "Now how did I know you were going to say that?"

"I don't know," Kevin said. "How did you know?" He leaned forward slightly on the throne, and its old wooden joints squeaked in protest.

"By the by," Marwick said, "that throne you're sitting on is priceless. Napoleon sat in it once during his conquest of Italy. I bought it at a Sotheby's auction . . . it was either that or one of Liberace's pianos."

He's got to be making fun of himself, Kevin thought. But Marwick seemed serious and content in his own little cloud of pipe smoke and luxury. "How did you know it would be Peter Pusecki?" Kevin repeated.

"Because he was so different from the others. So, he disappeared, did he? And the federal government sent you to find him. You, being a diligent young man, scoured his college records and found out that he came from this area and that I was responsible for getting him into Yale. And you'd like to know what I found to be so remarkable about him."

Kevin nodded. "He disappeared a while ago. Anything you can tell me about him will be helpful."

"Well, I suppose I should do my bit to help find him. Let me see." He tilted his head back and rocked fairly vigorously. Finally he stopped rocking and leaned forward. "He showed up for his Yale interview dressed like a street urchin. Blue jeans and a T-shirt—I thought he was coming to mow the yard. I asked him the usual questions and he was a bit taciturn. There was no one particular scholastic subject that fascinated him. He considered sports and extracurricular activities to be a waste of time. He hadn't traveled and he had had not noteworthy work experience. He disliked speaking about his parents and would just clam up when I pressed him about his home life . . ."

"And why was that?"

Marwick threw the question back at him. "You tell me? Why would a boy like Peter, whose parents were uneducated and very poor, dislike speaking to a stranger about them?"

"Because he was ashamed of them?" Kevin tried.

"Actually, I think it was because he was proud of them," Marwick said with a gleam in his eye. "I find that the hardship cases I interview who are ashamed of their parents blame them for their shortcomings as much as they can. Silence in such a case is a sign of love and pride. Peter took a look at me and at my house, and he knew his parents had no place here, so he left them back in Edgewater."

The maid walked in with a tray of cucumber sandwiches and two glasses of ice water. She put the food and the drinks down and left without a word.

"So was that what impressed you so much?" Kevin asked. "His reservedness?"

Marwick picked up a cucumber sandwich between his thumb and index finger and sampled a corner of it. "Reservedness?" he repeated, pleased with the word. "If you don't mind me saying so, you speak well for a federal agent." He popped the rest of the sandwich into his mouth, chewed, and swallowed. "No," he said, "I was intrigued that a young man could come out of a family like that and a school like that and do so well on standardized tests. He hardly seemed, however, like Yale material. I don't know how familiar you are with Yale, Mr. Randall, but there is a certain—shall I say sophistication—to the place. A person who doesn't know how to study, dress, carry himself, or speak in public will not do well there."

"I'm sure you're right," Kevin said without irony. "But you did recommend him, so something about him must have impressed you."

"I saw him glancing over at that checkers set," Marwick explained, pointing at elaborate checkers pieces that were set up on a low table. "So I asked him if he'd like to try a game. And what do you think happened?"

"He won the game?"

"Two out of three," Marwick admitted, getting up and walking to a bookcase. He returned with a volume called *Checkers for the Serious Player,* and Kevin glanced down and saw that the book had been written by Hieronymous T. Marwick.

"Beginner's luck?"

"I was the lucky one. Or perhaps he just let me win one of the games."

"And that was the reason you recommended him so strongly to Yale?"

Marwick smiled broadly, as if preparing to tell a valued secret. "There was one other reason. Please, follow me."

They walked down a long hallway to what Kevin assumed was Marwick's study. Large signed photographs of Kingman Brewster, A. Bartlett Giamatti, and Benno Schmidt hung above a fifteen-foot glass-topped half hemisphere of a desk. On the wall opposite the desk, spotlighted by its own little lamp, was a small and very beautiful Monet. "My prize," Marwick said, "and the final part of all my Yale interviews. For fifteen years I've been bringing the students I interview into this study and asking them for their reactions to this painting."

Kevin examined it closely. It was an impressionistic sunrise or sunset—it was difficult to tell which. Yellow and orange light played through soft clouds of white and pink. Something about the painting seemed unsettling, but Kevin couldn't quite identify it.

"Some kids just go blank and can't say a word about it," Marwick said. "Some manage a few sentences about color and texture. And occasionally I get a budding art historian who delivers a brilliant analysis of this painting within the larger context of early impressionism."

"And Peter?"

"Walked in and studied it for about ten seconds," Marwick remembered with the hint of a grin returning to his face, "and then he told me I had it hanging upside down."

Kevin looked at the painting again and realized what had been bothering him. The whole pattern of the flow of the clouds and the play of the faint sunlight seemed oddly inverted, but since the painting was so impressionistic it was very difficult to determine with any certainty. "Did you know?" Kevin asked.

"Only an utter ass would buy a Monet and hang it upside-down by mistake," Marwick grunted. "It was my own private little joke. For years the very brightest students had come in and gone on and on about this painting without catching onto my little game. I always told myself that if any student ever had the vision to see that it was hung wrong and the sheer nerve to tell me during a Yale interview, I would get him in no matter what. Peter didn't hesitate even a breath, he just came out with it."

A cuckoo clock in a corner of Marwick's office opened and the wooden bird popped out and cheeped the hour. Marwick glanced over at the clock, puckered his lips, and cheeped back. Then he looked at Kevin and raised one eyebrow, challenging him to rate the extent of his eccentricity. "I don't have much more time to give you," he said. "Do you have any more questions?"

Kevin wanted to ask Marwick if he really believed his upside-down painting test was a valid measure of a high school student's intelligence, but resisted. Perhaps Yale should spend more energy interviewing its own interviewers.

They began to walk back down the long hall, past a suit of armor and a giant stuffed grizzly bear and Mayan wall hangings. "If you were trying to figure out where this unusual young man disappeared to, where would you begin?"

"In his home," Marwick said without hesitation. "Deep secrets usually sprout from seeds that are sown years before in the home. And in this particular case, there must have been something out of the ordinary in that home to produce such an unorthodox fellow."

Kevin nodded and started toward the door.

"But I must tell you," Marwick added suddenly, stopping him with his voice. "I got the impression that the young man who saw through my little trick was a fairly accomplished gamesman himself. If he doesn't want to be found, I don't think you're likely to find him."

"You may be underestimating federal agents," Kevin told him. "We too may not be exactly what we seem."

Chapter 13

The tiny one-story house stood on a street so dreary and cramped that the wooden buildings seemed to lean on one another for support. Garbage and old newspapers flapped about in the wind like a flock of angry birds. Farther down the block, a Doberman wandering from yard to yard turned and snarled in Kevin's direction. Nothing about the neighborhood's houses relieved the drab grayness of their walls and grassless lawns. Several hundred yards away, a sewage conduit spilled out into the Hudson; an acrid odor hung like an invisible cloud above the leafless trees and low rooftops.

A fading sign on the front of the house proclaimed: JOSEPH PUSECKI, LOCKSMITH, JEWELRY, WATCHES REPAIRED, KEYS DUPLICATED. Kevin walked up the rickety wooden steps and rang the bell. There was no response. He rang it again, this time leaning on it for several seconds. Footsteps sounded faintly inside the house. They approached the door and stopped. "I'll have it for you by Friday," an old man's voice promised fearfully.

Kevin knocked with his knuckles. "I'd just like to talk to you."

His words produced a long silence. The river wind twisted

around the house, and it seemed a miracle that the frail wooden structure didn't collapse in a heap. "I'll have it by Saturday at the latest. Go away. I'm not opening the door for nobody," the old man's voice declared.

"My name is Kevin Randall. I'm not here to collect money. I just want to talk for a few minutes."

"About what?"

"About your son, Peter."

Two bolts were drawn and the door was opened on a chain. When an old man peered out through the crack, Kevin saw that he held a chisel in his right hand. "What do you know about Peter?" The question was delivered as a gruff challenge.

"I'm trying to find him and I'd appreciate a few minutes of your time."

The old man made no move to open the door. He examined Kevin carefully, taking in every detail of his appearance. The hand that held the chisel was thick and muscular, and crisscrossed with hundreds of small scars from nicks and cuts. Kevin guessed the man's age at about sixty. "Your name again?"

"Kevin Randall."

"Irish?"

Kevin nodded.

"You a cop?"

"I work for the government trying to find missing people."

"Irish make the best cops," the old man said, finally taking the chain off and opening the door. "I got no problems with the police. It's the other side I got problems with."

The house seemed to be in perpetual twilight. Lightbulbs were far apart and covered with shades. Drawn Venetian blinds hung over the windows so that only an occasional slant of sunlight filtered through the slats. Dust covered the floor and the tabletops and lent the interior of the house a dank mustiness.

"My wife, she's sick," the old man said, pointing to a closed door in explanation. "She sleeps best during the day, don't ask me why. This is where I work." He opened another door, and Kevin saw a small room dominated by several large drills and presses. He led Kevin through a kitchen barely ten feet square that apparently doubled as the dining room, and then ushered him into what looked like a shrine.

On a far table, two long white candles burned beneath a hand-somely framed print of one of Raphael's Madonnas. A carved wooden Christ on the Cross faced the Madonna from the opposite wall. On the table, in front of the white candles, sat a young man's high school graduation picture. The boy's expression was not happy or sad or serious. His face was very complicated—for, although his broken nose gave him a gentle sheeplike look, there was a definite tigerish set to his jaw. He was tall and broad-shouldered, and the strength of his physique was obvious even under his graduation robe.

"That's my son." The old man nodded, seeing Kevin's interest in the picture. "That was a day. I was so happy I couldn't sit still so I stood up all during the ceremony. Here are some more pictures." He gestured toward a thick black-bound photo album that sat on a corner of the table.

The first photo was of a skinny boy of six or seven holding a stringer of sunfish. Kevin skimmed through the pages watching Peter pass through early adolescence and begin to fill out and grow tall. Most of the shots had been taken on formal occasions—there was an annual posed Christmas morning shot and numerous photos com-memorating birthdays and yearly class photos. The last picture in the album was the same graduation snapshot that had been blown up and framed.

"You want to sit?" Peter's father pointed toward a green sofa beneath the carved Christ. The old man sat next to Kevin. "You wanted to talk?" he asked. "Then talk. You got questions? Then ask." He spoke without eagerness to answer, or bitterness at having his memories disturbed, or even curiosity at what had brought Kevin to his house after two years. His voice was flat, and if his words held any subtext at all it was a grim undertone of utter resignation.

Kevin waited a long beat. Having come this far and spent so much time and effort finding his way to this small shrine of a room, his instinct told him not to rush into the heart of the matter. "Have you always worked out of your home?" he asked the old man.

"For twenty years I had my own shop," he replied with a trace of old pride. "A good shop. With two local boys to help me. And Peter made three."

"Did you live here then?"

"No, above the shop. It was small but it was clean. And the air was good. You want tea? A beer? We don't have much to offer . . ."

"Thanks, I'm fine," Kevin told him. "What happened to the shop?"

The old man made an unconscious downward circling gesture with his hand and lowered his voice slightly as if talking about the honored dead. "Lost it six years ago to the creditors. Nothing I could do. That was the beginning. And this . . ." He moved his scarred hands around as if to encompass the entire rickety house and ailing woman in the next room and the picture of the lost son on the table beneath the Madonna. "This is the ending."

The silence sat between them for a while—Kevin, who knew grief as an old companion, saw that Peter Pusecki's father seemed to have a great familiarity with it too.

Finally Kevin went over and picked up Peter's graduation picture. He brought it back to the sofa, hoping to restart the conversation. "So after he graduated from high school, Peter went off to Yale," Kevin began. "Did you go with him?"

"No," the old man said, looking at the picture as he talked. "Peter wanted us to come, but his mother and I told him to go by himself. Make friends, learn his way around. Plenty of time for us to come later." The old man smiled at Kevin. "So many rich boys there—I didn't want to get in his way at the very beginning."

"But you did keep in touch with him?" Kevin asked. "Letters and phone calls?"

"My wife wrote. I don't write letters. Peter didn't write letters either. Twice he came home for a weekend."

"From the few letters he did write, and from the times you talked to him on the telephone or he came home for a weekend, did you sense that anything was wrong?"

The old man thought the question over, rubbing his index finger slowly down along the side of his nose. "No, nothing seemed wrong. He was young, in a new place, so he was a little confused. And he was in love."

"Did he tell you that?"

"My wife knew."

"He told her?"

The old man shrugged at such an idiotic question. "Doesn't a mother know when her son is in love for the first time?"

"And when he . . . disappeared . . . the police came and talked to you?"

The old man acknowledged that they had with a faint bunching of his eyebrows. Kevin had the feeling that he was treading on sacred ground, but he had to move forward. "They probably asked you if there was anyplace that Peter might go to if he was very confused and needed to be alone for a while."

"They asked. There was noplace."

"No other relatives? Or a place he had seen and liked a lot during a trip, or a cabin in the woods. . . ?"

"You think we can afford cabins in the woods?" the old man asked. "No family, no trips, nothing. Okay?" A faint irritation had suddenly crawled into his voice, as if he had put up with enough personal questions and his patience was beginning to wear thin.

Kevin spoke in a respectful whisper. "But Peter must have gone somewhere." The old man met his eye as he continued. "And you, his father, must have some clue to where he went."

"Peter is dead." Kevin and the old man both turned to look at the frail woman standing in the doorway. She wore a flannel housecoat and slippers, and carried a tray with two opened Budweisers and a bowl of peanuts. As she set the tray down on a small table in front of the couch, she then turned to her husband and said something in Polish.

"My wife feels bad that we don't have better things to serve a guest," the old man said.

"Thank you for the beer," Kevin said to both of them, and

took a drink. It was ice cold, and the long swallow cooled his throat. "Why do you say Peter is dead?" he asked the woman.

Her face was a mask of suffering. An inner light of human kindness could be glimpsed in her eyes, and occasionally her lips approached a smile and then backed away. "He would have written to me," she said simply. "He was a good son and I was his mother. He would have known that not hearing from him would kill me."

The old man went to his wife, put his arm around her shoulder, and stroked her fine white hair. "Shush, nobody's dying here."

"I'm dying, and it feels good to die," she said, her eyes on the painting of the Madonna, which seemed unnervingly lifelike in the candlelight. Then she looked at Kevin and said, "You shouldn't come here to bother us. We have enough troubles."

Kevin stood up to face her. "I don't want to add to your troubles," he told her. "I want to find your son."

"To find my son you will have to pass into another world," she told him with absolute conviction. "I think I will find him before you will."

"Was there anything strange about his birth or early childhood?" Kevin fished desperately, aware that the interview couldn't continue too much longer. "Or when he was in grade school? Anything that set him apart from his friends? Anything unusual that he did or said?"

The couple looked at each other, and for a second Kevin felt a silent communication pass between them. Finally she answered, her voice quivering as it grew louder, "No, No, NO, NO!"

The old man touched his fingers gently to her lips and she quieted instantly. "My wife is not well," he told Kevin. "You should go."

"How much money do you owe?" Kevin surprised himself by asking. His fingers were already wrestling his wallet from his front pocket.

The woman's eyes watched him raise his wallet, but the man looked down at the sawdust on the floor. His lips tightened and his face twisted into a frown. When he spoke it was to dismiss Kevin and his offer. "We don't take charity," he said. "We get by. Come, I'll let you out the door."

"Was there something you wanted to tell me, Mrs. Pusecki?" Kevin asked, suddenly a bit desperate. "It felt like there was."

She looked at him blankly, and her husband took Kevin's arm to tug him toward the door. In the doorway, out of earshot of the woman, Kevin again took out his wallet. This time the old man watched him. "How much?" Kevin asked.

The old man hesitated and looked back down the hall. His wife had returned to her bedroom. He raised all five fingers on his right hand. Kevin pulled fifty dollars out of his wallet and handed the money to him. The old man took the bills and tucked them into his back pocket. He looked directly into Kevin's eyes for a long moment, and his unspoken gratitude showed clearly.

"Was there something else?" Kevin pressed in a whisper. "Anything?"

The old man opened the door to let Kevin out. "No," he whispered back. "There was nothing. Anna is right. Our Peter is dead."

Chapter 14

Kevin drove back to New Haven in a windstorm that slowly built into a concert of the elemental forces of nature. Drumrolls of thunder reverberated as cymbal clashes of lightning licked the landscape.

Plausible yet contradictory theories flashed through Kevin's mind as he drove through the downpour. Could Peter Pusecki have gone off with his Yale girlfriend to start a new life among the idle rich? Had Peter himself been a victim of the murderer two years ago, and was his decomposing body stuffed in some dark closet or shadowy cellar? Or, most likely of all, had he simply fled the rain and academic pressures of New Haven and started life anew in some sunnier spot a half a continent away?

There was the Pusecki–Shahrzad connection, but then Yale isn't such a big school and perhaps it was just a coincidence that two of his suspects had once come to blows. Shahrzad was not only mysterious and dangerous, but according to Bradley Sutton he harbored violent feelings toward women.

And as for Van Dorn and Amy Strong, while they both had their eccentricities Kevin had to admit that there was absolutely no hard evidence linking them to the crimes. Hearing the thunder warnings in the near distance, Kevin tried to throw off his doubts about his investigation and concentrate on getting back to Yale in one piece.

By the time he reached New Haven, I-95 was two inches deep in water and traffic crawled. At home at last, he found messages from Jack Hobbs and Ron Christopher on his answering machine. Even before he got Jack Hobbs on the line, Kevin guessed what must have happened.

"I've been away, following a lead," Kevin told him. "I thought you never wanted me to contact you again."

"Everything's changed," Hobbs said. "A head nurse at the Yale-New Haven Hospital was murdered in the medical school library."

"When?"

"Yesterday, in the early evening. She was killed brutally—the resemblance to the murders two years ago was too direct for anyone to ignore. Romano told me to get in touch with you. He's under incredible pressure—there's talk of bringing in the National Guard to patrol the campus."

"No one saw the nurse's attacker?"

"Nope, same as always—it was another perfect crime." Hobbs paused and then couldn't control himself. "Have you found anything out? Any leads at all?"

"I don't know," Kevin told him honestly. "So far I've got a couple of interesting suspects and a lot of dead ends."

"Well, if you need anything from the police, or if you get any leads, call me or Romano right away."

Kevin hesitated, then asked, "Could you ask Romano to find out anything he could for me about a Yale student named Ali Shahrzad?" Kevin spelled the name out letter by letter. "He was away from Yale for nearly two years, and he's come back this semester to continue his degree. His name was on the list you gave me. I'd love to know where he went and what he did while he was away. If the New Haven police have any contacts with Interpol, it might be worth seeing if they have anything on him."

"Will do," Hobbs promised. "Anything else?"

"There's a woman named Amy Strong who teaches self-defense classes at the Women's Center and also for the New Haven police. She was on that list, too. Since she teaches New Haven cops, I wonder if Romano has heard anything about her—even rumors."

"I'll ask him. Anyone else?"

"Not right now. But I'll let you know," Kevin promised, and hung up.

Ron Christopher wanted to meet right away. The reporter pressed Kevin for names of details about his investigation, and it was all Kevin could do to get him to agree to wait until a lunch meeting the following day.

Finally Kevin called Bradley Sutton, Peter's freshman roommate. After the reporter's intensity, he was almost relieved to hear Bradley's cool, aristocratic voice answer the phone. "Bradley Sutton speaking."

"This is Professor Kevin Randall. I talked to you and your girlfriend a while ago about Peter Pusecki."

"I remember. I'm afraid I'm a bit busy now . . ." Bradley Sutton gasped a bit as he spoke, and Kevin heard a feminine giggle in the background.

"I wonder if you could do me one last favor, and then I won't bother you again. Could you give me the name of Peter's girlfriend—the one who you told me transferred to Penn. I've forgotten if you mentioned it. And if you happen to know who her best friend was at Yale, I'd like that name too."

"Jennifer Lawrence." Sutton tried to speak normally, but as his breath got shorter and shorter, his words came out faster and faster. "If you should happen to come across her, please give her my regards. Ahhh . . . Jennifer's closest friend at Yale was her roommate, a wonky drama school type named Mara Resnick. She's still around—I bump into her sometimes. . . . *Oh, baby.* . . . I think she tranferred to a psycho single in Ezra Styles. Oh, *Baby!* . . ." Bradley Sutton moaned suddenly and hung up the phone.

Kevin paged through the *Yale Directory* and soon found that Mara Resnick lived in Ezra Styles, B entryway, room 37. She didn't have a phone number listed, so Kevin pulled on a jacket, grabbed an umbrella, and headed off into the wet night.

Most of the Yale residential colleges are old and Gothic and graceful. Morse College and Ezra Styles College are exceptions. They are concrete-and-rubble disasters that Eero Saarinen designed for Yale University in the early 1960s. The two residence halls looked cold and chillingly lifeless. But they both have proportionately more single rooms than the other colleges, so students who want privacy often try to transfer to them by claiming that they need single rooms for psychological reasons. The lights from several of these so-called psycho singles dotted the massive concrete façade.

Kevin climbed the stairs of B entryway and knocked on Mara's door. There was a long silence. "Yes?" a timid voice asked.

"Mara? Mara Resnick?"

"Yes?"

Kevin tried to sound like a school official on urgent business. "My name is Kevin Randall. I apologize for coming by so late but I'm helping the university investigate a matter of the utmost importance, and if you could give me a few minutes . . . We're looking for an old roommate of yours—Jennifer Lawrence."

She opened the door. Mara was lithe and thin, with the body of a dancer and a playful, slightly owlish face. Her eyes were very bright, and her tiny, rounded chin gave her features a quality of warmth.

"I'm a professor in the English department," Kevin said, conscious of the late hour and trying to allay any fears she might have.

"I know," she said. "I took your survey class last year. Please come in."

Her small single room was a masterpiece of neatness. On the walls, Degas dancers pirouetted in exactly arranged frames. The bed was neatly made and covered with a magnificent patchwork quilt. A small golden Star of David hung from a silver chain above the mantel. Two intertwining willow branches rose out of a blue vase on her desk. There were no movie posters, notebook pages, cans of beer, bottles of wine, or any of the other junk that one commonly associates with college students' rooms.

Despite her timid appearance, Mara didn't seem at all uncomfortable about being alone with Kevin. She closed the door and gestured for him to sit down on the room's small couch. "I liked your class," she told him.

"Thank you. When did you take it?"

"Last year. Spring semester."

Kevin winced at what she must have seen of his teaching. "I was a little off my game that semester."

"We could tell." She smiled. "I still liked the class. And I learned a bit." She sat down next to him on the couch. She was wearing a pink leotard that clung to her skinny body as if it had been painted on. Her skin was very fair, and the effect of the luminous eyes gleaming out from that pale face was quite striking.

"I wish I could tell you why we need to get in touch with Jennifer so badly, but I'm afraid it's strictly confidential," he told her. "She herself has done nothing wrong."

"Jennifer never did anything wrong," Mara said, and it was impossible to tell whether her tone reflected envy or admiration.

"We've tried all the normal university channels for getting in touch with her . . ."

"Don't feel bad. Her parents won't tell anyone where she is. I've talked to her father six or seven times in the last few months, and all that he'll say is that she's studying art somewhere in England. He says that I can mail letters to him and he'll forward them, but he won't give me or anyone her address."

"Why?"

"He says she's recovering—getting herself back on the right track—and that he doesn't want anyone from her past to contact her and possibly impede her recovery. Those are his exact words—he doesn't want anyone to impede his daughter's recovery. I've sent him a few letters for her, but there haven't been any answers. For all I know, he shreds them the moment he gets them." Mara stopped and looked at Kevin quizzically. "I assume you know what she is trying to recover from?"

"Just the barest details," Kevin muttered. "Something about a love affair gone awry."

Mara tucked her bare feet under her thighs—her long legs seemed to bend into all sorts of unusual angles. "It was more than a love affair," she told him. "It was a love knot. They were completely tied up with each other. When she wasn't with him, Jennifer seemed like she was sleepwalking. Peter was exactly the same way. It got so that you couldn't talk to them when they were apart because they had this glazed-over quality, and you couldn't talk to them when they were together because they spent all their time in his or her bedroom with the door closed."

"It doesn't sound like she was much fun for you as a roommate," Kevin observed.

Mara shrugged. "Peter was a nice guy," she admitted. "Very smart, very gentle, and very for real. At Yale it's easy to find smart, and it's not that hard to find gentle, but guys who are for real are scarce."

"So what happened to the love knot?" Kevin asked, trying to sound as if he didn't really care and was merely asking for the sake of politeness.

"Don't ask me," Mara told him. "He flaked, she flaked, he flaked even worse, she brooded day in, day out, he disappeared, and she transferred to Penn. They were both taking an intro psych class, and I think they fought about some piece she was reading or writing for the class. I probably saw more of what was happening between them than anyone else, and I didn't understand it one bit. It was like Peter just came unglued, and Jennifer didn't know how to deal with it so at a certain point she just ran."

"What was it about the psychology class that made them fight?"

"I have no idea."

"Where did she run?"

"First to Penn," Mara said. "I visited her there. She seemed a little bit happier, I guess. Then to the University of Wisconsin. She stayed there for only two months. Then to Grinnell in Iowa. And finally she went to Berkeley. That was the last place I talked to her."

"She was moving west," Kevin said, thinking out loud. "Trying to get away from something."

"Whatever she was doing, it was ludicrous for her to even try to be happy at some of those schools. I mean, some of them don't have a decent art gallery around for a hundred miles." Mara paused, to readjust her legs.

"She was keen on art?" Kevin asked.

"Jennifer had this absolutely incredible art background. Before she met Peter, all of her passion was for sixteenth-and-seventeenth-century European art. Especially the English portrait artists—like Gainsborough and Reynolds and Hogarth and . . . I forget all their names. She had prints of their work up all over her room. That's why she came to Yale in the first place—because of the Center for British Art here. Imagine her trying to be happy at a small college in Iowa!"

"Tell me, did you ever hear her mention a boy named Ali Shahrzad?"

Mara looked at Kevin quickly. "Is Jennifer in some kind of danger?"

"No, but why do you ask?" Kevin deflected the question. "Is Shahrzad dangerous?"

Mara nodded. "Jennifer was afraid of him. He'd fallen madly in love with her at prep school, even though they'd only gone out for a month or so. He wouldn't let her alone. Her father finally had to threaten to have him arrested for harassment."

"But that was old stuff, from their high school days," Kevin objected.

"Jennifer was convinced that he was still after her. She claimed he only came to Yale because she came here. She told me over and over again never to let him in and never to trust anything he said. And you know about the fight he had with Peter?"

"I hear they nearly killed each other."

"That's an understatement."

Kevin decided to try a long shot. "Do you know if Jennifer ever had any contact with the Women's Center?" he asked. "Or does the name Amy Strong ring a bell?"

Mara thought, and then began to shake her head. Suddenly she caught herself. "Come to think of it, I believe Jennifer took that class."

"What class?"

"Our first month at Yale a girl was raped in her own dorm room. A bunch of girls from our entryway enrolled in a class at the center to learn to defend themselves."

"And Jennifer was one of them?"

"I'm pretty sure. But I think she dropped the class halfway through."

"Do you remember who taught the class?"

Mara shook her head.

"Could it have been taught by Amy Strong?"

Mara shrugged. "That sounds familiar."

"Do you remember why Jennifer dropped the class?"

"I guess she just didn't have the time to keep up with it. I really don't remember very clearly."

"Thank you very much for all your help," Kevin said, standing. "I guess we'll have to convince Jennifer's father if we want to contact her."

"Forget trying to convince her father of anything," Mara told him. "He's this big Wall Street mogul type, and he's absolutely inflexible." She stood and led Kevin to the door. "You seem better now than you did when I was in your class," Mara said. "I worried about you."

"Thank you," Kevin said.

"I used to say prayers for you," she whispered, and opened the door.

"And for Jennifer?" Kevin asked, stepping out into the hall.

"No," Mara said. She looked thoughtful. "Although if she's gotten tangled up with Ali Shahrzad again, maybe Jennifer needs my prayers."

At nine-thirty the next morning, as he was leaving to jog around the campus, Kevin was surprised to find Sam Curson, his friend from the anthropology department, standing on his doorstep. Curson was dressed for a morning of golf and refused Kevin's offer to come inside. "We tee off at ten," he explained. Then: "Where the hell have you been?"

"Busy," Kevin told him.

"I've gone by your office half a dozen times, but you're never there anymore. Is everything okay?"

"Fine," Kevin assured him. "Did you find out whether Van Dorn was at that conference in India?"

Curson looked around and lowered his voice. "I don't want it to get around that I've been checking up on him. Okay?"

Kevin nodded.

"It proved to be damn difficult to nail down, but a friend at NYU was at that conference and he said Van Dorn definitely delivered a paper on this day." He handed Kevin a piece of paper on which he had written down a date and a time. On the night that the girl had been killed on the twelfth floor of the stacks, Van Dorn had been on the other side of the world presenting a controversial paper. "Now then," Curson said, huffing, "do you care to tell me why it's so important?"

"Too difficult to explain."

"Career change? Are you becoming a shamus?"

Kevin was saved from further inquiries by the appearance of Jack Hobbs and Lieutenant Romano. They walked up the stairs to Kevin's apartment side by side, looking tired and grim. Curson took one look at them, shot Kevin a worried glance, and hurried off to his golf game.

Jack Hobbs, with his sleepy black eyes and heavy frame, cut an odd figure next to Lieutenant Romano, whose physique beneath his gray suit was lean and rock-hard and whose piercing blue eyes burned with curiosity and impatience.

Without a word, Kevin ushered them into his apartment. Jack Hobbs sat down on the living-room couch while Lieutenant Romano remained standing. "Coffee?" Kevin offered.

"With cream and sugar," Hobbs requested.

"Black." Romano bit off the syllable. He glanced around the living room, unabashedly studying Kevin's possessions.

Kevin returned with the coffee and set the cups down on the coffee table. Hobbs picked his up, blew on it several times, and then decided that it was too hot. Romano immediately drained a third of his cup—his thin lips seemed impervious to high temperatures. "You were right," he said to Kevin in a flat, even voice. "Sorry I didn't listen to you."

"You threw me out of your office," Kevin reminded him.

"Anyway, we want your help now."

"That's right." Jack Hobbs hurried to defuse the tension. "We should have been working together on this all along. Let's start now."

"Jack tells me that you've got some suspects," Romano said.

Kevin was silent for several seconds. "Nothing definite or even remotely incriminating," he finally admitted.

"Well, this Shahrzad character sounds pretty damn suspicious to me," Romano told him. "We ran a complete check for you. He's been arrested for violent behavior in six different states and in France, England, and Italy."

"Did you find out where he's been for the past two years?" Kevin asked.

Romano looked frustrated and angry, while Jack Hobbs supplied the answer. "We can't find a damn thing on Shahrzad during the past two years. No record of him leaving the country, but nothing on him in America either. It was like he vanished."

"And Amy Strong?"

"That's one of the reasons I came over here," Romano said. "She's been helping us handle this mess—organizing student patrols and coordinating them with our police patrols. So if she's in any way a suspect herself . . ."

"She has access to all security information right now," Jack Hobbs finished for him. "If she wanted to use that information to beat our patrols, she could do it in a second."

Kevin nodded and thought for several seconds. "I don't have any reason to think she's not what she says she is. Still, you might want to watch her closely."

"We are," Romano muttered. "Now what I need from you are the names of any other suspects and the progress you've made so far. Let us pick it up from here."

Kevin sat very still, watching Romano sip his coffee. It was tempting to share the little information he had. Since they were professionals, maybe they could help him sort it out. The electric clock on the wall made one tiny ticking sound as the hour hand reached the ten. "No," Kevin finally said.

"Why?" Romano matched him monosyllable for monosyllable.

"Because this is something I want to carry through on my own. If I'm on the right track, I'll do as good a job as you will."

"And if you don't, if you screw up, innocent women may be killed," Romano observed grimly.

"Close down the campus," Kevin told him. "There's a killer loose and until we find out what's going on, my best advice is to just shut down."

"You want me to tell Yale University that one insane creepo killer is too much for us to handle, and they should close shop?" If Romano's voice hadn't been so serious, it would have been derisive.

Kevin nodded. "There won't be any more murders that way."

Romano finished his coffee, put the mug down on the mantel, and walked over to Kevin. Standing only six inches away, the policeman let his blazing eyes and serious countenance work to maximum effect. "Why won't you tell me what you've learned?" he demanded in a fierce whisper.

"You didn't help me—why should I help you now?"

"I helped you, Kevin," Jack Hobbs said, rising and turning the intense two-man stare into an even more intense triangle. "I risked my career for you. Twice. You owe me."

"I'll tell you what I know when I'm ready," Kevin said. "Right now I don't trust the police. I think you'll make another mistake."

"We won't," Romano promised.

"You made a mistake when you closed the book on the murders two years ago. You made a mistake when you threw me out of your office. You'll make another one."

Romano controlled himself with a great effort. His voice, when he spoke, seemed to escape from his mouth in regulated gasps, like gas being released from a pressurized cannister. "I hurt your feelings when you came to see me. So now you're gonna pay me back. And for that childish revenge, innocent people may have to die. Is that what you want?"

Kevin felt his shoulders grow rigid with fury. "Yes, I want something," he shot back. "Pure and simple—revenge. He killed my wife, and I want him. This time I'm not going to give you the chance to fuck it up."

Romano's hands shot forward and grabbed Kevin's shirtfront. Kevin grabbed him back. Stepping between them, Jack Hobbs tried to pry them apart. For several seconds Kevin and Lieutenant Romano remained locked in each other's grip, staring into each other's eyes, and Jack Hobbs for all his strength could not separate them. Then, as if they sensed something about each other, the lieutenant and Kevin let go at the same moment and stepped apart.

The lieutenant smoothed down the front of his gray suit with his palms. "You're stronger than you look," he said to Kevin after a time.

"If I find out who the murderer is and where he is, I'll come to you," Kevin promised him. "We'll take him on, together."

"I'll find him before that, on my own," Romano said with a grunt.

"I hope you do," Kevin said. "I don't want any more women to die."

Chapter 15

"Please, have another oyster," Ron Christopher urged, spooning a ladle full of shellfish onto Kevin's plate. The hot seafood antipasto at Tony and Lucille's Restaurant was, Kevin felt, very possibly the best dish served in New Haven. The cauldron of zesty seafood gave off a garlicky smell that made nearby diners glance over. A nearly empty bottle of Chianti Classico sat on the table by Kevin's glass. Ron Christopher was doing none of the drinking, very little of the eating, most of the talking, and all of the paying. "My paper will be happy to pick up the tab," he assured Kevin, "so go ahead and order something else if you want."

"I think I've had enough," Kevin said, wiping his mouth with a corner of his napkin. "And we should talk business. I take it you want something from me."

The wine the sommelier had poured for Christopher at the beginning of the meal stood untouched. His face was as eager, as nervous, as ferretlike as ever. "We made a deal," he said, plunging in. "I helped you and, in return, you promised to help me."

"I don't have anything for you yet."

Ron Christopher leaned forward and his nose twitched eagerly.

"I have a hunch about you," he said. "When you first told me the current murders were connected to the ones two years ago, I was skeptical. But you turned out to be right. And the tip you gave me checked out. Everyone I ask about you tells me you have one of the best minds at Yale. I think you just might crack this wide open, and if you do I want the story."

"And what do I get?" Kevin asked.

"My full cooperation, and the resources of my newspaper. You give me something to check on, and I'll find it fast. That would be valuable for you, wouldn't it?"

As Kevin sipped his espresso, the caffeine jolted him out of his wine-induced lethargy. "Jennifer Lawrence," he said. "She was a freshman here two years ago. She transferred to Penn, then the University of Wisconsin, then Grinnell, and finally to Berkeley. Can you check for me and see if any crimes were committed against women in those colleges' libraries in the past two years?"

Ron Christopher's excitement showed in his face. "You really are onto something, aren't you?"

"After Berkeley she vanished," Kevin said. "She may have gone to England to study art. Her roommate said her special interest was seventeenth-century British portraits. She comes from a rich New York family and they could have sent her anywhere. Think you can find her for me?"

Ron Christopher nodded. "Just don't forget—" he began.

"I promise that if I do find the killer, you'll get an exclusive story," Kevin said, getting up from the table. "Thanks for the dinner."

Christopher was busy making notes. "I'll have this for you in a day or so," he promised.

Kevin walked back toward the Yale campus through the cold dusk, enjoying the way the last light softened the leafless winter scenery. As he took a shortcut down a narrow side street, he became aware that a car was following him. He turned—it was a black Cadillac with California license plates. It rolled to a stop a few feet from him and Fahmi got out of the driver's side. Another very tall man, whose facial scars were visible even in the fading twilight, got out of the passenger side. The two men approached Kevin.

"Ali wants to talk to you," Fahmi said. "Please get in the car and we'll take you to him."

"Where is he?" Kevin asked, instinctively backing away.

With remarkable speed, the tall man looped a long arm around Kevin's neck so that from a distance, it would look as if they were old friends greeting one another. Kevin felt something hard and cold between his shoulder blades, and realized that it was the barrel of a revolver. "Get in the car," the tall man said softly. He spoke with a French accent, his voice flat and empty of emotion. "We do not want to hurt you."

Kevin allowed himself to be marched toward the car and deposited in the backseat. The tall man sat next to Kevin, keeping the revolver on him while Fahmi drove the big Cadillac through the dark streets.

"Where are we going?" Kevin asked.

"Silence," the tall man commanded without raising his voice. "Your questions will be answered when we arrive."

The Cadillac plowed through the darkness for a long time, and then lights began to appear again. Kevin knew Connecticut well, but the twisting ride through the darkness with a gun pointed at his heart had left him thoroughly disoriented.

The Cadillac came to a stop on a quiet street outside a restaurant whose sign proclaimed it to be the Star of Persia. The restaurant looked closed, and the street was deserted. "We are going to go in the restaurant now," the tall man said in the same soft voice. "You will be silent and come with us."

Fahmi opened the back door on Kevin's side. The short, balding driver helped Kevin out and retained a hold on his right arm, while the other man slid out quickly and grabbed Kevin's left arm. Holding Kevin securely between them, they marched him toward the restaurant. He could not have put up much of a struggle against the two of them, even if he had wanted to, so he allowed himself to be led silently up to a back door.

The small, bare, storeroom that they took him to had a heavy door with an air lock, as if it had once been refrigerated. A folding chair in the middle of the room was obviously meant for Kevin. For some reason he felt that sitting would put him in a particularly vulnerable position and tried to resist their gentle pressure to seat him. The tall man put a hand on Kevin's shoulder and roughly shoved him down into the chair.

For perhaps ten seconds the three of them waited in silence. Then the door to the storeroom opened and Ali Shahrzad walked in accompanied by an old man. As soon as they entered, Fahmi and the tall man bowed to them slightly and stepped back.

The old man was wearing a dark silk tweed sports jacket over a bright-blue linen shirt. His face had deep lines, and something about the way he walked directly in front of Kevin and stood staring at him suggested he was used to wielding power.

Ali broke the silence. "Professor Randall, if you are really a professor and if your name is really Randall, I would advise you now to speak the truth."

"I'll be happy to," Kevin assured him.

"Why have you been looking into my past?" Ali Shahrzad asked quietly. He was wearing a tight black short sleeve shirt that accentuated his muscles.

"Who said I've been. . . ?"

"You lied to me about Bradley Sutton," Shahrzad cut him off. "You went to the Calhoun dean's office and tried to get the office worker to talk about me. You called other professors searching for information about me. This morning you met with two policemen, and this afternoon the police sent my name to every police department in the United States and to Interpol."

Shahrzad stepped closer. When he moved, the muscles beneath his shirt writhed like snakes.

The fragile old man stood next to him, watching with flintlike eyes that Kevin was sure had witnessed dozens of interrogations.

Kevin looked from the young man to the old man and back again. He opened his mouth but did not speak.

The ancient one spoke for the first time, in a language Kevin didn't understand.

"Do you understand Persian?" Shahrzad asked. Kevin shook his head. "He suggests that we begin by breaking your fingers one by one," the young man explained.

The room had grown warm with the five bodies. "May I stand up for a minute?" Kevin whispered. "I'd like a second to think."

"Stand and think then."

Kevin walked to a corner of the storeroom and tried to think, but his mind kept returning to the scars on the tall man's face. Finally he turned, took a deep breath, and began to explain.

He told them the entire story: what had happened to his wife Anne, how the murders had started up again, what the list of suspects meant, how he had uncovered the connection among Jennifer Lawrence, Peter Pusecki, and Ali Shahrzad, and finally why he had asked the police to run a check on Ali's name.

When he finished there was five seconds of silence. Then Ali Shahrzad gave a low chuckle. The old man glanced at Ali and then he too smiled.

"You don't believe me?" Kevin asked.

"You think that I became a mad killer because Jennifer Lawrence broke my heart?"

"Something like that?"

"She was a wonderful, foolish girl," Shahrzad said, "but she was not enough of a woman for me to kill for." He paused to glance at the old man, who nodded. "But I have discovered a woman worth killing for," he continued, speaking slowly. "She is a woman of infinite beauty that she has retained even after being despoiled. She is a woman with a soul thousands of years old, and one day I will kneel and kiss her. I speak of Persia, my native country, Professor Randall, and of the cause of national liberation to which I have dedicated my life."

"And the past two years?" Kevin asked.

"For the past two years I have been engaged in what we shall call a secret mission that no one in this room needs to know anything about. I assure you I was not mourning Jennifer Lawrence or stalking young women in libraries."

"I believe you," Kevin said. "Although the police did say you haven't left the country."

"Not under my own name or my own passport," Ali Shahrzad

agreed. "But we have no need to talk of that. Do you have any other questions?"

"Peter Pusecki and the fight."

"My mistake." Shahrzad grunted. "The last thing I wanted to do at that time was to get involved with the police." He broke off for a second, grinning. "But then when we are not yet twenty, perhaps we are all to be forgiven for letting our passions make fools of us. The fights of my childhood and the romances of my childhood are over now. The fight of my adult life has begun. Anything else?"

Kevin shook his head.

"Well then, the question is what we do with you."

Fahmi and the tall man took a few steps closer so that Kevin found himself facing four men.

Shahrzad turned to the ancient and said, "He has caused us great trouble, and he may have found out things he should not know. I suggest we kill him."

The old man looked up at Kevin as if he were conducting a second interrogation with only his eyes. He spoke then, using English for the first time, and his words sounded very smooth and measured. "What do you teach, Professor Randall?"

"English," Kevin answered, feeling a quivering of fear deep in the pit of his stomach. "Romantic poetry."

"Poetry?" the old man repeated, bemused. For a few seconds he was very far away. The tall man with the scars took out his revolver and held it loosely in his right hand, watching and waiting. "I used to write poetry when I was young," the old man finally said. "Many, many years ago, in a different country. Love poetry."

"So did I," Kevin told him.

"To your wife, who was murdered?"

"Yes."

"Where did you meet her?"

"England. She was very lovely."

For a second the old man's face softened. "Are you familiar with the *Rubáiyát of Omar Khayyám* or Naishápúr'?" he asked.

"Only with Fitzgerald's translation."

"It is a beautiful poem, don't you think? I wonder if you happen to have committed any of the quatrains to memory?"

The storeroom was suddenly very silent as the four men watched Kevin. He dug through his memory, trying to pull out a verse. His heart thumped wildly. When Kevin tried to speak, he found that his tongue was sticking to the roof of this mouth. His recitation came out in a half whisper:

> *Yet Ah, that Spring should vanish with the Rose!*
> *That Youth's sweet-scented manuscript should close!*
> *The Nightingale that in the branches sang,*
> *Ah whence, and whither flown again, who knows!*

The ancient man inclined his head slightly. "I do not wish to have the blood of a poetry professor on my nephew's hands. If we let you go, this entire interlude never took place. Do you understand me?"

"It never took place," Kevin agreed.

"And you will stop looking into Ali's past? I assure you that he is not the person you are seeking. Please relay this to the police.

"I will. I don't think he is either," Kevin replied.

The old man looked directly into Kevin's eyes for fifteen long seconds. Then he turned to his nephew and said, "Let him go." He walked out of the storeroom. Shahrzad muttered something to the man with the gun and followed his uncle.

The gunman looked surprised by what had just happened. "You are very lucky," he said in his flat, dry voice.

"I don't really think I am," Kevin answered. Then he said, "Please take me back to New Haven."

Chapter 16

Ron Christopher needed a full day to check the police records and campus news agencies at the four colleges Jennifer had fled to. Kevin passed the time by following up several small leads.

He learned that Jennifer Lawrence and Peter Pusecki had both taken an introduction to psychology class taught by a Professor Holtz. Kevin called Holtz and got a copy of the list of suggested readings that the psychology professor gave to his freshman students every year.

At the medical school library, security had been tightened to the point where it took Kevin ten minutes at the front desk to get into the stacks, and patrols marched by every half hour or so to ask if he'd heard or seen anything suspicious.

After several hours of digging, Kevin found that one of the readings on the list, a transcription of a guest lecture given at Yale and entitled "A Case Study of General Retrograde Amnesia in a Preadolescent" was missing from the stacks. The lecture had been given by a Dr. Clement Blake.

"This lecture transcription is missing," he told one of the librarians. The elderly woman had thinning reddish hair kept back with a pin and a smile that the decades had done little to dim. She punched the title into the computer and nodded sadly.

"I'm afraid that item has been missing from our collection for a long time."

Kevin frowned. "It's crucial for my dissertation," he told her. "And I need to read it as soon as possible. Is there any way you could give me the name of the last person to check it out, so I could call him and see if he knows what happened to it?"

"We're not supposed to release that information."

"I won't tell anyone." Kevin flirted with her a little bit. "And if I find it, I'll bring it back to you. Please. . . ?"

She took a green half pencil and, after glancing at her computer screen, wrote JENNIFER LAWRENCE in capital letters. "Here's the name of the culprit," she said, handing it to him. "Good luck."

"Thanks," Kevin said. "You be careful not to work alone at night."

Her slightly nervous grin thanked him for his concern. "With the new library hours, no one will be here after dark," she told him. "Look." She held up a memo from the head librarian, announcing that at the suggestion of New Haven Police Lieutenant Romano, the library hours were being curtailed indefinitely.

At home, Kevin called Professor Holtz again. Explaining that he didn't have his own copy of that particular lecture transcription, the professor suggested that Kevin call Dr. Blake at Rutgers University.

The office secretary for the Rutgers Department of Psychology explained that Dr. Blake had died of natural causes over a year ago.

Next, Kevin called Mr. Robert J. Lawrence at the Wall Street offices of Lawrence, Cartwright, & Dobbs. He rolled through two secretaries in no time flat and then fought his way past a very tough administrative assistant by repeating that he was a federal agent involved in a homicide investigation.

The administrative assistant put him on hold for a few moments, and finally a polite voice answered.

"Mr. Lawrence? Mr. Robert J. Lawrence?"

"Yes? I am Robert J. Lawrence."

"Sorry to disturb you at work, but you've probably heard about what's going on at Yale—the library murders. I'm Lieutenant Romano, New Haven police, and I'm in charge of the homicide investigation. We think your daughter may have some critical information. I need to talk to her."

"I'd like to help but I'm afraid my daughter is recovering from a very serious illness and can't be disturbed."

"I appreciate that," Kevin said. "And I can assure you that no one is going to harass her or ask her anything that could upset her. I'll talk to her myself—I just have one or two harmless but important questions to ask her."

"I said no."

"Look, pal," Kevin snapped, trying to imagine how Romano would handle this. "Maybe you didn't hear but this is a homicide investigation. I don't care who you are or where you work, either you cooperate or I'll have you charged with—"

Without waiting to hear the rest of it, Robert J. Lawrence hung up the phone.

———————————————————

Duroc was waiting for him. The team had left, and the master swordsman had turned off the side lights so that only the center fencing strip was illuminated.

"You look much better, my old friend," Duroc said, clapping Kevin on the back.

"I am."

"I was surprised when you called."

"I've been thinking about a puzzle all day," Kevin told him. "Maybe a little exercise will help."

"Let's see if you can still dance."

Kevin held his saber up, and the bright overhead lights cast a long thin shadow across the wooden floor. Duroc's saber shadow crossed Kevin's as the old coach held up his own weapon with a smile. "And now," he said, "on guard!"

They clashed again and again, sabers darting and probing and slicing, their feet dancing nimbly up and down the strip. Kevin had been jogging every morning and keeping to a fairly healthy diet and low alcohol intake, and he was surprised by his own good showing. He couldn't find an opening in Duroc's guard very often, but at least he furnished his old coach with a few tense seconds.

Duroc was as quick and graceful as ever. Time after time he flashed in and scored points before Kevin could react.

Just when Kevin was ready to drop from exhaustion, Duroc lunged a bit too eagerly and Kevin responded with a flawless reposte. It had been his favorite move in his heyday, and the simple but difficult to execute motion came back to him. First, he parried Duroc's lunge, and then in a silvery flash he thrust directly back in the line of attack. Duroc grunted with surprise as Kevin's saber found its mark on his padded fencing jacket. He stepped back, raised his mask, and grinned. "At least you haven't lost that."

"No, but nearly everything else." Kevin laughed.

Kevin took fifteen minutes to walk the four blocks from the gym to Trumbull College. As he limped through the night air, every muscle in his body screamed in protest, but the totality of pain and tiredness was rather pleasant. As he was crossing Tower Parkway, Kevin saw the marchers.

There must have been two hundred of them, nearly all women, some wearing placards that read "TAKE BACK THE NIGHT" and some of them merely holding candles. They were chanting: "One-two-three-four, we won't live in fear anymore, five-six-seven-eight, stop the killings, we won't wait."

Kevin stood on the curb and watched them pass. Most were students, some looked like graduate students or young professors, and there were several older women marching along stiffly but with great purpose. Near the head of the column Kevin spotted Amy Strong. She was holding a white candle in her right hand, and in her left hand she held a sign that read: "Two have died already—we deserve to live free from fear!"

As she passed Kevin, she looked over at him, and their eyes met. In that second Kevin knew that she was exactly what she said she was and that she was as eager to put a stop to the murders on campus as he was. That left only Peter Pusecki, and Kevin realized that his next trip would be back to New Jersey, to a small town on the banks of the Hudson River.

The marchers disappeared around the corner onto Grove Street, their candles dwindling into pinpoints of light that were ultimately swallowed up by distance and darkness. The last echoes of their chanting rode toward him on the night wind and then faded into silence.

The next morning, just as Kevin was getting ready to leave, a very excited knock sounded on his front door. When he opened it, Ron Christopher burst in.

The small reporter was far more animated than Kevin had ever seen him. His glasses were askew and his cheeks were flushed red. "You were right." He gasped. "You were right. I *ran* here to tell you."

"About the four colleges?"

"Yes." Ron Christopher leaned against the door jamb and thumped his chest with his palm, as if encouraging his overextended heart to keep beating. Kevin led him in and got him a drink of cold water. The reporter soon recovered enough to talk.

"A female student was killed in the main library at Penn twenty-one months ago, just after Jennifer Lawrence transferred there. When she moved to the University of Wisconsin, a librarian was found brutally beaten and died without recovering consciousness. Jennifer transferred to Grinnell, and thirteen months ago a female professor there reported being disturbed in the stacks by a man she didn't see but whose footsteps and behavior seemed threatening to her. And at Berkeley, at the very end of last semester, a female graduate student was found in the basement of the library stacks with her head bashed in." He stopped, exhilarated and at the same time appalled by the grim list he had just reeled off. "So now you have to tell me what you know. I'll drive myself crazy speculating if you don't."

"Try to hang on a bit longer." Kevin felt his own excitement rising at the reporter's news. At last the two-year interval was beginning to mean something.

"Then I'm going to write an article on the other murders in other college libraries. I'll be the first reporter to have noticed the pattern."

"If you do, you'll be sacrificing a major story for a very minor one," Kevin told him. "I don't want us to tip our hand in any way."

"That's not fair," Christopher protested vehemently. "I checked it out—it's my story."

Kevin shook his head.

"How long is it going to take for you to find what you're looking for?"

"Not too long. You can speed up the process. Did you find out where Jennifer Lawrence is studying art?"

Christopher shook his head angrily. "Someone's gone to a great deal of trouble to cover her tracks. The only thing I've got for you is that she flew from San Francisco to Paris two months ago, first class, on Pan Am."

"That's helpful," Kevin said, pulling on his raincoat. "She's probably in England, but check France if you don't find her there."

"I'll keep checking," the reporter promised. "I'll find her for you. Where are you going now?"

"To New Jersey," Kevin told him. "To ask an old couple a few more questions about their son."

"I'll come with you," Ron Christopher offered. "I'll drive for you, pay any bills, whatever . . ."

"You just find Jennifer Lawrence for me," Kevin told him. "And I promise you the newspaper scoop of the decade."

Chapter 17

The street was as dreary as Kevin remembered it—the same acrid odor hung over the closely set wooden houses and the same mangy dog trotted up from the bank of the river, to sniff at the garbage cans.

This time Mrs. Pusecki opened the door, and when she recognized Kevin, mixed feelings of gratitude and suspicion played out across her heavily lined face. The gratitude won out at first, and, giving him a tiny smile, she whispered, "Thank you for helping us the other day."

Kevin bowed his head.

Then her suspicion took over. Instead of inviting him in, she drew her housecoat tighter and demanded, "What do you want?"

"Can I come in?"

She answered him with an almost imperceptible shake of her head.

"Please, I just have two questions I want to ask you," Kevin told her, "or your husband, if you prefer. Then I'll go and I promise you'll never see me again."

"You think I should let you in because you gave us money?" The word money was spit out like a profanity.

It was Kevin's turn to shake his head. "Not because of that. Let me in because you love Peter and want to find out what happened to him."

"Peter is dead," she said fiercely, the three words snapped out with absolute finality.

"Who is it, Anna?" The old man's voice came from down the hall, behind her. She tried to push the door closed, but Kevin grasped the knob and held it with just enough force to keep it open. The battle over the door played out in silence, and while the woman clearly had little chance of overpowering Kevin she doggedly kept straining at it as if she could close it by sheer willpower. In a few seconds Mr. Pusecki ended the battle by whispering something in her ear, and she drew back into the hallway a few steps.

"Please, I'd like to ask you two questions," Kevin said.

"When you ask questions, you make us . . . feel sad."

"I know," Kevin said. "I'm sorry. But I have to. Please." He begged the old man with his eyes, and after one long beat of hesitation Mr. Pusecki opened the door for Kevin to enter, and led him down the long hallway, through the tiny kitchen, back into the shrinelike family room. Two new white candles burned beneath the Madonna, casting flickering shadows over Peter's graduation picture.

Kevin sat down on the green couch, while the old man remained standing. Mrs. Pusecki came into the room, as she had during his last visit, bringing two opened Budweisers and a small bowl of peanuts. She handed Kevin one of the beers, gave her husband the other one, and put the bowl of peanuts down on the table in front of the couch. The old man put his arm around her, and she drew close to him, tucking her chin against his scarred hand as if seeking both warmth and support.

"There's something about Peter's childhood that you're not telling me," Kevin said, looking up at them with an unwavering stare. "I don't mean to pry or to bring back painful memories, but I have to know what you're keeping back."

"There's nothing to hide," Mr. Pusecki said in a blunt, honest-sounding voice. His palm slid down his wife's chin and neck in a caress to settle on her left shoulder.

Kevin directed his inquiry to the woman. "Mrs. Pusecki, your son was a normal baby?"

"Yes," she said, her eyes fixed on the candle flames.

"And he had a normal early childhood?"

"Yes."

"And there was nothing that he needed to hide or that you needed to hide?"

As she shook her head, her husband shook his head too. "Peter was a good, normal kid," he told Kevin. "We can't help you find something that isn't there."

Kevin moved closer to them. On impulse, he took the old woman's left hand in his own and held it palm up, exerting a gentle pressure. He looked from her to her husband to her again, letting the silence wrap around them. Finally he spoke to her in a very low whisper. "Why do the pictures in that album on the table start when Peter was already six or seven years old? Why wouldn't he go swimming in gym class? What was there on his body that he didn't want his friends to see?"

Kevin saw the old man's hand tighten on his wife's shoulder, as she opened her mouth to speak but then said nothing. Beginning with her head and then rippling down her entire body, she shook from side to side as if her desire to negate his question gradually turned into a shiver against something dark and cold.

"Where did you get Peter from?" Kevin asked in such a low whisper that it seemed to merely scratch the deep silence and leave it unfractured. "Who gave him the scars on his back? Please tell me, I beg of you."

Mrs. Pusecki looked at her husband. His jaw quivered slightly, and his eyes narrowed as if he wanted confirmation that she had made a decision. Kevin saw no change in her face at all, but her husband found what he was looking for there. When he turned to Kevin, the graveness of his expression was remarkable. "We promised each other never to talk about it. For fourteen years we haven't told anyone . . ."

"You never will have to again. Just point me in the right direction . . ."

The old man took a deep breath and Kevin saw him summoning his strength as his chest tensed and his neck tightened. "You're right," he finally admitted. "Peter wasn't our own child."

The old woman let out a groan, slumped slightly, and then rallied and staggered out of the room. Her husband went after her. Kevin heard them in the bedroom, whispering, and then Mr. Pusecki came back alone. "My wife . . . she's very upset," he told Kevin. "You have to go now. Listen, Peter was adopted—a doctor at the state hospital interviewed us many times, and when he finally gave Peter to us he said we shouldn't talk about any of this ever again. He said Peter had come through a terrible experience that he did not remember at all. . . . Here, take this. If you have any more questions, call him yourself."

The old man handed Kevin a very worn business card that read:

CLEMENT BLAKE, Ph.D.
DIRECTOR OF PSYCHOLOGY
CEDARTOWN CHILDREN'S HOSPITAL
CEDARTOWN, NEW JERSEY

Now, please, please, go."

"Thank you," Kevin said, slipping the business card into his wallet. The old man walked him to the door. "Is there anything else I can do for you?" Kevin asked as he prepared to step outside.

"Yes," Mr. Pusecki replied, without anger or meanness. "No matter what you find, what new questions you think of, what you do and where you go, don't ever come back to this house. Things are bad enough for us."

"You'll never see me again," Kevin promised him, setting off down the steps and out into the grim, gray street.

Kevin spent a while walking around Edgewater, thinking. In the late afternoon he walked along the river, watching the barges and tankers move slowly past, making their way into the port. When evening fell foghorns began to sound along the waterfront, like the hunting calls of prehistoric beasts. Few stars were visible through the murk, but as Kevin got used to the brilliantly lighted skyline across the river he started to find new constellations in the manmade galaxy.

He was sure he now knew the name of the killer. Perhaps the right thing to do was to march into Lieutenant Romano's office and tell him that somewhere around Yale a powerful young man named Peter Pusecki was hiding and waiting to kill again. The police department could find and circulate pictures of Peter. They could piece together the missing clues and figure out where Peter was hiding. . . .

But if they were as clumsy and obvious as usual, Peter would sense that he was being hunted and disappear for another two years, or three, or four. And then the killings might start all over again.

Kevin drove back across the Hudson and cruised down Broadway the length of Manhattan Island, skirting pockets of late-night pedestrians hanging out on Columbus Avenue or dotting Times Square, or seeking midnight meals in SoHo. He drove into the early-morning hours, when the prostitutes left their streetcorners to finally share their beds with only their own tired bodies and the all-night cabbies turned off their taxi lights and drove themselves home.

Kevin felt a growing certainty that if he did go to the New Haven police, they would want more proof than he had that Peter Pusecki was the killer. In fact, he had no hard evidence at all. The only way to make absolutely sure, Kevin decided, was to get the entire story. If he knew why Peter was doing what he was doing, and where he was hiding, a trap could be set and the young man could be caught or at least stopped.

The logical next step, then, was to find Jennifer Lawrence and untie the final knot. And though not going to the police disturbed his conscience, he found that his hunger for personal revenge was far stronger than any pangs of guilt.

Kevin arrived back in New Haven just as the stores opened for the day, and he drove straight to the *New Haven Register*. Ron Christopher was already at his desk, talking on the phone. When he saw Kevin, the reporter said a few quick words into the receiver and hung up.

One look at Kevin's face was all Christopher needed. "You found something out! I can tell!" he said excitedly.

"Yes, I did."

"Do you know who's doing it? Come on, do you?"

Kevin hesitated, then nodded.

The reporter exhaled, and his eyes grew large with excitement. "Who?" he finally whispered.

"Soon," Kevin promised him, "but not yet."

"You know, you're killing, making me wait like this," Christopher said. "I'm losing weight, I can't sleep, I even missed Sunday meeting the other day . . ."

"It won't be much longer," Kevin promised. "Did you find Jennifer Lawrence for me?"

Ron Christopher pointed to the hundreds of notes and phone numbers spread out all over his desk. "The Yale Center for British Art gave me a list of every college with an art program and every art school in England. I've been calling them one by one—I'm almost done."

"And?"

"Not a trace of her. I'm going to try the ones on the Continent next. It might help if you'd tell me how this girl is linked to the murders."

"I will," Kevin promised him, "when the time comes. Right now just keep digging."

Kevin went home, showered, shaved, and listened to four messages from Jack Hobbs and two from Romano that either begged or ordered him to report what he knew immediately.

Halfway through a breakfast of cornflakes, Kevin got an idea. Mara Resnick had said that Jennifer had a passion for seventeenth-century English portrait artists like Gainsborough, Reynolds, and Hogarth. Perhaps Ron Christopher had talked to the right people and asked the wrong questions.

The Yale Center for British Art had been one of Anne's favorite places in New Haven. Kevin felt a deep stab of nostalgia as he passed the street-level shops and climbed the steps to the glass doors of the museum that famed architect Louis Kahn had built. Anne had loved the spacious interior of the museum, with its two open interior courts illuminated by skylights.

For a while Kevin browsed through the exhibition galleries, remembering how Anne and he had wandered hand in hand through the subdued yet elegant rooms. But the white oak paneling, the linen-covered walls, and natural wool–carpeted floors that were designed to present a low-contrast background to the paintings made the museum so antiseptic and muted that suddenly Kevin felt mildly claustrophobic. He hurried out into one of the main open courts, where a tour was passing by.

"This Center for British Art houses one of the world's largest collections of the pictorial arts of Britain from Elizabethan times until the middle of the nineteenth century," a dowdy tour guide explained in rehearsed phrases. "The collection includes more than fifteen hundred paintings, twenty thousand prints, ten thousand drawings, and twenty thousand rare books. The Center was made possible by money given to Yale by Paul Mellon, B.A. nineteen twenty-nine . . ." Her voice trailed off as she led her tour group up ι staircase toward the second floor.

"I need to speak to someone who specializes in British portraits of the seventeenth century," Kevin told, an attractive young black woman at the information desk.

"About. . . ?"

"I'm a professor in the English department here," he said, "and I have a few questions about several paintings of the period. Is there somebody here I could make an appointment to see?"

She thought for a second. "That would be Dr. Davidson, the assistant curator. Hold on, I'll see if he's in."

She dialed a number and spoke a few quick words into her desk telephone. "You're lucky. He's in and he'll see you right now. Just take the stairs up to the fourth floor and look for the faculty offices."

When Kevin reached the fourth floor, a small, jovial man with ruddy cheeks and a warm smile accosted him with a wave. "Excuse me, I'm Arthur Davidson. Are you the chap who wants a word with me?" His Oxford accent stung Kevin a bit—for two years he had done his best to avoid upper-class Britons.

"Kevin Randall, thank you for taking the time."

"Not at all, not at all. Many people come to look, but few stop to talk. What can I do for you?"

They strolled along the top floor's observation deck, beneath the skylights. Kevin studied the baffles and filters used to diffuse the sunlight and screen out direct, harmful rays. "I have sort of an unusual question to ask you."

Dr. Davidson smiled pleasantly. "Then I shall try to give you an unusually good answer."

"Actually," Kevin admitted, "I don't even know how to phrase the question."

"Have a go at it," the museum official encouraged.

"Well, let's say a person loved British art, particularly seventeenth-century portrait art. And let's say that person had suffered an upset of sorts, so she went off to England. If she wanted to be able to study the paintings and the artists that she loved the most, where would she go?"

"That's easy. She'd go to London," Dr. Davidson said without any hesitation. "She'd rent a flat somewhere between the National Gallery and the British Museum, and she'd be all set."

"But suppose she couldn't go to London," Kevin pressed. "Suppose she was living in fear, perhaps had a breakdown, and she wanted to avoid large cities. Is there a place she could go to recuperate that would still cater to her interest? Maybe a small city or even a town with an unusually fine museum, or a private collection . . ."

"There are several small cities that have superb galleries. Of course, the Ashmolean Museum at Oxford comes to mind right away. And I suppose there are a few credible museums at that funny little school down the road," Dr. Davidson said, revealing where his school loyalties lay.

"No universities," Kevin told him. "She fears colleges even more than she fears big cities. This is a girl who wants rest and privacy."

"She's a bit picky, this girl, if you don't mind my saying so,"

Dr. Davidson observed. "No cities, no universities—doesn't leave us much to work with." He stopped in front of a print of Hogarth's "The Rake's Progress" and stood before it, stroking his temples in contemplation. "This young woman of ours wouldn't happen to have unlimited money, would she?" he finally asked.

"As a matter of fact, she's rich beyond words."

"Well, you should have told me that going in," the assistant curator reprimanded Kevin gleefully. "It makes your difficult question quite simple. She'd go to Cheltenham."

"Chelten-where?"

"Cheltenham Castle. It's probably the most expensive and exclusive rest home in all England. The castle itself is a marvelous thirteenth-century edifice that has been completely modernized. The grounds are magnificent, there's a medical staff on hand, and the castle has one of the finest private collections of British portraiture in the world."

"You've been there?" Kevin asked.

"Several times. They brought me over twice to get my thoughts on American-owned pieces they were considering acquiring. Also, I gave a lecture there once on the revival of English sculpture in the seventeenth century." Dr. Davidson smiled at the memory, and then his face saddened a bit. "It's too bad the gallery is closed to the public, because they really do have a most extraordinary collection."

"Is there any other place like Cheltenham?" Kevin asked. "A second choice that our friend might also have considered recovering at?"

"Not if she had the money for Cheltenham and she knew what's what about portrait art. You sound as if you're considering taking a trip. . . ?"

"I am," Kevin admitted.

"I don't want to discourage you, but there is something you should know," Dr. Davidson said. "You'll be wasting your time and money unless the woman we've been speaking about specifically asks to see you. Otherwise, you'll never get near her."

"The security's that tight?"

"Tight isn't the word. It took me an hour to get past the guard-house, and I had been invited to lecture there."

"Well, I think I'll try anyway," Kevin told him. "The fact that the security is so tight is actually a very good sign. And I have a connection in England who should get me through the door."

"And I repeat, old fellow, you'll be wasting your time trying. No matter whom you know, Cheltenham isn't the kind of place you can just waltz into."

"Thanks for the warning. My connection is a very good one so I think I'll give it a shot anyway. You've been a great help."

Dr. Davidson beamed. "My pleasure, and good luck to you on your odd little adventure."

Back in his apartment, Kevin called the airline to make a reservation for a direct flight from Kennedy to Heathrow. He packed quickly and haphazardly, throwing warm sweaters and wool socks into his leather suitcase as he happened to come across them. The scale of his gamble in going all the way to Cheltenham with no hard knowledge that Jennifer Lawrence was there thrilled him. It all seemed to fit: it was a top-notch rest and rehabilitation home, the security was apparently airtight, and it had a terrific collection of paintings Jennifer loved.

He sent a brief cable to Lord Barrington-Mayfield announcing his visit and the time his plane would land.

Finally, when he was packed and ready, he wrote down everything he had unearthed since his first New Jersey visit. In a covering letter, he instructed Laura Donovan to put this report with the first one he had given her and to turn them both over to her brother-in-law, Jack Hobbs, if Kevin didn't contact her within two weeks. He mailed the letter to her on his way out of New Haven, wondering how Hobbs, and Romano would try to continue the investigation if something did happen to him. Perhaps Interpol could get access to Cheltenham, but from the way Dr. Davidson had described the place, Kevin doubted it.

It raised Kevin's spirits to be leaving New Haven once again. The cold Long Island Sound drizzle spattered his windshield. He knew that in an hour or so, when the temperature sank a few more degrees, the cold rain would turn into an icy sleet. As he steered the rented black Plymouth onto I-95 and headed for New York and Kennedy Airport, the thought occurred to him that New Haven was one of the few places in the world whose climate made the prospect of a London winter sound attractive.

Chapter 18

Kevin landed at Heathrow Airport at three o'clock in the morning. After clearing customs, he walked out the arrival gate and was pleased but not entirely surprised to recognize Poole waiting for him. Wearing a long gray overcoat that seemed distinctively English, Lord Barrington-Mayfield's aged valet stood alone, away from the crowd, as if too much contact with the hoipolloi might reflect badly on his distinguished master. His bearing was stiff, circumspect, and his tone when he addressed Kevin was polite and decorously understated. "Welcome back to England, sir. Allow me to carry your bags."

Kevin protested, but the aged servant, whose thin frame was an angular combination of sinew and bone, hoisted Kevin's suitcase and traveling bag as if they weighed nothing at all. A few minutes later Kevin found himself in the backseat of a vintage Rolls-Royce sedan, watching as the headlights of the speeding car fleetingly lighted two bright circles of English countryside. "Why north? Why not Gloucester?" Kevin asked, wondering why the lord had abandoned his family seat for his much smaller country house near Nottingham. At first the servant gave no answer, and the only sound was that of the wheels on the dark highway.

"His lordship shuns Gloucester," Poole finally responded solemnly. "I expect you will understand why he prefers solitude."

"I do. How long has he been in seclusion?"

"These two years."

"And his daughters?"

"They visit him regularly."

"He hasn't traveled abroad?"

"Not a day's trip away." Poole clearly considered Kevin to be family—the lord's reserved old servant and guardian would never have opened up even this much in front of an outsider.

"And how is the lord then?"

"You'll find him greatly changed, I should think," Poole said sadly. After that, he drove in silence, and Kevin opened the car window a crack, settling back on the leather seat to let the smells and sounds of England remind him of happier times.

Dawn was just breaking when Poole turned the car up the tree-lined side road to Mayfield House. The windows were all dark and everything was eerily still. The Victorian red-brick mansion glowed grayish in the first light of dawn, while the hulking ruins of the ancient abbey behind it still seemed shrouded in night shadow.

They entered the house through the principal corridor where the portraits were hung one above the other in Victorian fashion, so that generations of Barrington-Mayfields looked down on Kevin, an austere and silent audience. Poole left Kevin in a small sitting room while he went off in search of his master.

The carpet in the room was in a peculiarly sober yet striking tartan pattern; so were the curtains and pelmets. The chairs and settees were upholstered in leather. A fire burned low in the stone fireplace, and as Kevin warmed his hands in front of it he looked around at the trophies of the chase hung along the walls. The antlers seemed to shift and turn in the dim light, as if the heads had come back to life in the darkness and now, shot through by the first rays of morning light, were in the final paroxysms of fruitless struggle to avoid returning to being merely daytime wall decorations.

Kevin awaited his father-in-law's entrance with a certain trepidation that brought back memories of their first meeting. Then he had been a young American scholar asking a peer of the realm for the hand of his favorite daughter. Initially he had received the cool reception he had expected and feared, but within minutes Kevin had felt the nobleman begin to soften toward him. Their friendship had grown and strengthened all during the happy years he and Anne had spent together. Now he had come again to this country house to find Lord Barrington-Mayfield apparently nursing his grief in seclusion. Kevin had little doubt that his presence would stir up all of the painful memories of Anne that her father had been trying to put to rest for the past two years.

Poole returned. "His lordship sat up for you most of the night and finally fell asleep in his study." The servant lowered his voice as if to impart a secret. "He sleeps so rarely that I'd rather not wake him."

"Let him sleep," Kevin agreed. "I'm tired myself."

Poole led him up the grand staircase to the second floor, and then down a long hallway to a door that waited half open. At the sight of the open doorway, Kevin felt an odd sense of disquiet. Poole announced, "My wife's lighted the fire for you and provided you with all you should need. If there's anything wanting, just ring and I'll come at once." As Kevin followed Poole through the doorway, he realized with a sinking heart what disturbed him about this room. Anne and he had come to Mayfield House once and had stayed in this very room. Kevin recognized the gilded Louis XVI four-poster bed with its silk canopy. "There wouldn't be any smaller rooms . . . this one feels a bit drafty?"

"With the fire going, it should be warm enough soon, sir," Poole explained. Then he smiled sadly and admitted, "His lordship lives here alone for long periods so we only keep a very small staff. The other wing of the house has fallen off a bit . . . but if you would prefer another room I'll have Mary begin to fix one for you immediately."

"This will be fine," Kevin told him. "It's already getting warmer."

Poole withdrew, and Kevin found himself alone with his memories in the ornate bedroom where he and Anne had shared two particularly passionate nights. He undressed slowly and lay down in the lavishly decorated bed. His head sank into the goosefeather pillows, and when he closed his eyes the only sound he heard was the gentle gossip of the small woodfire as it told its secrets to the flagstone hearth. From New Haven to Kennedy Airport to Heathrow Airport to Nottinghamshire Kevin hadn't dozed at all. Suddenly the long miles began to weigh him down into the sweet abyss of thoughtlessness.

Kevin slept far longer and more deeply than he had in two years. Again and again he seemed to sense Anne's soft body beside him on the bed, and he reached out for her beneath layers of blankets and layers of dreams. He imagined he felt her gentle breath inhaling and exhaling warmly against his cheek, and the certainty of her nearness that these tactile hallucinations gave him lent his dreams a tincture of honeyed bliss. In his dreams he tumbled slowly downhill through an endless field of wild grass, and the slow-motion somersaults of this midnight journey were given a magical sweetness such as Kevin had never known because of his dreamstate conviction that Anne was beside him, tumbling down the same endless grassy slope.

Kevin woke suddenly and at first was totally disoriented. The curtains had been drawn over the windows, and the canopy above the bed screened out what little daylight had managed to find its way into the room. His right arm encircled one of the large pillows, holding it to his chest. When he realized where he was, and that the dream had merely been a dream and the pillow was merely linen stuffed with goosedown, Kevin was seized by a despair as cold and penetrating as any he had known over the past two years. Icy fingers of certainty that he would never see Anne again in this world drained the sweetness from his dreamy afterglow. It took Kevin long minutes of struggle to shake off the paralysis of despair enough to stagger to his feet.

An hour later, showered, shaved, dressed, and greatly recovered, Kevin descended in search of Lord Barrington-Mayfield. Poole met him on the landing. "Good morning, sir. I hope you slept well?"

"So well that I may have worn out the patience of my host."

"I'm afraid you have missed him," the old servant admitted. "But not for long. Every afternoon he goes for a long stroll over the grounds by himself, but he always returns at sundown. He said to tell you not to wait for him to eat. He often skips the evening meal entirely."

Kevin dined by himself on the long table in the main dining room. The table could easily seat fifty guests, and Kevin felt odd and small eating alone at it. Poole served up a fine feast of poached trout with dill, followed by a marvelous leg of venison roasted in a sweet mustard glaze. Kevin was just finishing his coffee when he heard Lord Barrington-Mayfield's uneven footsteps approaching. He turned and suppressed an audible gasp only with a great effort.

Lord Barrington-Mayfield had aged ten years in the past two. Kevin remembered the Englishman's face as having been uniquely strong and proud with a high forehead, eyes that would have been haughty if they had not been so kind, and a fierce slab of chin that was almost Churchill-like in its proclamation of British bulldog valorousness. Now that same face was a map of grief from the white hair down the continent of tragedy-wrinkled forehead to the soft sea of sunken cheeks. Only the Englishman's flashing brown eyes were as proud and unyielding as Kevin remembered them.

"Well met, Kevin Randall," Lord Barrington-Mayfield said, extending his hand.

Kevin stood and took it in his own. "I'm sorry to be foisting myself upon you without invitation or warning."

"Your apology should not be for coming, but for staying away for so long," Lord Barrington-Mayfield said graciously. "And since I see that you have finished your dinner, may I suggest that we talk in more comfortable surroundings?"

"I haven't played in two years," Kevin said, sensing what his father-in-law had in mind.

"Neither have I," Lord Barrington-Mayfield admitted. "That should make for an even game, don't you think?"

Leaving the dining room, they walked through the library and entered that large section of the ground floor that had been constructed as the male domain. Glancing about as they passed through the smoking room and the gun room, Kevin was reminded that mid-Victorian society with its false sense of chivalry had been inordinately restrictive of women. In all of English history there had probably never been a period in which so many different activities were considered unsuitable for nicely brought up women. This attitude had necessitated a virtual partitioning of the house so that the men could continue to enjoy the pastimes of the day.

The Englishman led Kevin into the billiard room, past the billiard table, to sit down facing one another on opposite sides of the elegant chess table. The tabletop was of hand-polished rosewood, and its black and white pieces were carved from Ceylonese ebony and African ivory. Kevin felt a bit humbled by the knowledge that Basman, Wallis, Miles, Keane, Stean, and the other leading grandmasters of twentieth-century English chess had at one time or another sat in the chair he now occupied. A picture of the incomparable Gligoric, signed "To Lord B, a damned fine player and my dear friend," hung at eye level a few feet away.

"Shall I tell you why I've come?" Kevin asked, eager to convey to his host all that had happened.

"No, let's play first and talk after," Lord Barrington-Mayfield replied. In his aristocratic code of behavior, eagerness or any other strong manifestation of emotion was unsavory and a sign of weakness. He held out two closed fists, and Kevin tapped the right one, which obediently opened to reveal the black pawn.

Kevin didn't even need to look at the board to know his opponent's first move. It was one of Lord Barrington-Mayfield's endearing eccentricities that even though he had once been a world-class player, throughout his entire life when he had the white pieces he always played the English Attack. Kevin responded with his king pawn, his opponent fianchettoed his king bishop, and the game soon developed into the traditional struggle for control of the center.

More than an hour later, Kevin smiled and knocked over his own king in resignation. "I don't know why I even bother trying."

"Nonsense, nonsense. If you had studied the openings and middle-game theory just a bit more, you could have been winning tour-

naments instead of writing books of literary criticism. Now then, I
have something I want you to try." He got up and hobbled over to
his liquor cabinet. Lord Barrington-Mayfield, a highly decorated
RAF pilot in World War II, had lost his right foot and half his leg
when he was shot down over Germany. When Kevin first met him,
the Englishman had walked so easily on his prosthetic limb that his
limp was almost imperceptible. Now, as he crossed the floor bearing
a private reserve bottle of port, the older man's body dipped notice-
ably with each step.

"I drink to your health, sir," he toasted Kevin formally yet with
a smile.

"And to your own," Kevin replied with equal gravity and equal
warmth. "And now I have a strange story to tell you."

Lord Barrington-Mayfield settled back in his tall armchair, his
glass of port in his hand. Simply and sequentially, Kevin told him
everything that had happened from when he had seen the headline
about the new Yale library murder in the newspaper more than a
month ago, to yesterday when he had arrived in England to search
for Jennifer Lawrence. As Kevin's narrative progressed, Lord Barrington-Mayfield's normally reserved countenance took on a look of
consternation. By the time Kevin finished, the Englishman was sitting forward on his chair, and his deep brown eyes flashed twin
fires.

"Good Christ," he whispered to himself when Kevin stopped
talking. "Those murders at the four colleges, place the answer
beyond any doubt."

Kevin sipped his glass of port, his eyes remaining fixed on his
host.

"Well, Kevin, you've earned your dinner and your glass of port,
and a good deal besides," the lord said admiringly. "You found all
this out yourself? The police didn't help?"

"I went to them at first and they thought I was merely interfer-
ing."

"Understandably. Well, not to put it too strongly, if what you
tell me is true, it seems like we may be dealing with a bloody fiend."

"Quite literally, a bloody fiend," Kevin agreed.

"Then if other young women are in danger, there's not a moment to lose. I know of Cheltenham. It won't be the easiest place to get you in—it's a bit like a Swiss bank in how seriously it takes itself. But I went to Harrow with the fellow who now runs our Secret Service, and I expect he may be able to help." Lord Barrington-Mayfield paused and muttered half to himself, "Even if he is a bit of a fool."

Kevin nodded sympathetically, thinking of his old secret society acquaintance and CIA connection, Dan Roberts.

"There's a phone in the library. I'll make the call right away. Come, make sure the arrangements are to your liking."

The library was a wonderful room, redolent with the rich odor of centuries-old leather-bound books. Lord Barrington-Mayfield was soon talking on the phone with "Old Keble," as he called him. First he flattered, then he cajoled, and finally he negotiated, pausing at every point to make sure Kevin approved of what he was asking for.

"Well, that's set then," he declared, hanging up the phone. "Keble will be sending a car by for you in a bit. They'll take you straight to Cheltenham. It'll be cold there this time of year."

"Thank you for helping me. I couldn't have gotten in without you."

"Oh, I don't know." the Englishman brushed off Kevin's gratitude with a chuckle. "You seem to do fairly well investigating on your own. Frankly, I've got half a mind to join you . . . But then, my hunting days are over. I'd only hold back the chase."

"You would still do honor to any chase, sir." Then Kevin summoned his courage and whispered, "Forgive my saying so, but it's a shame to see such a heroic and vital life ending on such a resigned and mournful note."

Lord Barrington-Mayfield stood still and smiled peculiarly, surprised by Kevin's gallantry and daring. "Damned if you aren't an odd one for an American," he finally muttered. "The car will be here for you quite soon. Kevin Randall, let's talk."

Kevin waited.

"My father died in World War I. My mother was killed by German bombs two decades later. Both my brothers fell at Dunkirk, fighting in the suicide division that held the line so that the miraculous evacuation could succeed. My dear wife died of a rare disease after battling it for years with great courage and enduring almost unimaginable pain. After her death my greatest solace was Anne, my favorite daughter, who was very like her mother. I don't need to tell you what happened to Anne, and I can see by looking at you that your grief these past two years has been at least equal to my own." Lord Barrington-Mayfield paused in his extremely uncharacteristic account of his personal misfortunes and looked Kevin right in the eye. "I don't tell you all this because I want your sympathy, but rather because I respect you as a man and would not have you think me a coward. Napoleon had several opportunities to leave St. Helena, but he had lost too many battles and he was just too tired. My surrender has also been one of weariness."

"I would never think you a coward," Kevin assured him, "but how do you pass your time here all alone?"

"I read," Lord Barrington-Mayfield answered. "The poets who were the most miserable are by far the most soothing. Lately I've been reading George Gordon."

Kevin grinned—Lord Barrington-Mayfield was the only person he knew who referred to Lord Byron so familiarly. "What of Byron?"

"Mostly the poems of the separation." The Englishman tilted his head back and recited:

> *Fare thee well! and if for ever,*
> *Still for ever, fare thee well:*

"Good stuff, but easier said than done. Of course, perhaps it is more fitting to read George Gordon in the billiard room than in the library."

The Englishman's reference to the rumor that Byron had begun his notorious affair with Lady Frances Webster atop a billiard table amused Kevin. "I'm sure Lord Byron gave equal time and had equal pursuits in libraries."

"No doubt. By the by, I finally got around to reading your last book. It's rather well done I should say."

Kevin bowed slightly.

"And now you should probably go up and pack your bags. But before you go—one thing more. I would like to give you some paternal wisdom. Revenge is not an honorable ambition for a gentleman."

"I'm an American teacher, and there's not a drop of blue blood in my body," Kevin shot back almost resentfully.

"Nonetheless, you're a gentleman and you'll find what I'm saying quite true. Grudges and vendettas and bitterness nourished within the heart will turn to poison and destroy you." The older man's brown eyes gleamed as if this particular bit of wisdom had been hard won. "Justice is a quite acceptable end, but revenge is honorable only in certain rare cases."

"Such as?"

Lord Barrington-Mayfield thought for a very long time. "In my whole life," he confessed, "there have been a lot of men I've run afoul of who I've disliked for one reason or another, but I can think of only two cases where I have truly felt justified in hating a fellow man and desiring to spill his blood. One was Adolf Hitler. I would have run him through on sight."

"And the other?" Kevin asked.

Lord Barrington-Mayfield drew himself up, and when he spoke his voice came out straight and sure as a cannon blast. "If you need anything in seeking the maniac who dispatched my Anne—money, firepower, influence—I lay all that I have at your disposal. And I trust that if you ever do come face to face with that cur, you will give him a swipe or two for your bride's grieving father."

Chapter 19

Kevin arrived at Cheltenham in pitch darkness.

A pleasant woman dressed in a white hospital jacket met his car at the front entrance and showed him up to his small, fastidiously clean room on the second floor. The castle was completely still and silent, and the woman, whose white hair belied her vigorous and otherwise youthful appearance, took great pains to open and shut the door noiselessly. When the two of them were safely inside his room, she smiled and said, "This is highly irregular for us, Mr. Randall. There is a great fear among the board of directors that your activities here may reflect badly on Cheltenham's reputation for privacy and security. On the other hand, we simply could not refuse what is, I gather, a matter of national security."

"I shall be very discreet," Kevin promised her.

"I trust that you will. As was requested, none of the guards or members of the medical staff have been informed of the reason for your presence. Everyone will think you are just a new patient."

"Thank you. I appreciate your cooperation."

"As loyal subjects, it seemed we could do no less. I am Marjory Worsley, assistant director of operations. Here is my card. I can be reached at this extension twenty-four hours a day. Do not hesitate to wake me up—I fall back to sleep quite easily."

She held out her right hand and Kevin shook it once politely. "Thank you again for your cooperation," he muttered.

"And thank you again, in advance, for your discretion," she replied, and walked out the door.

The next morning, when Kevin awoke, it took him several minutes to recall the previous night's drive and remember that he was indeed at Cheltenham. It was a bit disorienting to wake up each morning in a different English castle. He lay in bed for a time, studying his small and tastefully furnished bedroom while he wondered how he should proceed with his investigation. He sensed that he was very near to the final answer, and though the thought was exciting it also brought on a vague feeling of dread at what must come next, once all the pieces of the puzzle were in place.

Breakfast was still being served in the main dining hall when Kevin came down. The magnificent banquet hall's high ceilings were crisscrossed by massive polished oaken beams; stained-glass windows let in a warm roseate light, and a large central crystal chandelier, supported by several smaller chandeliers whose candles had been replaced by candle-shaped electric lights, hung over a rectangular table of Spanish mahogany that ran the length of the great room. Smaller tables were placed in side nooks at pleasingly irregular intervals.

About thirty patients were still at breakfast. Some sat in clusters, enjoying their toast and marmalade as they discussed the morning's *London Times*. Others sat alone, sipping juice or tea or coffee, observing the way the warm morning light was patterned on the ceiling beams. A few patients were in wheelchairs, but most of them appeared ambulatory and in fairly good health.

Kevin chose a seat by himself, at a corner of the large banquet table that provided him with a sweeping view of the rest of the hall. His breakfast was quickly brought to him. As he spread the thick orange marmalade on the still-warm sides of toast and began to eat, he studied the patients. They were mostly an older lot—many in their sixties or seventies. Only five of the patients in the hall looked as if they could possibly be in their twenties, and none of those five looked even remotely like the beautiful twenty-year-old daughter of an American multimillionaire.

Kevin spent the morning touring the grounds. Within the fenced-in perimeter there were three very different and quite marvelous gardens. A stream flowed through the west corner of the grounds, and around the edges of that stream centuries-old oak and elm trees stood shoulder to shoulder. Even though they were leafless, their thick trunks grew so close to one another that it was difficult to see through them to the towering Norman castle.

The rose garden was of course bare and skeletal in the winter frost. Still, as Kevin walked through the network of trellises, he could appreciate what a complicated masterpiece the garden was, and how lovely it must be when the first pink and red and white buds opened to the spring sun.

Finally there was a maze. It was a garden of tall evergreen bushes that grew on both sides of ten-foot-high red-brick walls. Wandering into the twisting and turning paths of the maze, Kevin soon found the center clearing. In the middle of that clearing, a small white gazebo stood beside the placid waters of a lovely fountain and pool, which reflected the puffs of cloud in the sky overhead. A bronze swan in the center of the fountain twisted its long neck as if it were scanning the water for fish. An intercom, mounted near the gazebo, had a small sign posted next to it explaining that patients had only to shout and a guard would quickly come to lead them out of the maze. It took Kevin nearly half an hour to find his way out on his own, and by the time he safely made his escape it was lunchtime.

On this day, the midday meal was served buffet style in the castle's conservatory. The relative newness of the conservatory's walls and the modern curve of the glass ceiling dictated by its steel supports led Kevin to conclude that this wonderful circular room had originally been an open-air courtyard. Now, geraniums in full bloom, sweet-smelling calycanthus, beautiful heliotrope, and long-fingered ferns turned the large space into a perfumed bower of mid-winter magic. Artfully simple marble tables were spaced through the large room, and servants hurried amid the flowers bringing lunches to hospital guests.

Kevin walked through the fragrant indoor garden, trying to look as if he were deep in thought, while he covertly scanned the patients sitting at lunch. He began to think that he had struck out once again; Jennifer didn't seem to be at any of the marble tables. And then in a corner of the garden, beneath ivy that cascaded down from the ceiling like a green waterfall, he spied two girls. They were using a flat white rock as a table, and sat half hidden in the ivy as if they relished being in their own secret world.

Kevin sat down on a bench and fought not to stare.

The Japanese girl was perfect. Her amber skin, coal-black eyes, delicate figure, and most especially the exquisite understatement and control of her every look and gesture bespoke centuries of asthetic refinement. She wore a short black skirt and a white cotton shirt, and her precise movements as she ate barely rippled the strands of ivy that brushed her arms.

The other girl was more than perfect. The tiny flaws in her appearance added immeasurably to her overall beauty by giving her budding girlish femininity a mature womanly depth and warmth. Her full lips neither smiled nor frowned; her large doelike eyes were both innocent and wary; her chestnut hair braided down her back and tied with a thin blue ribbon was girlish yet peculiarly regal; and even the way her bare arms again and again crossed her breasts and stomach in a gesture that was at once defensive and accepting, all combined to give her nymphlike appearance a beguiling undertone of hard-won wisdom and sad experience. What struck Kevin most forcefully was that this twenty-year-old Mona Lisa was shamelessly flirting.

She was eating a round red apple while looking directly into the eyes of her lunchtime companion. She pierced the skin of the apple in tiny bites, and then her pink tongue flicked out to lick up the sweet juice. Kevin simply could not pull his eyes away. Finally she felt his glance and looked across the room at him. He turned away quickly, knowing that it was too late. He stared down at his lunch for the rest of his meal, not trusting himself to look at her, and when he stood up to leave the two girls were gone.

That afternoon Kevin explored the interior of the castle. He began at the oldest part of Cheltenham, where many of the doorways and gateways still featured the perfect semicircular arch, hallmark of Norman architecture. The sixteenth-century chapel was magnificently preserved, and Kevin sat for a time in one of the pews staring directly up at the roof of the nave vaulted with ornamental carvings depicting the Battle of Bosworth Field.

Next Kevin passed through the armoury where sixteen full standing suits of armor stood guardlike, a platoon from antiquity. Helmets and breastplates and swords and doubleheaded axes hung one above another on walls that reached up twenty-five feet to the high ceiling.

The art galleries connected the unrenovated section of the castle to the part that had been modernized and made a rest home. Hall after hall of paintings beckoned, each one filled with pictures hung at eye level, above a neutral green carpet. Kevin recognized several Van Dycks and Gainsboroughs, and saw that he was indeed in the presence of one of the world's great private portrait collections. His attention was so caught up by the masterpieces that he very nearly blundered into the two girls who sat staring up at a particularly stunning Edwardian painting of a fox hunt. The Japanese girl glanced at him quickly, but her companion, whom Kevin had decided must be Jennifer, was sketching the painting and never broke her concentration. Kevin gave them wide berth, passing around them in a twenty-foot semicircle that just barely allowed him to see the quality of Jennifer's sketch.

After leaving the gallery hall so as not to tip his hand, Kevin found himself in the main library, which was obviously quite a favorite with the patients. Several sat in stuffed leather armchairs and on three-hundred-year-old settees, lost in costly volumes they had selected from floor-to-ceiling shelves. Leopard, tiger, lion, and bear skins were strewn over the polished floor of the library giving it a wild and slightly exotic flavor.

Kevin returned to his room and dialed Marjory Worsley. She answered on the first ring. "I'd like a chart of the patients' wing, with their rooming assignments," he told her. "That way I'll be far less likely to disturb the wrong patient."

As he had hoped, given such a reason, she was more than happy to comply, and within twenty minutes a diagram of the first two floors of Cheltenham was in his hands. The patients' names were written in in black pen. He found Jennifer Lawrence and noted with surprised satisfaction that her room was directly beneath his own.

Kevin dallied through both servings of dinner waiting for Jennifer to show up, but neither she nor her Japanese companion ever appeared. They also stayed away from the evening's scheduled activity, a lecture on the early British social documentary filmmaker John Grierson, which Kevin managed to sneak out of during an intermission.

He returned to his room and dressed completely in black from head to foot. For a time he paced nervously back and forth, rethinking his plan. Tonight he would try to verify that Jennifer was sleeping in her own room, alone. The next morning, very early so as to catch her at a time when all of the other patients in the castle were still fast asleep, Kevin would knock on her door and politely but firmly demand to speak to her. Lord Barrington-Mayfield's old Secret Service chum had provided Kevin with impressive credentials, which he could show her if need be.

There came a rising whisper as the pressure of the evening wind slowly increased against his window. At the stroke of ten o'clock, Kevin stopped pacing and hurriedly left his room.

No one saw him slip down a side staircase and out into the shadows. The darkness swallowed him totally—he could not even see his own right arm or hand in its black sleeve and glove. Moving in the narrow lane between the shrubbery and the outer wall of the castle, he edged along step by step, counting off the windows. At the edge of the third window he paused and looked around. All was silent and still. He took the final step to Jennifer's window and peered inside.

Jennifer appeared to be dancing. She was standing in the center of the bedroom, which was lighted only by two candles in holders on her desk. Her face was flushed, and her half-closed eyes did not even try to focus on anything but seemed to swing wherever the momentum of her dance pointed them. She was wearing a full-length black evening gown. As she swayed back and forth to her own inner music, she tilted her head back and her body writhed as if an electric shock were slowly traveling down her spine.

Without breaking the rhythm for even a heartbeat, she reached back and unzipped her gown. The movements of her body soon shook her dress down her torso and legs, till it lay in a satiny puddle on the floor. Next she lowered her chemise revealing her naked body inch by inch—the already taut breasts, the flat stomach, and the dusky diadem of pubic hair.

Kevin glanced around nervously. The moon was hidden by the clouds, and all the castle windows were dark. Reassured that he had the cold, black night to himself, he turned back to the window.

Jennifer's hands went to her breasts, and she moved the tips of her fingers in slow circles. Her half-closed eyes opened once and then closed completely, and the look of pleasure on her face changed to one of desire as she teased her nipples with greater and greater pressure. As her right hand slid down her breast and stomach, she bit down on her lower lip.

Watching in the shadows, Kevin was amazed to find himself growing firm and then rock hard. He hadn't had a strong erection in nearly two years.

Then the Japanese girl appeared, naked, from a corner of the room that had been hidden from Kevin's view. She stepped up to Jennifer so that their breasts touched and their stomachs were flat against one another, and she kissed her on the lips.

Jennifer lay down on her bed, and her Japanese lover nimbly got on the bed so that her head was above Jennifer's spread knees. And as the two girls began to make love to each other in the candlelight, Kevin stifled a moan and sank down into the shadows beneath the windowsill.

———————————————————————

The Anderson twins had never felt bound by rules.

They were big and blond and their identical looks had allowed them to break hundreds of regulations all during their childhood. They had even cheated on their SATs. Bonnie did the math sections on both exams while Meryl did the English sections—then they switched papers. When they were fourteen, they had gone out on first dates together, had lost their virginity on the same night when they were sixteen, and had roomed together during their first three years at Yale.

Alone now in the vast library, they sensed each other's nervousness. Meryl gave a little chuckle, saying, "This was your idea, after all."

"It was a good idea too," Bonnie said defensively. "How else were we going to finish the poly sci papers so we could enjoy the weekend? And you have to admit it was fun hiding out when they searched the library before closing it for the night." She shivered and hunched her shoulders. "It's just kind of creepy to be here all alone. . . ."

Meryl put a sympathetic hand on her twin's shoulder. "Let's get to work. By the time they open the doors tomorrow morning we can be nearly finished. Imagine trying to lock us out of the library on the Thursday before Princeton Game weekend!"

For an hour they worked together on their papers on the Cuban missile crisis. They had intentionally chosen complementary topics so that they could research in tandem and save time. After an hour, Bonnie put down her book and stood up.

Meryl saw her hesitate. "Afraid to go alone?"

Bonnie nodded. "I feel weird needing company to go to the bathroom. But you have to admit, this silence is over powering. Listen . . ."

For ten seconds the two young women listened to the complete silence of the empty library stacks, a silence unbroken by any movement or sound except for the almost inaudible crackle of electricity through the coil of the lightbulb that glowed above their desk.

"Come on," Meryl finally said. She picked up their flashlight, clicked it on, and began to lead the way towards the bathroom. Bonnie grabbed the large knife they had brought almost as an afterthought—how they had giggled over bringing it, but it didn't seem very funny now—and followed her sister and the flashlight beam that opened up a tunnel of light between the shelves of books.

"In you go," Meryl said when they reached the small bathroom. She saw Bonnie hesitate and look at her pleadingly. "I don't want to watch you pee." Still Bonnie hesitated. "Oh, you're such a coward," Meryl gave in angrily.

They entered the bathroom and Meryl pulled the door shut behind them. Bonnie reached over and locked it. The windowless white tile bathroom held only a sink, a toilet, and a metal trash can. The wall around the toilet was covered with graffiti complaining about the sexual inadequacies of Yale men.

Bonnie undid the snaps of her jeans and slid them down to her knees. And at that moment they both froze as there came a gentle knocking at the door.

The twins looked at each other. "If we say anything, we announce our presence," Bonnie whispered, so frightened she could barely stand.

"Whoever it is didn't knock at random. He must have seen us come in. Maybe it's a guard."

"At this time of night? In a locked library?"

"Maybe it's a police patrol."

The knock sounded again, just a bit more insistently, two clean and almost friendly raps.

"Who is it?" Meryl called out, and her usually strong and sure voice quivered and almost broke.

The only answer was the deep, complete silence of the empty library. It was a silence so oppressive that the two girls instinctively realized the futility of shouting for help. Above them, below them, and around them were millions of volumes that would completely muffle even the loudest screams.

"Are you the police?" Meryl tried again. "Someone from the library? We know we shouldn't be in here—answer and we'll come out."

Again, silence was the only answer.

Bonnie handed the large knife to her sister. "You'll be better with it," she whispered.

And suddenly, the overhead light of the bathroom went out. Bonnie screamed once, and then regained control in the pitch darkness.

"Meryl?"

"I'm here."

"Hold me. I'm afraid."

"I'm not going to let anything happen to you. Remember, we have this knife." Twin hugged twin in the darkness.

And then the crashing started. The door to the bathroom was made of solid old oak. It held firm under the first few furious assaults, as an outside body threw itself against it. Then there was a silence that lasted perhaps twenty seconds.

Bonnie wept and Meryl kissed her. "Don't cry, Bonnie. If he comes through the door, I'll get him with the knife. Please don't cry."

"I've never been so scared."

"Please, please stop crying."

And then the crashing came again, louder and even more furious. This time it was the splintering crash of a large and heavy metallic object being pounded against the door over and over with increasing fury.

The wood splintered. The door buckled. Meryl let go of her twin and threw herself against the door to hold it shut. The hammerlike blows continued, and Bonnie joined Meryl in trying to keep the door shut.

There was a three second pause—a nightmare silent beat—as the outside body summoned its strength. Then there came the thumping charge of the shoulder again, and this time the weakened door burst inward sending the two girls sprawling on the tile floor.

Bonnie blacked out for a moment. She came back to consciousness when a hand gripped her long blond hair and yanked her up with such fury that her feet almost left the ground. She screamed and tried to twist away, but the hand got an even more secure grip on the side of her head and bent her down till her cranium came in contact with a hard object. Somewhere in the depths of her fear she realized that that hard object was also screaming and shaking to get loose, and that it had to be Meryl's head.

And then the force began to grind their heads together. Bonnie glimpsed a light shining internally, as if her brain was bursting into flame. She bucked and kicked and scratched to get loose, but the force that pushed her skull against her sister's skull only increased. The internal light grew brighter and brighter, till even in her death screams Bonnie was dazzled. And then her skull caved in, and as she made the journey from life to death she was even closer to her twin sister than she had been when they had fought their way out of their mother's womb.

It finally quieted, and Err dropped the two lifeless bodies onto the white tile floor. Blood and bits of brain and tissue hung from his hands.

Over? the scared voice asked.

Yes, it's quieted now, Err answered, feeling tired the way he always felt when he managed to quiet the rage that built up inside of him day by day, hour by hour, minute by minute, until it rang like an alarm clock and he had to do something, anything to quiet it.

After the rage came the tiredness, and the urge to creep back down, down, to a safe place to sleep.

There had never been a time when there was not this rage, and there would never be a time when it would not be there, because she had kept them in darkness and done such things to them, that as they waited for her to return all they could do was comfort each other and feel the fear build and build until it spread itself around their world like a fire, dying and flaring up, destroying everything in its path.

Chapter 20

K evin did not rap on Jennifer's door early the next morning. He did not seek her out at breakfast, or hunt through the conservatory greenery for her at lunch.

In fact, as lunch was served in the conservatory, Kevin stood alone by the river in the west garden, his mind whirling like a child's pinwheel in a strong wind. Plagued by guilt, all night he had roamed the grounds in a feverish state, at times wracked by a re-awakened desire for life and love that he could scarcely believe, at times skewered by a self-hatred so pervasive that he nearly threw himself off the castle ramparts to have an end of it.

Dawn had not brought him peace. Here he was in England—in an English castle of all places! Territory sacred to Anne's memory. He had come all this way to avenge her death. Less than two days ago he had been in the company of her father, and they had been kindred spirits in the shared certainty that neither of them would ever be able to recover from the tragedy of Anne's death. He was here for a reason, a purpose, a mission, he reminded himself. There were a few important questions he had to ask the American girl, and then he could leave her and this castle forever. But when he tried to remember what those questions were and how he should phrase them, his mind kept returning to the image of Jennifer in the conservatory taking tiny bites out of a red apple and then licking out the sweet juice. Jennifer dancing . . .

It was a bright wintry day. The sky above was whitish with thin clouds that floated across it in an infinite pattern of curlicues, like shorn fleece. Around noon the fleece began to drift down so that the castle grounds were soon as white as the sky overhead. Kevin let the large snowflakes melt into his hair and clothes, and the cold wetness felt pleasantly reviving.

He followed the river for a while, watching the thick white flakes sift onto the thin skin of ice that lined the banks. Then he turned back toward the castle, passing through the rose garden. The falling snow was clinging to the trellises, turning the bare garden into a gleaming wonderland of unusual white shapes.

As Kevin neared the brick maze, he was surprised to hear the faint but unmistakable sound of a cello being played with exquisite mastery. The music came from within the maze, so Kevin entered the winding well-hidden paths and was soon completely lost amid the twists and turns. He let the music be his guide and was moved by the bittersweet sadness of the melody. Stepping out from the final blind turn into the central clearing, he suddenly stopped in his snowy tracks.

Jennifer Lawrence sat on a wooden bench inside the roofed gazebo, her cello braced between her knees. She wore a flowing red dress that brushed the floor of the gazebo, and a white sweater that seemed the same texture as the falling snow. The gazebo was still very much in sunlight, and Jennifer appeared oblivious to the white flakes that cascaded down on all sides. She looked up and saw Kevin watching. The melody of her song trembled but did not break.

When their eyes met in that initial look, a current of pure electrical attraction flowed back and forth. Kevin fought against it and he could see that she did too. The melancholy cello music was somehow steadying—the sad song seemed like a third person there with them, an old chaperone who helped keep the moment from getting out of hand.

Rooted to his spot at the edge of the clearing, he stood watching her small hand move the bow gracefully back and forth. Her long chestnut hair was not braided as it had been at lunch the day before—it was loose and hung down across her white sweater touching the polished cello. She finished the sad piece she was playing without taking her eyes off Kevin. As the last note quivered in the air he felt that they were both afraid to be alone together without the music as a mediator. She put the bow down and managed a polite smile.

Kevin had intended to be strictly businesslike, but he surprised himself by saying "That piece you were playing was lovely. I didn't recognize it." He walked closer to the gazebo, brushing snow off his shoulders. The bronze swan in the fountain gleamed with white flakes on its sculpted feathers.

"I wrote it myself, over the last two months," Jennifer admitted hesitantly. "You're the first person who's heard it. Thank you for listening."

"I am the one who should thank you." Kevin knew that he should switch the conversation to his purpose, but when he glanced down at her bare neck and narrow shoulders he heard himself say, "You must be cold sitting out here. Would you like to borrow my jacket?" He stepped in, under the roof of the gazebo, and took off his wool jacket.

She rewarded him with a smile. "Thank you for offering, but I enjoy the cold." She hesitated a beat, and then her face hardened almost imperceptibly. When she spoke, the warmth and friendliness were gone from her tone. "And now I suppose I should ask why you've been following me."

"Have I been?" Her question and tone having broken the spell, he found he could think rationally again.

"Yes," she said, "you have. You were staring at me at lunch yesterday. When I looked back at you, you tried to hide it. You tracked me down in the art gallery yesterday afternoon, and then took a detour and hurried away without speaking. And—" She broke off and sat looking up at him.

He stepped farther into the gazebo, until he was in front of her. "Yes?" he asked. "Go on."

"And if I'm not mistaken, I saw the moonlight glinting off a pair of eyes outside my window last night." She said this last sentence without blushing, although her voice dropped down to a loud whisper.

"But if you saw me and didn't cry out, you must have wanted me there?"

"Don't judge me too harshly," she requested unexpectedly. "I used to be quite innocent."

"Me too."

His reply seemed to confuse her. For a few seconds she studied his face, as if she were trying to read the small print between the lines of pain that had etched themselves into his still-handsome features. "I repeat my question," she said. "Why have you been following me?"

"Would it be enough of an answer for me to tell you that I've come all the way from New Haven to ask you some questions? Or had you already guessed that?"

Her lips trembled slightly, but otherwise she managed to preserve an expression of great calmness. "In that case I've been expecting you for a long time," she said. "And I've already decided to answer them. What do you know, and what do you want to ask?"

"I know that during your freshman year at Yale, you fell in love with a young man named Peter Pusecki," Kevin said in an even voice. "I know that he had a dark secret in his past, and that he had scars down his back. And I know that sometime during that first semester he may have begun to remember where the scars came from and that knowledge led to madness. I don't know exactly why he began to remember right then, whether it was something in the Yale environment that set him off or something else . . ."

"It was an article we read for our psych class. It made his bad dreams much worse," she interrupted. "He would cry out in his sleep. Finally he told me that he wanted us both to drop the class, and we argued about it. And then he had the fight . . ."

"With Ali Shahrzad?"

She nodded. "You seem to know everything. Yes. I'm convinced the violence of that fight and particularly the blows to Peter's head made him much, much worse. Ali and Peter beat each other very badly before the police broke it up. After the fight, Peter began to spend a lot of time by himself, talking to himself, almost in some kind of a trance."

"Where did he go?"

"To the libraries," she said. "And the more time he spent there, the more he began to come apart."

"Until," Kevin said gently, "he eventually went mad and killed two young women in the stacks of those same libraries."

"That's not true!" she interrupted furiously. "Peter could never have hurt anyone."

"I also know," Kevin ignored her protests, "that you suspected what was happening and transferred to Penn and then to the University of Wisconsin, and then to Grinnell, and finally to Berkeley. I suppose it really doesn't matter whether you fled from fear or horror or heartbreak. What is important is that he followed you." Kevin paused to give his question the needed emphasis. "What condition was he in?" he finally asked her. "How did he manage to follow you across the country in such a state? Did you help him?"

She appeared greatly upset. She shook her head no to his question, but wasn't capable of speaking.

"So he tracked you. Did he have lucid moments? Could he operate in the outside world?"

She nodded, anguished. "At first it wasn't so bad," she whispered very low. "Then it got worse and worse and worse. Sometimes he was almost himself, and rambled about going back to Yale and being a student again. Other times he would disappear for weeks."

"I know that at each of the colleges you transferred to, attacks occurred in the library stacks. Gradually you had to admit to yourself that your former boyfriend was becoming a murderous monster."

"Violent crimes occur on colleges campuses all over the world," she tried to argue, but there were tears in her eyes.

"And I know that at the end, when he found you at Berkeley, you decided to hide in a place where he could never track you down. So your father sent you here."

"If you know so much, what more can I tell you?"

Suddenly angry, Kevin bent down as if he meant to grab her. "Didn't it bother you to leave him on the loose? Didn't you know that other women were in danger? Couldn't you have guessed that when he couldn't follow you he would return to New Haven and begin killing again?"

She buried her head in her hands as if to shut out all sunlight and slid a few inches away from him on the bench. "I loved him, I still love him," she said hoarsely, without taking her hands from her eyes. "No one loves anyone the way I loved him. You don't know half of what we felt for each other so you can't judge me. I couldn't . . ."

Kevin reached down and clamped his hands around her wrists. With a wrench, he pulled her palms from her eyes. She resisted only for a second, and then looked up at him, a fierce pride beginning to kindle in her eyes.

"He's come back to New Haven and begun to kill again," Kevin told her. "He's killed at least twice—maybe more by now. You're not protecting your lover any more, you're shielding a monster." Kevin's fingers suddenly tightened around her wrists so that she whimpered slightly. "Jennifer, where is he?" he demanded.

She shook her head.

"He has a secret place somewhere, doesn't he? A place in New Haven, or around in the surrounding countryside. A place he took you to because he loved you and trusted you, and wanted to share a secret. Maybe you had trysts there—maybe it's locked away in the deepest corner of your heart, but you have to tell me." Kevin felt every muscle in his body tense as he repeated the question with tremendous energy and directness: "Where is he?"

She shook her wrists free and pushed him back a step. "Who are you?" she whispered half to herself.

Around the gazebo, the snow fell in thick patches of white, like a flock of white birds descending.

"Who are you?" This time her question was addressed directly to him.

Kevin found himself momentarily without an answer. "I'm Kevin Malloy Randall," he finally replied.

Now she was in full control, her dark eyes flashing with anger and pride as they dared him to justify himself. "Who are you?" she asked again. "You're not a cop. You don't talk like a cop. You don't act like a cop. Who are you?"

The ferocity in her face completely overawed him. "I'm an English professor," he said lamely.

She stood up to face him, looking directly into his eyes, as if she would drive him away with the sheer force of her will. "You've found all this out. You've tracked me here. You want me to betray the one person who loved me more than anyone in the world. Who are you?"

When Kevin finally understood the depth of her question, the power of the moment seemed to shift instantaneously from her to him. His reply came out from a private place deep within him. *"Sanguis mactati sum!"* he said in a tone that would have been accusatory if it had not been so solemn. She tried to turn away, but he held her by the shoulders so that she had to look at him and repeated: *"Sanguis mactati sum!"*

"I don't understand Latin." Her whisper was barely audible.

"I am the blood of the butchered!" he told her. "Your boyfriend killed my wife!"

She gasped and started, but he held her fast.

"He killed her horribly, brutally, cowardly . . . in a dark place where no one could hear her screams for help. And now he's back, killing again. *Where is he?*" His fingers dug into the soft skin of her shoulders even as his eyes poured liquid fire into hers.

Trembling, she shook her head from side to side as if to deny that this could really be happening. Kevin's grip grew tighter.

Jennifer looked back into his fierce eyes. Instead of answering his question, she bit her lower lip till blood came. When Kevin saw the blood, he lost all control of his actions and drew back his hand to hit her. Then, instead of striking her, he was amazed to find himself kissing her, and even more amazed to find her kissing him back passionately.

With a near-maniacal spurt of strength, she burst free. Kevin dived after her, his outstretched hand catching her right heel and tripping her. She fell onto the floor of the gazebo, her red dress fluttering as she tumbled.

Kevin bent to help her up, but instead of letting him raise her up, she drew him down with her onto the floor of the gazebo. Her arms locked behind the small of his back, pulling him tightly on top of her. Then her hands moved up to caress his shoulders as her lips found his own. She kissed him thirstily, desperately for several long seconds while their bodies pressed together. Suddenly, without warning, her caressing hands folded into small fists that pounded on the back of his neck. Her lips continued to kiss him even as she opened her fists and her nails raked his neck and shoulders.

He seized her dress at the neckline and pulled. Buttons popped off and snaps came unfastened. The heels of her feet joined the heels of her hands in pummeling him. She squirmed free and began to crawl away.

He caught her by the hips and twisted her onto her back again. For a second the struggle mysteriously ceased, as she looked up at him and he looked down at her. They were both panting. She glanced at the nearby intercom with its posted sign explaining how lost guests needed only to yell and a guard would come. But she did not try to summon help. Instead, she reached up and with shaking fingers unclasped his belt and drew it through the loops.

"Where is he?" Kevin's voice rasped, his body poised above her.

Jennifer opened her mouth and then closed it again. He reached out and gently stroked her cheek.

The temporary truce ended in a struggle far more furious than the one that had preceded it. She bit his hand, and he pinned her down with his body weight. He palmed her taut breasts under the sweater with a force that made her gasp. Then his right hand swept down across her body, pushing up her dress even as he reached beneath it to tear off her panties, and she moaned.

As they struggled, Kevin was dimly aware that there were actually four people rolling and battling in the snow. Anne was on his back, pulling his head up from Jennifer's kisses. And though he was betraying his dead wife's memory, the savagery of what he was doing was very much a bolt of revenge.

Peter was also there, in the snow, fighting with and for Jennifer. Kevin felt Peter's presence when Jennifer broke off her passionate kisses to bite and claw at him, and most especially in her refusal to open her legs to him even though her arms were wrapped around his back, clasping him to her.

She resisted, resisted, and then suddenly her thighs fell wide apart. He didn't move. Their eyes locked, then without breaking the stare, Kevin moved his body slightly forward and in one smooth motion planted himself deep inside of her. A shudder convulsed her body. Her legs stapled him to her so tightly that he lost his breath. As soon as her shuddering convulsions passed, the grip of her thighs eased and her hips began moving, faster and faster. She grabbed his hair and forced his lips to her own, and her tongue danced into his mouth.

Her uneven panting became one long ascending moan that rose to a summit so close to both pleasure and pain that it was impossible to tell whether she was approaching rapture or agony.

Kevin was lost in the body beneath his, far past the realm of thought. His strokes became faster and more frenzied, and his hands slid beneath her buttocks, pulling her upward, impaling her even more deeply. A sensual kaleidoscope of colors turned inside his closed eyes, flashing from yellow to orange to bright red, and with the onset of bright red the dam broke and he pumped inside of her, feeling her let go almost at the same moment in a series of spasmodic contractions.

For a long time after that they lay without speaking or moving, their loud panting alone fracturing the snowy solitude. Her arms and legs were still around him, pressing him to her as if she were now desperately afraid of losing something.

The tears came to him first. Tears of shame over his part in what had just taken place; tears of bitter regret for having moved so much farther away from Anne; tears of great emotional and physical release.

Watching him cry, Jennifer cried too.

"I'm sorry . . ." he began, but she put her index finger to his lips and shushed his apology.

They lay in complete silence for a while as she seemed to be summoning her strength. Finally she put her lips to his ear and whispered, "The tunnels."

"What?"

Her confession came out in a string of gasping breaths that were not intended for the outside world, but were whispered deep into the shell of his left ear. "Below Yale . . . there is a huge tunnel system. It connects the colleges . . . the libraries . . . and the oldest secret societies." She stopped for several seconds to clasp him all the tighter, as if only their physical closeness allowed her to whisper this information. "There are old steam tunnels, new steam tunnels, and passageways that were built when Yale was a training center in World War II. Peter told me about them. He found the tunnels and explored them. That was where we would go—"

She broke off then, and tears ran freely down her cheeks. He stroked her burning cheeks with his palm and licked the tears away. She summoned her last bit of strength: "Peter would take me there when we wanted to be alone together. He had a mattress down there, deep underneath Sterling Library. We would walk down with only a flashlight—otherwise it was completely dark. That was his secret place, our secret place . . . my lover's and mine."

Her final words caught in her throat and she choked on them. Kevin kissed her eyes closed, sealing the lids shut with his tongue. "All right," he whispered. "That's enough for now."

Her eyes remained closed as she asked, "So are you going back to New Haven now, Professor Kevin Malloy Randall? Now that your investigation is complete?"

"Yes," he said. "Yes, I am. Immediately." It was his turn to breathe secrets into her ear, and his hotly whispered words made her tremble. "I thought it was all over for me." His whisper became still more searing. "Come back to New Haven, Jennifer, and we'll see this through together. And when it ends, if it ever ends, let's help each other to live again. It will never be the same . . ."

"No," she agreed, "it will never be the same. And I couldn't stand to stay in New Haven."

"Neither could I. We'll go wherever you want."

"To the ends of the earth," she said, like a child.

"We'll take a little hut at the ends of the earth," he agreed, as his fingers traced the curves of her cheeks. "And every night we'll make violent love beneath a tropical moon. And you can pound on my back with your fists and flay my neck with your nails, and in the mornings when the fishing boats put out into the breakers you can play your cello as I sit behind you licking the salt spray from your neck."

In the long silence that followed she looked directly into his eyes, and finally kissed him gently on the lips. "I have something in my room that you should see," she said. "Come."

The transcription of Dr. Clement Blake's lecture was short and concise. Kevin read it through, as Jennifer sat staring out the window. Every once in a while she turned to look at him, as if she were making sure that he was really there.

The lecture—"A Case Study of General Retrograde Amnesia in a Preadolescent"—began with Dr. Blake explaining that retrograde amnesia occurs when a person forgets things preceding the event that caused the amnesia. Usually such amnesia is selective and lasts only for a short time. People commonly forget names or destinations, and then remember them a few days later. But occasionally the amnesia may be general—so that the sufferer's memory is wiped clean.

In very rare cases, according to the article, patients may experience general amnesia for extended periods of time, resulting in fugue states. For example, a prominent nineteenth-century American, the Reverend Ansell Bourne, wandered away from his home one day after a severe shock and acquired a totally new identity. A second shock, years later, brought him suddenly and completely out of his fugue state and he became the Reverend Ansell Bourne once again. He remembered nothing of the time he had spent away from home.

Dr. Blake then turned to the case he had just handled in a small New Jersey town. It had been, he wrote, by far the worst case of child abuse he had seen in his thirty-five-year career. A woman named Edna Roberts lived in a dingy house at the very edge of the town. She had lived there for decades, a tough old loner who didn't bother anybody and whom nobody bothered with. She appeared in town only to buy books at rummage sales and garage sales, and to buy food for herself and dog food for her dogs. Except that, as it later turned out, she didn't have any dogs.

She had two little boys. They were the two sons of her only daughter, who had died giving birth to the second boy, leaving them fully in the old lady's charge. There was no record, according to Dr. Blake, of who the boys' father was or what had happened to him. Apparently she kept the boys tied up in her dark cellar like two animals, fed them just enough dog food to keep them alive, and tortured them unmercifully. And no one in the town had an inkling of what was going on—to those who bothered to think about her, she was just a strange old woman who loved to read.

"I wonder what she did with all the books?" Kevin asked Jennifer.

"Maybe they muffled the screams," Jennifer replied without looking up. "Or maybe she just liked to read."

Kevin went back to the article. One day, according to Dr. Blake, the old woman cut and burned the little boys so badly that one of them died outright and the other was near death. She then poured gasoline all over her little library and herself, and struck a match. The inside of her house rose up like a Roman candle, and by the time they put the fire out both the old woman and the younger of her two captive boys were burned almost beyond recognition. Most of the above information, Dr. Blake explained, had been pieced together from the remains of the house and the severe scars and flesh wounds that crisscrossed both boys' bodies. She had scalded them and branded them, cut them with knives and lacerated them with needles. The dead boy's body was found next to hers in the cellar, a rope and leather thong collar around his neck.

But somehow, the elder of the two boys, named Eric Roberts according to a birth certificate, was found alive in the ruins. He had revived and struggled free during the fire. The first firemen on the scene pulled him out of the cellar more dead than alive. Both of his arms had been broken, he was so badly malnourished that he looked like a sack of bones, and just before the firemen had reached him a beam had fallen and knocked him unconscious.

Eric was brought to the New Jersey State Hospital where for two months he lay in a coma as they waited for him to die. But after sixty-two days, he opened his eyes to the world again. Within hours he began looking around blankly at the nurses and doctors, and in a few days he was eating and beginning to put on weight.

At first Dr. Blake and the other doctors thought the boy had sustained some serious brain damage. He didn't know how to do anything—he couldn't eat or speak or even walk. But gradually his condition was diagnosed as a very rare case of general retrograde amnesia, resulting in a permanent fugue state.

According to Dr. Blake, who quoted numerous sources and examples, Eric Roberts's young mind was so malleable and his dissociative reaction against the hell he had been tortured in was so strong that his fugue state became his permanent state of mind— he would never remember or return to the way he had been before the night of the fire. His memory for the rest of his life would begin with the afternoon he opened his eyes in the New Jersey State Hospital.

Under Dr. Blake's direction Eric was retrained and reeducated to the level of a normal five-year-old boy, and placed with a carefully selected family. The family was instructed not to discuss the adoption with anyone and not to pry into the circumstances of their child's past life that had left him with scars all over his body.

Kevin finished the article and was surprised to find that while he had been caught up in it, Jennifer had been reading it over his shoulder. He looked at her. "So Eric Roberts became Peter Pusecki?"

"Peter was a wonderful, gentle, brilliant man," she said in a low voice.

"I'm sure he was," Kevin agreed. "You both read that article for psych class, and he started having bad dreams?"

"He always had nightmares," she told him. "They just seemed to get worse."

"And then he had the fight with Ali Shahrzad?"

She nodded. "I thought they were going to kill each other. It was horrible. Peter got a cut on his head that took forty stitches to close. He was never the same after that fight. It was like he kept forgetting . . ."

"Or remembering," Kevin finished. "It depends on how you look at it.

She put her hand in his own. "I don't want anyone to hurt Peter," she said.

"No one can," he told her. "Peter is gone forever. Eric Roberts has taken over and gone back to the place with the books. He's striking out with a child's rage at the woman who tortured him and his brother. He's striking out blindly, and he's doing it with a powerful grown-up body." Kevin squeezed her hand and released it. "We've got to get back to New Haven as soon as possible."

Jennifer looked sad for a moment. Then turning, she walked to her closet and took down her suitcases.

Midori did not speak.

She helped Jennifer pack in silence, folding the blouses and dresses with exaggerated care, stacking them artfully in one of Jennifer's suitcases. Whenever Jennifer looked at her guiltily, hoping for any conversation at all—even angry condemnation—Midori turned away and continued folding and packing.

When they finished, Midori pulled the suitcase shut and fastened the clasp. "That should hold safely," she announced, her voice muted, strange.

"Midori," Jennifer pleaded.

"Now, do you have any more bags to pack?"

"Don't let us part this way."

"You should go to sleep soon. You'll want to be rested for your flight."

Jennifer sat down on her bed, staring silently up at Midori until the Japanese girl finally gave in and looked at her. "I think you probably saved my life," Jennifer told her.

"Thank you for trying to make me feel important."

"I love you. I really do."

"And that's why you're leaving me? Because you love me?"

"I have to go back to New Haven," Jennifer declared defensively. "I have no choice."

Midori sat down lightly on the bed next to her. "I know," she whispered. She let her long fingernails make tiny tracks into the soft skin of Jennifer's shoulder. Then she pulled away. "My anger is not for you. It's for myself. It was selfish of me to keep you here for so long. Your father saw what was best for you. And so did you, but you stayed with me. I knew too, but I couldn't find the strength to let you go. Now let me kiss you one last time." It was a light, long kiss of farewell.

Midori ended the kiss and stood up. "Now," she whispered, "follow your destiny. I know it will be very painful going back, but I wish you happiness in the end. *Go yukuri*, Jennifer-*san*." Midori bowed once, very deeply and formally, and then turned and hurried out of the room so that her friend and lover would not remember her for the tears of weakness she was about to shed.

Part Three

The Tyger in the Night

And what shoulder, and what art,
Could twist the sinews of thy heart?
And when thy heart began to beat,
What dread hand? and what dread feet?

What the hammer? what the chain?
In what furnace was thy brain?
What the anvil? what dread grasp
Dare its deadly terrors clasp?

When the stars threw down their spears,
And water'd heaven with their tears,
Did he smile his work to see?
Did he who made the Lamb make thee?

Tyger! Tyger! burning bright
In the forests of the night,
What immortal hand or eye
Dare frame thy fearful symmetry?

—William Blake,
from "The Tyger"

Chapter 21

The snow followed them from Cheltenham.

Kevin drove Jennifer into New Haven late Thursday afternoon through a storm that had already covered College Street with nearly two inches of powder. The city green was a gleaming white rectangle broken only by the three churches. Jennifer sat next to him in the front seat, muffled up against the bitter cold. She had been silently brooding for nearly the entire plane flight and car trip, and now that they had reached New Haven her mood became even more pensive. She seemed to need to touch Kevin constantly, as if to reassure herself that he was really there. On the plane she had leaned her head against his shoulder, when they had disembarked she had linked a single finger with him, and as they pulled into New Haven she reached down to grasp a corner of his trench coat.

Once inside his apartment, she examined it with great interest, lingering over the pictures of Anne with special respect. He felt extremely uncomfortable when she picked up his old wedding picture and tilted it to the light, studying it with puzzled fascination, like a gypsy reading a fortune in tea leaves.

Later, while Jennifer took a hot bath, Kevin leafed through the newspapers that had piled up outside his door. When he read about the twins who had been slaughtered, he jumped up and paced the room several times before calming down enough to finish the story. From the current newspapers, he gathered that Yale had become a university under siege. The libraries had been closed, football players and other athletes had formed student patrols to crisscross the campus looking for signs of trouble, and a large deployment of New Haven police had been indefinitely assigned to protect the students. Newspapermen and other representatives of the media from around the country had apparently flooded into the city to follow the terrible case.

He threw out the newspapers to spare Jennifer, who emerged from her bath looking rejuvenated. She walked over and put both her arms around him, nestling her wet head against his chest. His fingers stroked through the cool dampness of her hair, and for a short while they sat on the couch in each other's arms, watching the snow fatten the limbs of the trees outside his window.

Later he called the police station and was told that Lieutenant Romano was away working on the case. Kevin left a message that he had returned and that he would come to the station the next morning at ten o'clock. The officer who took the message said he doubted that Romano would be able to make a meeting on such short notice since he was extremely busy these days, but he would make sure the lieutenant got the message. The policeman's doubts turned to incredulity when Kevin added almost as an afterthought that Romano should make sure an expert on tracking with police dogs was present at the meeting.

That night Kevin and Jennifer did not make love, but lay in each other's arms as the ghosts that tormented both of them flitted and whirled around the bedroom. "When will you begin?" she whispered after several hours of tense silence.

"Tomorrow morning. Better to get it over with quickly."

His reply seemed to calm her, and she finally lapsed into a light sleep. At first her sleeping breath was steady and her body lay warm and still against his own. But about three in the morning Kevin felt her begin to stir restlessly in her sleep, and her even breathing soon became so irregular that he was tempted to wake her. She spared him the trouble by suddenly gasping and sitting up in bed, her eyes opening from sleep to gaze wildly about the room.

When Kevin very gently put his arm around her she jerked away from him with a start, but relented and sank back into the haven of his embrace. "Just a bad dream," he promised her, sensing the depth of her fear.

"No," she whispered back very softly, and the certainty of her reply hung in the darkness of the pitch-black bedroom. "He knows I'm here."

Kevin tightened his arm around her. "How could he know?"

They lay back down on the bed, and she buried her head in his chest. "I don't know," she whispered back. "He found me at Penn, and I knew when he had come. He found me at Grinnell, and at Berkeley, and each time I sensed it when he was near. And he's near us right now."

"Believe me, it was just a bad dream," Kevin told her, hating the uncertainty in his own voice. Sleep was impossible for both of them after that. They lay in silence listening to the wind brush the snow against the windows. When the wind intensified a bit more there came tapping sounds that Kevin had heard many times before and knew to be a tree branch blowing back and forth so that it scraped his rooftop. Nevertheless, on this night the sounds were uncannily like footsteps, as if a large person were walking back and forth across the roof searching for a skylight or other entryway. Remembering that his apartment was less than fifty yards from Sterling Library, Kevin held Jennifer all the tighter. He decided that he would never leave her alone in his apartment.

When morning finally arrived, Kevin, who hadn't slept a wink all night, felt his fears and forebodings disappear. He was suddenly filled with an intense excitement and a desire for immediate action. Over breakfast, which was only two cups of coffee, Kevin asked Jennifer to accompany him to the police station. "Your presence will add credibility to my story. And you may be able to help us pinpoint the places in the tunnels we should concentrate on."

"I've told you where he is, I've told you about his condition the last time I saw him, and I've come back to New Haven to be with you," she answered. "I'm not going to go to the police station and start drawing Xs on the map. You might as well ask me to load their guns for them." She shivered as she said this last line and looked down at the coffee in her cup as she sipped it.

"But I can't leave you here . . ."

"Do you know anyone in New Haven who is totally unconnected to this . . . thing, whom I could stay with?"

First he called the English department chairman, Charles Lansbury. Lansbury's wife answered with the information that her husband was in Boston delivering a lecture and wouldn't be back until the weekend.

Kevin next tried two friends on the faculty who lived in suburbs of New Haven, but both of them had already left home fearing that the commute would take longer than usual because of the snow.

It was nearly 9 A.M. The meeting at the police station was fast approaching, and Kevin couldn't think of anyone else to call. Finally he dialed Laura Donovan. She answered on the first ring, and recognized his voice instantly. "It's so good to hear from you. I've been thinking about you a lot." Her warm voice was filled with concern. "This . . . terrible case has been in all the newspapers lately."

"I need a big favor from you," he told her. "I have a . . . friend . . . kind of a witness . . . who's involved in the case. She's afraid of being left alone. Can she stay with you for a few hours while I talk to the police?" Kevin felt oddly guilty asking Laura, but he saw no other alternative.

"You don't even need to ask," Laura told him. "My school is closed today because of the snow, so I'm going to stay at home and work on a 'Teach Yourself Conversational French' class I've been taking on tapes through the mail. If she doesn't mind listening to me garble pronunciation, she can stay as long as she likes."

As Kevin and Jennifer walked the few blocks to Laura's apartment through the morning blanket of fresh snow, he was struck by how silent and empty the Yale campus seemed. The first morning classes were already in session, and normally droves of students would be hurrying off to libraries or to Science Hill, in small groups or by themselves. Now the place looked like an academic ghost town. The few students who did pass by walked in groups of three or four and seemed extremely wary.

Kevin also could not suppress the feeling that he and Jennifer were being watched and followed. He knew there was no way Peter could have known that she was back in town, or that she was with him, but several times the sensation of being followed became so strong that he could not stop himself from glancing around. Once as he spun and looked up, he fancied he saw a moving shadow duck back among the other shadows of a rooftop. These irrational imaginings angered him. With an effort he regained control of himself and did not turn around again all the way to Laura's apartment.

Kevin noticed, as he introduced the two women, that Laura's eyes widened slightly when she saw Jennifer, who looked even more elegant, young, and vulnerable than usual.

"I don't want to put you to any trouble," Jennifer said. The fact that she could be so cordial and soft-spoken when she was obviously terribly frightened and overwrought seemed to win over Laura.

Her face softened with concern. "Don't be silly, you're welcome to stay as long as you like. Come, you look pale—would you like some tea?"

Before he left, Kevin maneuvered Laura alone and asked if she had a weapon.

"Of course not," she responded with a laugh. "I'll keep the door locked and we'll be just fine."

"You have the New Haven police number? Call if anything suspicious happens."

"I will. Your little witness is very nice. She's made you happy?"

"Yes," Kevin admitted. "Yes, she has."

"I'm glad," Laura said, turning away. "Now go on to your meeting. Go on, leave. Out!"

The snow fell around him, the cold blew over him, as he made his way across icy rooftops and then down fire escapes to dark alleys, staying invisible, keeping to the shadows . . .

Jennifer . . .

Jennifer who had caused pain by leaving, such pain that he had searched all over for her, borne the darkest darkness and braved the loneliest loneliness . . .

Err? Don't . . .

Hush.

Don't . . .

Err took control and hushed him then.

In and out, upside down, through the dark alley, keeping to the shadows, and they are all the same because they all cause such terrible pressure, the woman who comes by night and the woman who left by day, a ringing singing stinging that needs to be stopped, quieted, crushed, ripped, beaten into silence.

"Those are my terms," Kevin said. "And it's an all-or-nothing proposition. Either you accept them and we work together, or I will tell you nothing."

Walter Green, the New Haven chief of police, was in the room. He was a well-built black man whose face seemed open and friendly but whose tight lips never parted to emit a sound. Throughout the meeting he seemed inclined to watch and let his lieutenant do the negotiating.

Lieutenant Romano looked as if he hadn't slept in weeks. His usually crisp movements were a bit fuzzy, the dark grizzle on his chin attested to his lack of time to shave, and even from a distance of two feet Kevin could smell the long nights of coffee and cigars on his breath. Still, he was a battler, and like a good prizefighter in the late rounds he came out swinging in this meeting with reserves of energy and determination.

"Don't try to push us," Romano growled. "Two more girls died because you had to try to do this thing your way."

"No, they died because you couldn't find the killer," Kevin told him. Romano didn't like that at all—his jaws locked to contain the explosion that wanted to burst out of his mouth. He looked as if he were chewing on gunpowder. "None of you could find him," Kevin continued, looking around the table at the other men in the room. Standing near Green, the silent police chief, was Jack Hobbs, who had apparently become Romano's legman in the investigation. He looked at Kevin with enough hostility to make it amply clear where his loyalties lay. Next to Romano sat a short man with a peculiarly long face who had been introduced to Kevin as Sergeant Donaldson, the department's canine trainer. Finally, there was a Connecticut State Police special investigator named Banning, a tall young man with a professional athlete's build and flint-colored eyes.

"What do you think you know?" Banning asked simply and directly, cutting through the old animosities that wound around the room.

"Everything," Kevin answered him with equal directness. "I

know who is doing this, why he's doing it, where he is, and how we can catch him."

The tension in the long silence that followed his announcement was palpable. Chief Green was the only man in the room who didn't seem to feel it. He continued to study Kevin with his friendly, relaxed look, as if he were watching Kevin play a game and were trying to guess how to lay a sidebet.

"What are your terms?" Romano finally asked, breaking the silence.

"I want to help set the strategy and I want to be in on the actual hunt. I'll bow to you guys"—Kevin nodded at Romano and Green—"in tactical police-work details, but this is a personal thing for me and I don't want to end up standing on the sidelines."

"What's this hunt you're talking about?" Donaldson asked.

Kevin ignored him. "Second, we move quickly. If possible, I'd like to go after him this afternoon."

"Why?" Romano wanted to know. "If you know where he is, why not just wait an extra day or two, handpick the men we'll need, and really plan the operation?"

"We move as soon as possible for my own reasons," Kevin said, thinking of Jennifer and her fear. Sensing the hostility of the other men to his answer, Kevin added, "Yes, I know where he is now, but I also know that he's very capable of leaving Yale. That's why the murders here stopped for nearly two years. He crossed the country before—killing all the way to California—probably traveling only at night and eating God knows what—and he could do it again."

"Why did he come back?" Jack Hobbs had invested so much in the case that he couldn't contain his anger.

Kevin shook his head. "Either I tell you everything or I tell you nothing. My last requirement is that we restrict the number of people who know what we're planning. If we flush the quarry out too early, or let him hear the sounds of the hunt, I guarantee you he'll vanish. We're not chasing a normal fugitive, so normal police procedures and precautions won't be sufficient. Those are my conditions."

Banning was the first to speak. He addressed himself to Romano, as if Kevin weren't there. "Is he for real?"

Romano glanced toward Jack Hobbs and then nodded his head very slightly.

"Well, if he knows what he says he knows, maybe we'd better play along." Banning shrugged.

Walter Green slowly stood up. Since he hadn't moved or spoken throughout the entire meeting, his action at this critical moment drew everyone's eyes. "I have a question," he said to Kevin in a resonant voice that filled the room. "Even if we say we'll abide by your terms, how can you trust us? What do you expect as a guarantee?"

"Your word," Kevin told him. "And his." He pointed at Romano. "I don't like him, but I trust him."

Police Chief Walter Green hesitated only half a beat. He was obviously a man used to making quick decisions, and after studying Kevin's face a few seconds more his thin lips twisted up in a peculiarly grim smile. "Like my friend on the state police force, I believe that if you know what you say you know we should work with you." He looked right at Kevin. "You have my word."

Romano had a much harder time making the promise. The vow seemed to stick to the roof of his mouth so that he had to peel the words off one by one with his tongue. "We'll do it your way," he finally managed to say. "Now tell us what you know."

Kevin told them the full story from beginning to end, changing only the intimate details of what had happened between him and Jennifer. He talked steadily for at least twenty minutes and nobody in the room moved during that time, except Donaldson, the canine expert, who occasionally ran his hand over his long face, wiping off invisible sweat.

When Kevin finished, everyone began to move very quickly.

Jack Hobbs hurried off to locate a contact named Fish. He was a local architect who had done renovations and repairs on many of the Yale buildings over the years, and who knew everything there was to know about the campus. He had helped the police department before.

Chief Green and Banning had a whispered discussion over jurisdiction, and apparently the police chief was able to convince the state policeman to let the city force mount the operation.

"I can see we're going to need every trained dog we have," Donaldson told Romano. "I'll get on it right now. We have a dozen, and we can probably borrow at least ten more on short notice if we need 'em." He left in a hurry, apparently very excited that his dogs would be playing a big role in such an important case.

While everyone was busy with his different errands, Romano walked over to Kevin and held out his hand. His palm was as dry as the leather of an old catcher's mitt. "You're really a thick-headed son of a bitch," he muttered, unable to keep the admiration from his voice. "That was some story you told us."

"Coming from a mean bastard like you, that means a lot." The two men held the grip a long moment, staring at each other with mutual hatred and respect.

"I'll be arming my men with semiautomatics," Romano said. "Do you need a gun? Can you shoot?"

"Thanks," Kevin told him, "but I already have a weapon."

And at that moment a young patrolman ran in, out of breath, with the news that a woman had just called the police emergency number hysterically pleading for immediate police help. She had begged to talk to Kevin Randall or Jack Hobbs, but before she could give her address or tell what the emergency was, the line had gone dead.

Chief Walter Green, Lieutenant Romano, and Kevin were soon in a police car speeding toward Laura's apartment. The snow had started to fall again, and the police car with its lights flashing and siren blaring skidded around every corner. Even before the car braked to a stop, Kevin jumped out the door and bolted through the front doorway of Laura's building.

He raced up the stairs three at a time, flight after flight, remembering how slowly the elevator moved. The footsteps of hurrying policemen thudded behind him. The front door of Laura's apartment had been knocked in and the heavy wooden door lay flat on the hallway carpet. Kevin ran into the hallway, and as he did he heard footsteps retreat into the living room, then stop altogether. He darted toward the sounds, but found the living room empty and the large window by the couch wide open. The afternoon breeze blew the light curtains inward, depositing stray snowflakes on the carpet.

Kevin ran to the window and looked in all directions. A narrow ledge five feet below window level led around the side of the building to a fire escape. Barefoot prints and drops of blood led away along the ledge to the corner of the building. The falling snow was already beginning to fill in the footprints and whiten over the crimson patches of blood.

Kevin raced through the apartment, a foul, musty odor in his nose and mouth, his blood pumping from fear at what he might find. Romano and Walter Green ran in from the hallway just as Kevin reached the bathroom door, which had been battered but was still in one piece and was still locked.

"Jennifer?" he called. "Laura? It's Kevin." He pounded on the locked door with his fist.

The silence lasted only a second, but it seemed interminable. "Kevin?" Jennifer called back, sounding very frightened.

"Yes, and the police are here too. Open the door."

Fingers fumbled at the lock from the inside, and Kevin had a moment to thank God that Laura's building still had very thick old doors with sturdy locks.

Then the door swung open, and Kevin saw Jennifer held a scissors in her hand like a knife, while Laura stood next to her, brandishing a long nail file. They dropped their weapons and sank into each other's arms at the sight of Kevin and the police behind him. They both seemed frightened out of their wits, but were very much alive.

Walter Green questioned them in the kitchen, as policemen searched the building and the surrounding area. Laura explained, in a surprisingly steady voice, that they had been talking in the living room when they had heard the doorknob to the apartment turning back and forth. Then, with no further warning, there had been a series of very loud crashing sounds, as a large body threw itself against the front door again and again.

While Jennifer dialed the police number, Laura grabbed the biggest cleaver in her kitchen and stood by the door, waiting. The crashing stopped suddenly, and Jennifer had just managed to get the police on the line when the phone went dead. Then whoever it was began at the door again with redoubled fury.

They knew the door wouldn't last long, so they planned a retreat into the bathroom. As soon as the front door splintered inward admitting a large body, Laura swung the cleaver with all her strength and heard a yelp of pain. Then Jennifer yanked her away and they fled into the bathroom, locked the door, and waited.

It was quiet for a few minutes—and they began to hope the cleaver had done some serious damage or had scared the intruder away. Laura hadn't really struck at a target or even really seen the person clearly; she explained that she had just swung blindly at a large shape and fled.

After a short while, the intruder began battering the bathroom door. It held against his first few assaults, and then the hinges started to give way. The two women armed themselves as well as they could and were preparing for the final fight when the intruder suddenly stopped. A few seconds later Kevin called to them.

As Laura finished her story, a young policeman hurried up to report that the intruder had gotten away through a back alley. Footsteps and traces of blood had been found as far as a block away, and then the trail had been covered over by the snow. Donaldson was on his way with the police dogs, but it seemed clear that the fugitive had not been too seriously wounded and that he had headed back toward the Yale campus at great speed.

Chapter 22

At the police station a friendly policewoman explained to Jennifer and Laura that she had been assigned to guard them, and invited them up to the women's lounge on the third floor. Laura wished Kevin good luck with her eyes and followed the police woman. Jennifer also moved away, but turned back after only a few steps.

She had been almost completely silent since he had found her holding the scissors in Laura's bathroom. When Kevin saw the look of foreboding on her face, he wasn't sure she was going to be able to let him go. But she only whispered: "Take care, and come back soon."

"I will," he promised, and she turned resolutely and walked away.

A command post had been set up in the largest conference room at the police station, and Fish, the old architect and expert on the Yale campus, seemed to be in charge. He was bumptious and bent, with a bald and wrinkled pate through which the outlines of his skull were visible. He continually moistened his lips with his tongue, and he seemed very happy as he hurried from table to table where maps and large architectural blueprints were spread out.

"Are you sure you can shut off all entrances to the tunnel system?" Kevin asked him.

Fish scowled at him. "Didn't I design the tunnels in thirty-seven and fifty-five? Ain't I fixed up the other ones hundreds of times?" He looked around, but no one contradicted him. "Give me two hours and I'll have all the entrances sealed. Then you can go get him."

Kevin drove back to his Trumbull College apartment to change to warmer clothes. While there, he telephoned Ron Christopher, telling the reporter to hurry to Harkness Hall. Then Kevin took out his best saber, which he had bought for several hundred dollars in Heidelberg and which he had used only in major fencing tournaments. It was a beautifully crafted weapon with an intricately designed haft and a razor-sharp edge. He slipped it through his belt.

The campus was completely deserted. The snowstorm and the fear that had gripped the Yale community over the murders kept everyone off the streets. All was silent and still in the muffled and blanketed town. Time itself seemed oddly frozen, and as Kevin looked around at the various grim Gothic edifices frowning down on the open expanse of Cross Campus it was easy to believe that, by imitating the great old universities of Europe, the founders and shapers of Yale had created a world that harked back five centuries into the dark past—an isolated little community with its own cathedral, its own town square, its own gentry and laborers, and now its own monster.

The "hunters" had assembled in a large classroom in Harkness Hall. Kevin saw the dogs first, with Donaldson moving among them, scolding and cajoling them to behave. They were all large German shepherds, with bells on their collars that tinkled whenever they moved. They sat, alert, off to one side of the podium, and appeared to be far better trained and behaved than any of the police officers in the room.

Ron Christopher was dancing around the throng of police officers and dogs like a dervish, taking pictures and talking to whoever would put up with him. As soon as Kevin entered the reporter ran up and began peppering him with questions.

Thirty of New Haven's finest, all armed with Browning nine-millimeter automatics, milled around the room nervously. Lieutenant Romano and Chief Green stood at the front of the room, talking to Fish back at the police station via walkie-talkies. The police chief handed Kevin a sheet of paper. Green seemed in high spirits. Since he sat behind a desk most of the year, he was obviously enjoying this return to action. "When Fish gives us the okay we'll enter the tunnels through four different entrances and sweep toward Sterling Library," he explained. Glancing down, Kevin saw that the paper was a Xerox of a detailed plan of the tunnel network with a route traced in red Magic Marker. "Jack Hobbs will lead the group that you're in. Frankly, I hate to use a nonprofessional like you in an operation like this, but I gave my word and I'm sticking to it. But when the action starts, I want you to leave it to the men who are trained. Understood?"

Kevin didn't say a word. The police chief gave him a long look and walked away.

They waited twenty minutes for the go-ahead from Fish. Occasionally the dogs snarled at each other, and Donaldson waded into them shouting vile imprecations.

Jack Hobbs stood off in a corner of the large room, by himself. The semiautomatic gun he wore looked small strapped to his massive frame.

Finally Chief Green got the message he wanted from the walkie-talkie and announced, "The tunnel exits are all sealed. Let's go!"

That announcement brought Jack Hobbs back to life. He walked over to where Kevin stood with the seven policemen in his group, and looked from one man to another, sizing them up in terms of toughness. He seemed to like what he saw. He glanced at Kevin last, looked at the sword on his belt and said with a grunt, "You ready?"

Kevin studied the bluff face with its big eyes that were usually friendly. Jack Hobbs had clearly been upset by the attack on Laura, and today his eyes blazed with anger. "Let's get this fucker," he said, and led them out.

Kevin's group—Jack Hobbs, the seven policemen, and three German shepherds—hurried across the campus to their designated tunnel entrance beneath Mason Laboratory. No one spoke on the walk through the snow. The only sounds were of the men's shoes crunching through the layer of ice above the snow, and the constant tinkling of the bells from the dogs' collars, designed to keep the four groups from mistakenly shooting at one another.

They entered the tunnels and at first they moved along quickly. The passage they traversed was more than ten feet in diameter, unobstructed, and well lighted. Three policemen, each holding a dog on a long leash, led the way. The other men followed in a fairly tight pack. Kevin noticed that the policemen kept their hands on their pistol grips, and he constantly found his fingers returning to the haft of his saber.

Before long they entered an older tunnel system where the ceiling lights were spaced much farther apart, and they had to turn on their high-powered flashlights. The whitish-yellow beams licked the stone walls as they moved forward. This tunnel system had many short culverts leading off to either side, which were slick from water that drained down from above. Each time they came to a side passage they had to stop and wait while two or three policemen and a dog broke away to investigate.

Then their route took them downward. The daylight that had occasionally filtered through grates to light their way and cheer their spirits disappeared. They entered a pitch-black tunnel so narrow they had to walk single file. The floor was damp with a cold, squishy, unidentifiable oily residue. Tiny footsteps scurried away at their approach, and several times their flashlight beams illuminated large sewer rats that turned in their direction and flashed sharp yellow teeth before scampering off into the darkness.

The methodical slowness of the search began to grate on Kevin. He had dreamed for so long of the moment when he would come face to face with the being who had caused him immeasurable pain. Now, with each step that moment drew closer, and yet his movements were restricted and the progress so slow that it was excruciating.

Earlier, when he had been waiting in Harkness with the other policemen for the go-ahead, different memories of Anne kept flashing into his consciousness, as if he were screening a retrospective of her most endearing moments. Now, as he walked through the black tunnel with his right hand on his saber hilt, he saw only one recurring image in his mind's eye: her body on a long metal tray in the New Haven morgue, waiting for him to identify her. Even as he had forced himself to look at her bruises and dislocated limbs, which testified to the agonies she had suffered, another part of his mind was furious that his wife should lie exposed stark naked on a metal tray in front of a bunch of strange men. In a way it had been that initial reaction of male protectiveness and jealousy, and his immediate realization of how absurd such feelings were, that had driven through his heart the numbing truth that Anne was really gone from the earth forever. As he relived the horror of that moment, Kevin's pace increased until he nearly stepped on the heels of Hobbs, who was in front of him.

The dogs caught the scent as Kevin's group began the third leg of its route. Almost instantly, all three German shepherds surged forward excitedly. The men holding their leashes had a hard time controlling them and soon all semblance of order was lost in the narrow passageway as cursing men and snarling dogs on twisted leashes bumped against one another.

The biggest dog actually yanked his handler off his feet and tugged him along willy-nilly across the stone floor. Kevin grabbed the leash away from the handler and raced along with the dog. They managed to separate themselves from the confused tangle and were soon far ahead of the rest of the hunting party. The German shepherd bounded forward in huge strides that made Kevin strain to keep up.

Twice as they entered long, straight sections of tunnel, Kevin thought he glimpsed a shadowy form fleeing before them in the distance. Both times Kevin felt a craving in the pit of his stomach that he had never felt before, a craving that made it much easier to keep pace with the bounding dog. It was a craving for blood on a startlingly bestial level that Kevin had not known existed within himself.

Faintly at first, and then more loudly, there came the sounds of men and barking dogs drawing near from other directions. The tunnels widened out again, and Kevin was surprised when Jack Hobbs came up beside him. Jack was plainly not a natural distance runner, and the effort of keeping pace had turned his face bright red. He gasped with each step and beat his right arm against his right side to unsnarl a painful cramp.

The four tunnel routes converged in a large subterranean chamber. At nearly the same instant that Kevin, Jack Hobbs, and the huge dog ran into the open space, Police Chief Green and his contingent of young policemen hurried into it from another tunnel entrance. Kevin's dog and the ones held by Chief Green's handlers surged straight toward a corner of the large room where a two-foot-square opening in the roof led to a narrow vertical shaft. The dogs stood beneath it, barking and growling.

Kevin shined his flashlight up the shaft. The thin beam of light showed dank crusty walls stirring with roaches and silverfish. The air beneath the shaft was noxious with the effluvium of insects. The shaft seemed to go up and up interminably, and Kevin's flashlight beam was soon deflected by various small and large overhangs.

Chief Green pulled out his map of the tunnels. As he tried to locate the shaft, State Police Investigator Banning's group arrived. Banning joined them at the entrance to the shaft, peering up into the darkness. "How could he go straight up that?" he demanded.

"Practice," Jack Hobbs muttered grimly.

"Or he had a rope hanging down it that he pulled up after him," Kevin suggested. He had already thought about trying to climb up the shaft after Peter, but had discounted it as physically impossible.

Romano arrived with his men a few minutes later. He could barely contain his impatience as he peered over the chief's shoulder, trying to make out the shaft on the complicated floor plan.

Chief Green straightened up from his map and when he spoke his voice rang through the underground chamber. "That shaft leads right up through the middle of Sterling Library," he announced. "It is a dumbwaiter shaft that opens onto every single floor."

"Then we've lost him," Kevin said bitterly. "By now he's slipped out into the streets of New Haven."

Police Chief Green shook his head, and there was triumph on his face. "Score one for old Fish," he said. "Since the chase was directed this way, he had me completely lock up Sterling. That library's built like a fortress, and when its doors and windows are barred and locked nobody can get in or out. And I have to admit I thought it was a needless precaution, but I took his advice, and the library is ringed with about twenty policemen."

"Then he's up there in the library," Hobbs whispered, craning his neck. "He's all alone, and he knows he's trapped."

For a long moment they were silent, imagining the one shadowy form moving somewhere on a floor far above them, among the millions of dusty volumes.

Gray police sawhorses kept the crowd back. The throng of students, townspeople, and reporters pushed against the barriers as if they could force out new information by mass pressure. Even though the bitter winter day grew darker and colder by the minute, the crowd around the gigantic library soon numbered in the hundreds. All stared expectantly at the search groups and dogs huddled near Sterling's stone walls.

For once, Kevin and Romano were on the same side of an argument, and since Romano was in a far better position to speak, Kevin stood a few yards away and listened to the lieutenant battle with his chief.

"He's a multiple murderer. We've finally got him cornered," Romano said, eagerness swelling his voice. "We have to go in after him. It doesn't matter what the risks are."

Chief Green answered in a low, politic, almost friendly tone, as if he were explaining something that should have been obvious to a stubborn child. "The sun's already setting. That library's huge and some of the floors have low visibility even in broad daylight. Sending men in at night to search through dark stacks and hallways for an insane killer would be a suicide mission."

"We'll find him," Romano vowed.

"We will anyway. When morning comes, I'll send in a hundred armed men. As for tonight, we have the place completely sealed off and surrounded. Let him stay up there by himself till dawn—it can only soften him up."

Chief Green tried to walk away, but Romano grabbed his arm and stopped him. The police chief clearly didn't like being restrained. His eyes flashed angrily, and Romano switched to a less combative tone. "I'm not saying that you should order men up there. I'm saying that you could get enough volunteers to mount the operation. With the overhead lights turned on and with flashlights, we'd be okay. We could use tear gas and masks . . ."

On the other side of the arguing pair, Kevin saw Jack Hobbs also listening intently.

The police chief pulled his arm free, and when he spoke his voice was razor sharp with authority. "I've been the chief of this force for two years and in that time we've only lost one man on duty. When I say we're not risking it, that means we're not risking it. Don't push me any more, Frank, or you'll regret it."

Chief Green walked away toward the police sawhorses to talk to the TV reporters, and this time Romano let him go. For a second Romano, Hobbs, and Kevin exchanged impatient and frustrated looks, then they turned away in different directions.

Kevin wandered closer to the great outer walls of Sterling and touched the cold limestone trim. It was like putting his fingers on the edge of an iceberg. He found himself running his hand along reddish stone, and the contact seemed to complete some sort of telepathic link. Suddenly Kevin felt in his fingertips the very presence of the killer trapped inside the Gothic fortress. Near him, two policemen with drawn pistols stood by the locked main entrance. Kevin tried to convince himself that the building really would hold its captive until the next morning, but all of his hunter's instincts rebelled against giving the prey so much time to find a way out of the snare.

By ten o'clock the three major networks had news crews just beyond the sawhorses. Ron Christopher was exultant in his privileged position inside the cordon, and several times spoke to Kevin. On this night of grim and silent waiting, Kevin found the reporter's questions annoying. He walked away from the crowd again to stand by himself.

Just after midnight Jennifer slipped under one of the sawhorses and ran over to Kevin. The policewoman who had been assigned to watch her trailed several feet behind. "I kept listening on the radio," she explained breathlessly. "I couldn't wait any more." She hugged him, and her warm breath defrosted his icy cheek. "Is he really in there?" she whispered, breaking away to look up at Sterling Library, which the moonless night had turned into an enormous and shapeless shadow.

"Yes," Kevin told her, feeling buoyed by her presence but at the same time wishing intensely that she hadn't come. "Don't you feel him too?"

She looked surprised by his question, surprised that Kevin had access to that instinctive knowledge. Finally she nodded, shivering. "Yes, he's there."

Crouched in the shadows on the third floor, aware that the whole building was sealed off, hearing the wail of the police sirens from the cars parked outside the main entrance, glimpsing the growing crowd outside and knowing that they were there for him. They wanted to drag him out. Into the light. That's what they were waiting for now. The light.

Insects that had fastened onto him during his climb up the stinking shaft nipped at his skin and slithered through his hair. The window again. The crowd was growing.

Dawn would come soon.

They would come with their dogs, their guns, in twos and threes, working methodically, one floor at a time, driving him upward until he had no place else to hide. What to do? Darkness, only darkness. Darkness as thick as the tongue of a man struggling for breath. Silence rooted in childhood. A vast space filled with books, ideas crouching on shelves, armies of them, but not the one he needed.

What to do?

Silence. It happened on a night as dark as this, beneath the same full moon. The leather collar around his neck. The sounds of her footsteps descending the stairs, slow, ponderous, she was holding something. The cries of his brother as they held each other and down she came toward them. Her face in the semidarkness of the cellar, a face savoring pain that was about to take place. In her hands she held a white-hot poker and a carving knife, and for a second in the darkness brother and brother screamed but there was nowhere to run, no place to hide.

The smell of burning flesh, sweetly nauseating, and the screams as pain gave way to pain, screams ripped through the throat as the knife broke skin, as the poker seared his brother's rib cage and then fell white hot across his own arms and shoulders, as hell rose up and engulfed them, and the face of hell was an old woman's face with no expression and eyes the color of freshly spilled blood.

Then darkness had fallen, and he had woken from that darkness into darkness to the thick smell of gasoline, and then a match had pierced the blackness, illuminating her blood-streaked face one last time, as she shrieked like the demon she was and dropped the match in the gasoline, and then . . .

Then . . .

The fire had come.

Flames sang and danced.

Flames.

Suddenly Err was moving quickly, ripping dry paper from old volumes, breaking glass bulbs to expose live wires . . .

They were waiting for daylight.

He would not wait.

Chapter 23

The first alarms rang at two in the morning. Jennifer was show-ing symptoms of frostbite, so Kevin walked her to a police medical van. As he returned, he saw a stir of activity among the policemen and heard the first faint ringings of the fire alarms from within the library. He stood for a moment, listening to their metallic clanging, wondering if Peter had set them off. The answer came almost instantly and caused him to dart forward through the police lines.

Chief Green looked amused by the steady clanging. "So he's pulled a few fire alarms," he scoffed to the small group that sur-rounded him. "If that's the best he can come up with, then I'd say he's pretty pathetic."

"And I'd say you're a fool," Kevin shouted in near despair, battling to get close.

The ring of policemen opened so that Kevin and Chief Green stood face to face.

"We had a chance to go in and get him." Kevin's voice was sharp with fury. "Instead you made us wait. You've ruined every-thing with your caution—look!"

"If you have a point to make, then make it. Otherwise I'm going to have you thrown the hell out of here."

"He was trapped all right, but he's figured out a way to get out of the trap! And now there's nothing we can do."

They looked at him uncomprehendingly for several long seconds. Then the silence was fractured as a young policeman standing about fifteen feet away pointed up at a third-story window and shouted, "Look up there! Flames! Fire!"

Orange and yellow tongues licked hungrily from inside several windows on the second floor.

"He's set the library on fire!" someone in the crowd behind the sawhorses bellowed.

"Damn him," Chief Green muttered in a loud whisper, punching his large fists together. "Damn him to hell."

Almost immediately the New Haven night echoed with fire engine sirens. Flames were now visible in the third-floor windows. The crowd surged forward as if to warm itself around the unexpected blaze. Policemen pushed them back.

A yellow-slickered fireman hopped off the first truck that pulled up and hurried over to Chief Green. They shook hands without much enthusiasm. "I've been following things on TV and I know who you've got in there," he said. "Sorry, but we've gotta go in."

"Can you keep the number of entrances your men make to a minimum?" the police chief asked. "We could try to watch . . ."

The man in yellow shook his head. "This is Sterling Library— the third largest library in the country. If it goes up, it'll cost millions and take God knows how many other buildings with it. We've got to do what we can to contain it now."

As if to affirm what he had just said, there came the sound of splintering glass as a fireman on a ladder swung a heavy ax through a window on the second floor and climbed inside. Up and down the front of the library, fire trucks pulled in and the firemen began unreeling hoses and scaling ladders.

Chief Green raised his arms to give an order to his men and then slowly lowered them in a gesture of impotence. That was when Kevin began to move. At first he didn't know why he was walking toward the main entrance, which a gang of firemen was now forcing open. Then he knew, and he increased his speed. "Kevin, stop," he heard Jennifer call, but he kept moving with fanatic determination.

He reached the door just as the firemen got it open. "Hey, you can't go in there!" one of them shouted, and made an effort to catch him. Swerving around the fireman, he threw himself through the doors and into the main hallway. It was pitch dark but he could feel the thickness of smoke in the air.

Kevin knew the library well from countless days and nights spent doing research. He blundered along, feeling his way down the glass display cabinets and knocking into objects every few feet. At the north staircase, he raced up the steps three at a time.

The fire alarms were much louder inside the library. They beat a regular clanging rhythm, like a racing metallic heartbeat. As Kevin reached the second floor and turned toward the front of the library, the smoke grew thicker and he could feel the heat from the flames. Drawing his saber, he held it in his right hand as he dropped to the floor and began to crawl toward the bank of windows that faced out onto High Street.

Since the smoke was the thickest at the windows where the flames were spreading quickly, that's where the firemen would be likely to concentrate their efforts. So Kevin was operating on the assumption that Peter either would simply slip out a window in the confusion or would try to knock out a fireman and take his uniform to make his escape. Either way, Peter would want to be where the most firemen were entering the library.

Several times the heat drove Kevin back. Whole walls of shelves were catching fire suddenly and roaring up in bursts of orange and red. Even skirting these conflagrations, and sucking up all the available oxygen at three inches above the floor, Kevin could barely move forward. Dante's *Inferno:* the thought flitted across Kevin's mind that the hell he had been living in for two years had finally taken substantive form. Here sparks shot out for no apparent reason, and heat slowly melted pride and willpower, amid the hiss of great ideas catching fire and the seared ash of what had once been lovely and valuable. And here any step Kevin took in any direction might bring him closer to his own doom.

At that moment, as Kevin cursed the reality of his own private hell, he saw his own private Satan for the first time. Twenty feet away a mostly naked man crouched above a fireman's body, wrestling his uniform off of him. His bare skin and crouching posture, glimpsed through a tunnel of smoke and flames that gleamed orange and red by turn, gave Peter Pusecki the aspect of a demon from hell. He glanced up just as Kevin saw him, and for a moment the fear and fury of the prey and the fear and fury of the hunter clashed. Then a curl of white smoke came between them. When it moved on, the fireman lay on the floor alone, his long-handled ax gone.

Holding his saber at the ready, Kevin advanced toward the fireman's body. The area to his right was a blast furnace that no one could possibly cross, so he was sure the attack would have to come from his left.

The attack came swiftly and savagely from his right. Peter dove through the roaring flames to surprise him. Kevin managed a quick sidestep so that the ax blade glanced off his left shoulder without cutting too deeply. But the force of the blow made him cry out and knocked him backward over the fireman's body. He lay for a second on the floor, stunned.

Looking up, Kevin saw that whoever and whatever Peter Pusecki had been in his earlier life, whatever sainted name he had been given and whatever sweet girl he had loved, he was now a true monster. Peter advanced slowly, dragging his feet, the way a child who has been chained in a basement for most of his life and suddenly set free might move. The few torn rags he wore did little to hide the way his massive frame had been ravaged. His body hair was matted with dirt and grime and caked with dried blood and human excrement. As Peter drew closer, Kevin saw the repulsive scuttling dots of vermin crawling over Peter's body and open sores. His wild black hair stuck out in all directions and his facial hair was so long that his mustache hung down over his mouth while his beard hid most of his thick neck. As Peter stood above Kevin for a second, looking down at him, the fire lighted the crags and valleys of his face, and his volcanic eyes. Slowly he raised the ax and brought it down in a crushing arc.

Kevin rolled to one side just in time, so the ax cut through thin air and clanged against the stone floor. From his prone position, Kevin slashed awkwardly upward, hitting Peter who bellowed as the saber traced a long bloody line from his temple to his chin. When Peter jumped back and screamed, the ax fell to the floor. Then, as Kevin staggered to his feet, Peter darted off down the fiery corridor, running in an off-balance stride that nevertheless covered a lot of ground.

Kevin chased him through the flames, hurtling recklessly through sheets of fire that singed his hair. Somehow he managed to find just enough oxygen in each smoky breath to keep his body going. The throbbing wound in his shoulder rendered his left arm next to useless, making it very difficult to run quickly. Peter headed straight for the north stairwell. Kevin pursued him up flight after flight, following his heavy footsteps as they fell unevenly on the stone steps.

At a spot between the eighth and ninth floors, the footsteps suddenly stopped. Kevin advanced very cautiously up the nearly pitch-black stairwell, listening for even the slightest movement. A faint glint of moonlight filtered in through a high window, providing only the slightest visibility. He had already lost a lot of blood from his shoulder wound, and as he crept upwards Kevin began to feel light-headed. That high above the fire it was easier to breathe, although the air was already thick with smoke. The only sounds in the stairwell were the ringing of the alarms, and the rasping of Kevin's breath from his long climb.

Without warning Peter dove down on Kevin from a hidden ledge almost directly overhead, and Kevin had no time to swipe with his saber before the heavy body smashed into him. The impact of the collision knocked Kevin backward so that even as the two men fought one another, they tumbled down the steep stone stairs. The back of Kevin's head slammed the edges of two successive steps, almost causing him to black out.

As they hit the eighth-floor stairwell, Peter ended on top. His powerful arms wrapped around Kevin's shoulders so that Kevin's face was pulled in against Peter's noxious-smelling bare chest. Summoning all of his remaining strength, Kevin bucked sideways and managed to shove the heavy body off, but before he could take advantage of his freedom, Peter smashed his knee into Kevin's groin. Black and red waves of nausea filled Kevin's eyes, and he felt his body being lifted like a rag doll and slammed backward into the stone wall. Peter's fingers closed around Kevin's throat and held him in a strangler's grip, his heels two inches above the floor.

Kevin brought his right hand up and tried to wrench away the hands, but the grip held and tightened. The smoke in the air suddenly seemed to be inside his head, clouding his thinking. Kevin felt his heels kick spasmodically against the stone wall as he started to slip into unconsciousness. With a final effort he raised his right hand around the arms that pinned him to the wall and jabbed his finger into Peter's left eye. His finger split the cornea and sank deeply into the eye socket, causing Peter to reel back with a scream of pain that seemed to shake the stairwell. Once again Peter suddenly gave up the fight and headed back up the steep stairs. Kevin limped after him, pausing at the point the collision had taken place to grope around and retrieve his saber.

Peter's retreating footsteps did not slacken as they climbed into the library's tower. Kevin forced himself to keep moving, though the light-headedness from loss of blood now made it difficult for him to keep his balance, and he was still in great pain from where Peter had kneed him. The stairs grew narrower and steeper above the fourteenth floor, and as Kevin negotiated the bend at the fifteenth floor he heard a crashing just ahead of him. Rounding the corner, he saw that Peter had forced open a wooden door leading to the roof. A square patch of starry sky shone down through the gaping hole.

Kevin climbed out onto the roof. The cold night air revived

him and cleared his head. The immense rooftop was blanched in white moonlight. A police helicopter, circling high above, swept a high-powered beam over the area, illuminating turrets and tangles of wire and piles of masonry.

Peter was nowhere to be seen. Spinning around to the center of the rooftop, Kevin saw a structure that he had heard about many times but had never quite believed was really atop Sterling. In the 1930s, when the library was completed, a tiny chapel had been constructed on top of the great library. Kevin approached it warily, and as he stepped inside the doorway a heavy metal pipe slammed into his chest, cracking one of his ribs and pitching him back out into the moonlight. Peter followed up on his blow quickly, running out of the tiny church to swing again at Kevin with murderous strokes.

The thousands of hours Kevin had spent on fencing strips saved his life; he managed to dodge most of the blows and parry the rest of them. Yet he was so stunned from the blow by the pipe and so weakened from the other injuries that he had sustained that he had to give ground constantly. Once, when Kevin did not move quickly enough, Peter's pipe fell on his already badly injured left shoulder. Tears of pain blinded him. He staggered back several steps and regained his balance only on the very edge of the rooftop.

Peter chased Kevin along the edge, his bloody eye socket giving him the look of a maddened Cyclops as he swung the pipe at Kevin's knees, trying to knock him off the roof. Sixteen floors beneath them, the lights of New Haven flickered. Kevin continued retreating until he backed into the corner where the edge of the roof ran up against the wall of the little chapel. He realized that he was trapped and would have to fight his way out, but he had so little strength left that he could barely hold the saber up in his right hand.

Peter, sensing victory, redoubled his attack. With a bloodcurdling shout he swiped the air three times with the length of pipe. Then he stepped back and raised the pipe high with his muscular arms, bringing it around with tremendous power in a blow designed to either crack Kevin's skull or knock him off the roof.

Kevin saw the blow coming and with a last gasp of energy brought his sword up to turn the pipe aside. Completing the movement that had always been his claim to fame as a fencer, he thrust directly back in the line of attack in a lightning riposte that had the full power of his body behind it. Peter, lurching forward to put his full weight into his blow, was impaled on Kevin's sword by his own momentum. The steel pierced his heart, continued on through his body, and out his back.

Peter looked down at the saber buried nearly to the hilt in his breast, as if amazed that such a thing could have happened. And then, as he swayed on the very edge of the roof, Peter's face underwent a miraculous transformation so that all the rage of the monster who had killed so viciously seemed to melt away. Instead, it became the face of a small child, frightened and confused, but innocent and very much a creature of God. As Kevin watched, that small boy in the brute's body fell backward and plummeted off the roof and down into the New Haven night.

Kevin walked to the edge of the roof and, peering down, could just make out where the body had landed near a crowd of policemen. A young woman emitted a scream so loud that it reached up to Kevin through the dark void, and he saw Jennifer run to the body and fall down next to it.

Despair filled Kevin and he was tempted to undertake the same downward journey in search of merciful release. He stood looking out over the rooftop, swaying tiredly, hypnotized by the lights of the snow-covered city beneath him. There was the rectangle of the old campus, and there the dark patch of the New Haven green with its three church steeples gleaming in the moonlight. His glance was drawn farther and farther out over the narrow streets of the sleeping port city to the sudden ribbon of blackness where the curved coastline outlined the edges of Long Island Sound. It was into that doorway of darkness that Kevin intended to step, but just as he was about to rock forward he stopped to listen. Very faintly in the inner sanctum of his own memory he heard the bittersweet cello music that Jennifer had played for him at the center of the maze in Cheltenham Castle. Each sad note seemed to fall down to him with a distinctive crystalline pureness as if stars were dropping one by one from the constellations high above. Remembering, Kevin was filled with such a deep sense of wonderment that he actually smiled as he turned back from the precipice and limped painfully toward the stairway.

A fireman coming onto the roof caught him as he blacked out.

Chapter 24

The small island of Hatsushima lies a hundred miles south of Tokyo, in the calm waters of Izutaga Bay. It is an island of fishing families who turn their homes into small *ryokan* inns to earn a second meager income. Six times a day the ferry arrives from the resort city of Atami, bringing mail and supplies and an occasional batch of revelers in search of an isolated place to get drunk and lose their inhibitions. Six times a day the ferry returns to Atami loaded with small fish that the Hatsushima housewives have dried and cured for the shops in the malls around the train station.

For a long time the islanders were curious about the American couple who leased an old house far out on a corner of the island. The woman was young and beautiful and the man was tall and distinguished-looking, and it was difficult for anyone to explain why such a pair would want to bury themselves among foreigners in that lonely place.

Occasionally the couple would take the ferry to Atami for a French dinner at the fabulous Seagull Restaurant or to see an exhibit of paintings at the MOA Museum or even just to sip strong coffee and nibble pastries at the chic Café du Chemin coffee shop where writers and artists from Tokyo gathered on weekend evenings.

Mostly, however, they stayed in their small house on the quiet island. They bought fish from the island market, and the fresh vegetables that the farmers brought down from their terraced fields in the center of the island, and every once in a while the man would buy a quantity of Asahi beer.

Some said they were criminals, fleeing either the law or their own tormented consciences. Others read the sorrow in their faces and suggested that they were recovering from a very private grief— perhaps the loss of a child. The most insightful of the villagers, an old fisherman named Enzo who drank too much, joked that they were probably just looking for a place where they could make love without being disturbed.

At night, when the village boys crept close to the house, they heard the woman crying and the man groaning in either ecstasy or anguish. And on the mornings after these sessions, the villagers always heard remarkably beautiful cello music drifting out the windows of the house. The fishermen listened to it at sunup as their boats rounded the point where the Americans' house lay. Something about the music made them look fearfully at the open ocean ahead and glance back at their receding homes with a new appreciation for what they were leaving behind.

In time the man and woman began to leave their house more often, walking hand in hand along the island's beaches. It was strange, since they had been living together for a while, but they suddenly seemed like a young couple falling in love for the very first time. And watching their growing love for one another and the way they frolicked on the beach, everyone in the village agreed that it would not be very long before the couple would leave Hatsushima to return to their true home far across the waves.